VIC LEGACY

by Matt Kaplan

Enjoy
the
Adventure!

Matt
Kaplan

Also by Matt Kaplan

The Science of Monsters

Science of the Magical

Printed in the United Kingdom

First Printing, 2019

ISBN 978-1-5272-4621-8

Matt Kaplan

P.O. Box 409

Hitchin, SG5 9FN, UK

www.somuchsciencesolittletime.com

Cover image by Sarah Hannis Illustration

This is a work of historic science fiction.

The historic events took place.

The majority of the historic characters existed.

The science is based upon the latest findings in psychology, cellular biology and neurology.

Full details can be found in the factual notes.

To Thalia. For believing in Victor.

Contents

VICTOR'S LEGACY

Part 1

Place: Imperial College, London

Date: January 20th, 2015

Time: 9:08pm

The delicate finger-like projections of the neuron gradually stretched outward. There, out in the darkness, they met those of other neurons and formed synapses, the very basis for memory formation.

Ida eagerly looked at the image on her microscope screen and compared it to a printout on her desk. Were the synapse junctions identical? Had the tiny transplant of hippocampus tissue from one mouse to another succeeded in generating the same synaptic connections? If yes, then the memories lost by the removal of the original neural tissue would be regained. Come on, she thought, come on.

It was then that the package landed on her desk with a thud.

"What is this all about?" asked Ida, looking up from her screen.

"Special project" replied Dixon with a smile.

Just perfect, she thought, yet another distraction from her ever helpful research supervisor.

"You do realise that I have a PhD thesis to finish and stroke patients to treat" she said with only a mild sense

13

that she was being a bit overly dramatic. Sure, while her success with partially regenerating the brains of mice that had their neurons destroyed by blood clots had been erratic, she had occasionally got some of the implanted neurons to take hold, grow and help the mice recover their lost memories.

"I'm also aware that you have three more years of funding to finish it, funding that I helped you secure. So, the least you can do is help me out with a few odds and ends" answered Dixon.

Ida rolled her eyes and briefly wondered if she would have been better off leaving Manitoba for a PhD spot in the USA instead of Britain. Sure, she would have had to endure hours on end of lecturing to sweaty undergraduates but that was starting to seem less of a nuisance than the never-ending random projects being thrown at her by Dixon.

"Okay, fine. Let me finish this and make myself a coffee. Then, I promise, I will get on to the wonder that is your special project" she answered with the best sarcasm she could manage.

"And I am sure the wonder you experience will be of the highest level imaginable" replied the Brit with sarcasm well honed from years of practice. He started to walk away but stopped as he reached the door.

"Out of curiosity, how is it going?" he asked.

"Well, it was going just fine until..." she replied acidly.

"No seriously, any luck with getting our little neuron transplant to stick" he asked.

"They are sticking for sure but I need to have the computer chew on the images to work out if the original neural network has been fully replicated or if we've again got some random new network being generated" she explained.

"Well, what does it look like to you?" he asked.

She turned to the image on her screen again and looked more closely at the network of dendrites and axons. He came close, looked over her shoulder and then glanced at the printout.

"Well, that network on the left shares some of the same connections as this network here" he said as he pointed to a region on the printed image in front of her. "But I'm not sure if it is an actual replication. Could just be coincidence that those two bits of the network look alike. Actually, the more I study it, the more I think you've struck out again" said her supervisor.

She put her head in her hands. Damn. If the network wasn't identical, the original memory would be lost. What the hell did she have to do to get the neurons to recreate their original network relationship after transplantation? She was presenting them with identical biochemical conditions, placing them right next to each other, priming their synapses to bind in just the right places. It was infuriating. Dixon patted her on the back.

"Don't take it too badly. If you were to crack this in your first year on the task, that would be unbelievable. It's going to take time" he advised. He strolled over to the door as Ida looked at the box he'd left on her desk.

"What exactly is this special project anyway?" she asked.

"Garage sale" he replied with a smirk.

Fantastic, another pack of oddball samples from a research centre that couldn't be bothered to label things properly and had forgotten what they had collected in the first place. She turned back to her screen to look at the cells.

"Don't leave it too long, a few things in that box are on ice" Dixon said as he left her to it.

Place: Boston, Massachusetts

Date: April 6th, 2018

Time: 11:56am

The woman and her son turned the corner of the street and plodded along at a steady pace. It was a sunny day for early spring but still bitterly cold. The woman pulled at a scarf around her neck to keep out the chill. As she did so, her glance fell upon her son taking his gloves off.

"Keep those on" advised Catherine.

"But it isn't really that cold" said Adam, loosening his scarf to drive the point home.

She gave him a withering motherly glare and was met by a look of passive resistance. It was the same stoic defiance that her eleven-year-old always used. Others found the behaviour unnerving, but Catherine, for her part, had grown used to it. His intensity was undeniably frustrating but fighting over the scarf and gloves was just not worth it. And besides, Catherine knew full well that she might as well stop. She would not win when he got this way. Fortunately she was saved by an excuse to avert her gaze as she glimpsed the sign out of the corner of her eye. 'Harvard Medical Plaza.' Breathing a sigh of relief, she turned towards the building.

"Will this one be like all of the others?" asked Adam.

"I sure hope not sweetheart. I sure hope not" said Catherine with a sigh as she opened the door.

17

The building had the familiar smell of antiseptic that every other building of this sort had. The elevators were laid out in exactly the same format. Four in a row with a large black board between them presenting the names and floors of the different doctors working there. All the same. Adam was certain this guy was going to be just as much a clown as everyone else. After briefly examining the board, Catherine stepped into the elevator. Adam followed reluctantly.

The hallway leading up to the office had door after door with names followed by obscure combinations of letters. DMR, FFA, ChB, MD... they all, as per usual, made no sense, but then came the three letters that always followed the names of people his mother took him to see. DPM... doctor of psychiatric medicine.

The pair entered a small, empty waiting room. The same sort of stale and crumpled magazines were strewn about on these coffee tables that were typically strewn about the tables in every other office. Bored and vaguely curious, Adam picked up a copy of the journal *Nature* and started paging through it. Yes, just as he had expected, stale. The first article was about artificially re-creating the electricity-generating cells naturally found in electric eels and using them to power the light bulbs on a Christmas tree in Japan. Christmas was months ago, thought Adam, why couldn't these doctors be bothered to put out recent material for people to read?

"What is it with you and trying to read this sort of stuff?" Catherine asked with a smile, "There are a few kid's magazines over there."

Adam looked quizzically at the magazine again but was broken from his thoughts as a door at the other end of the waiting room opened. A man in his fifties emerged.

"I'm so sorry if I kept you waiting" explained the doctor with a hint of an accent that Adam could not quite place.

"Not at all, we have only been here for a couple of minutes" said Catherine.

Adam watched the doctor's eyes sweep over him and lock on to the magazine in his hands.

"You can hold on to that if you want" said the doctor.

"No, that's okay" said Adam as he placed the magazine back on the table where he had found it. The doctor waved Adam and his mother in.

The sun's rays beamed through the windows across oddities on the psychiatrist's desk. Adam saw a clock running off water droplets, a small blue and white flag stuffed with fountain pens in a coffee mug, a photograph from what appeared to be the doctor many years ago with his family, presumably on a trip to Paris since the Eiffel Tower was in the background.

"I trust you found my office easily enough Mrs. Johnson" said the doctor.

"Yes, yes. Please, just call me Catherine" she said.

"Of course" said the doctor, now turning his attention to the boy. "And you must be Adam. I am Dr Wolstone."

"Hello" said Adam with a bit of hesitation as he sank into one of the office's leather chairs.

Catherine quickly sat down as well, putting her hand on Adam's arm. "Thank you so much for re-arranging your schedule to see us."

"It was no trouble. I've had a couple of cancellations today" said Wolstone as he wheeled his chair around the desk and sat down heavily in front of Adam and Catherine.

Wolstone's eyes darted towards Adam again. Yes, the child seemed to be sleep deprived, he had the look of someone who hadn't slept well for days but, in spite of this, the boy was extraordinarily intense in the way he examined the space around him.

Realising he was being watched, Adam caught himself staring at the blue and white flag in the coffee mug and immediately broke his gaze to start looking out the window at the sunny sky instead.

"We've met with so many people" explained Catherine, "and we were told that you might be a good fit for us. We are really hoping that you can..."

"I was very sorry to hear that Dr Hermann was unable to help you. He's good. Particularly with kids" said Wolstone.

"Yes, he suggested though that a specialty in child psychiatry might not be of much use in our situation" explained Catherine.

"Well, I will do what I can, but, as I am sure Dr Hermann told you, my area of expertise is dealing with acute stresses, almost always in adults. Most of my patients are veterans who have had challenging tours of duty with the military. Children... not so much" explained Wolstone.

The doctor noticed Adam gazing intently at the water clock. The boy was studying it in a way he had never seen anyone do before.

"I know, I learned all about your work on your website. It was very well written" said Catherine.

"So, Dr Hermann advised that there were dreams, bad dreams, but I know nothing more" said Wolstone.

"That's right, nightmares" replied Catherine.

"They wake your son up at night?" asked Wolstone.

"Not always, but when they do not wake him, he often talks about the dreams around the house and with people at school. As I am sure you can imagine, there have been a lot of calls from the teachers" she explained.

"The teachers are worried that his stories will frighten the other children" asked Wolstone.

"Not so much that, they are just..." she trailed off and gave the doctor a serious look. Adam, watched the two of them, he didn't understand why his mother tried using glances and facial expression to communicate with other people while he was around. He knew she was worried about him. It was annoying that she played these games rather than just coming out and saying it.

"Really, we've been at a loss on how to respond to it all for a while. The sleep disruption is what has caused us to take action though. He always has these dark circles under his eyes. We're worried about long term effects, you know, on his health" explained Catherine.

Wolstone made a few scribbles on his notepad as he digested what she was saying. Dreams were funny things. Wolstone knew they could be representative of current tensions, but occasionally reflected past experiences. With nightmares, particularly those of the reoccurring sort, they were often manifestations of early life stresses, but he would need more information to determine what those stresses might have been for this patient.

The possibility of abuse briefly floated through Wolstone's mind, but he immediately tucked it away. It was, of course, a potential reason for reoccurring nightmares, but the psychiatrist decided he would rather not explore that path until he had exhausted other options first.

"May I ask, have there been any traumatic events that have taken place in your lives during the past year?" he asked.

"None that I can think of" responded Catherine.

"Adam hasn't been in hospital or anything of that sort?" asked Wolstone.

"No" answered Catherine.

"What about during the past five years?" asked Wolstone.

"He fell off a ladder at the playground four years ago and needed a few stitches, but it wasn't like the bad dreams started then or even soon after that" explained Catherine.

Wolstone twirled the pen in his hand around with a small flourish.

"Ok, let me ask you a different question then, when did the nightmares begin?"

"Oh, gosh, they've been there ever since we got Adam, but they've been getting steadily worse" explained Catherine.

Wolstone's eyes immediately shot to his notepad and then over to the boy. Adam was barely listening to either the questions or the answers. A crease formed on the doctor's brow and a look of concern wrinkled his features as he gazed back at Catherine. People didn't 'get' children. That just wasn't the way such things were said. Catherine, for her part, seemed to know exactly what was on Wolstone's mind. Adam yawned; he'd watched this interaction so many times. It was getting old.

"It isn't a problem. We've talked about this a lot. Adam knows he was adopted when he was two" she said.

Suddenly things started to fall into place. No wonder Dr Hermann had passed this patient along to him. He must have thought the dreams were the result of some sort of stressful event that the current parents were unaware of. A stress that must have taken place at some point before Adam came to Catherine. Wolstone quickly realised the mother would be of no further help here. With that, he turned towards Adam. The boy was gazing right back at him, it was slightly unnerving.

"Adam, is there anything that you can remember before coming to live with your mother" asked Wolstone.

"No. I remember nothing" replied Adam as he quietly turned his attention towards the window.

They were the same questions from the same old doctors. This one wasn't going to be able to help him any more than the others. Suddenly, Adam felt a pang of sadness. He so desperately wanted to be able to sleep again.

"That's okay. I can't remember anything from when I was two either" laughed Wolstone, not quite catching the misery that briefly flickered across Adam's features.

"Can you remember your bad dream when you have it?"

"Yes, mostly" replied Adam, happy enough to give this doctor the same sort of chance that he gave everyone else.

"Would you mind telling it to me?" asked Wolstone.

"I can, but I don't want to upset you" answered Adam.

"Upset me? Please don't worry about whether what you say is going to bother me."

"Okay. It's just... it's just that a lot of adults get sad or angry when I talk about my dreams. I don't want to scare you" said the child with a gaze of unsettling sobriety.

To Adam's surprise, Wolstone met his gaze without even flinching.

"I can be brave" the psychiatrist replied, the accent in his voice strengthening ever so slightly.

And without any further prompting the boy began to speak...

Place: Norway

Date: 1940

Time: Night

The thick clouds blew wildly overhead as lightning lanced through the sky. Heavy rain pelted the deck of the warship as it rocked violently in the waves of the storm. Gunfire mingled with the screaming of sea birds echoed in the distance. In spite of the fact that Adam had been to this place so many times, fear gripped his heart just as fiercely as it always did. Familiarity was no protection.

He cautiously looked from side to side for... something. It was always astonishing to him that he felt fear so early in the dream when there was nothing yet to really be scared of. There were clearly battles far off but he wasn't involved in them. At least, he didn't think he was. The gunfire was obvious, but there did not appear to be any immediate danger. Then, as if moving of their own accord, his legs walked him towards a staircase leading down into the heart of the ship.

A large wave crested the side of the deck and he struggled to avoid losing his footing on the stairs as water rushed past. When he came to a bend in the passageway, voices echoed from down the hall. Not wanting to be discovered but still feeling the need to take a look, Adam silently poked his head around the corner. There, he spotted an elderly officer speaking with a guard no more than thirty feet away.

The officer's eyes and Adam's instantly met, but the officer gave him a knowing look and took no action to raise the alarm. If anything, he seemed to only engage the guard in a more intense conversation, as if trying to keep him occupied. Did this officer know him? He seemed familiar. Were they colleagues. Adam could not remember, but either way he felt pleased to have the guard distracted. He quickly crept across the corridor and slipped into a cabin.

The bed and trunk made it immediately clear that these were quarters, most likely those of an officer since there was only one bed and a bit of extra space to spread out. Movement in the bed forced Adam to suddenly freeze up. Somebody was asleep in here. Somebody who Adam somehow knew... and feared. A sheet slipped back as the figure moved revealing a pale face and blonde hair.

Guided by dread, Adam's hands took to the trunk. With remarkable dexterity, he used a thin metal bar and a wire to pick the lock on it in little time. It quickly opened and inside Adam found an aged leather-bound book and a small bronze box.

In seconds, he had them in his hands and was at the door. The guard was still facing the other way and in conversation with the officer, so Adam's legs went where they always did, straight towards the stairs.

His heart was pounding hard. This was where it always happened. The storm forced the boat to lurch to one side and Adam, as much as he knew the boat's extreme movements were coming, lost his footing. His body, along with the book and box, crashed to the floor. The guard shouted.

Soaked to the bone and dazed with terror he glanced behind him. The man with the blond hair and pale face emerged from the quarters in his nightclothes. He was carrying a revolver. Adam got off the floor, scrambled up the stairs and back on deck. The blond man followed.

Shouting unclear words lost in the chaos of the storm and gesticulating wildly with his gun in the pouring rain, Adam felt an undeniable urge to back away. Cradling the book and box in his arms, he searched for a quick escape. The fiercely foaming black water presented terrible appeal. One of his hands slowly grasped the railing and a foot followed upwards. The waters were to be his end and that somehow seemed for the best.

Then there was a deafening crack and pain ripped through his left arm. Blood poured from the bullet wound and, losing his grasp on the railing, he slammed to the deck. In moments, the blond, pale-faced man was charging him and reaching for the book and box. There was a violent struggle, but then it all ended in an instant as an inhuman arm lashed out at the man.

The arm's bluish grey hand latched on to the pale-man's throat with a vice-like grip. Adam was aghast as he looked closer. The hand's nail beds were blue, like arctic ice, the muscular arm was covered in a network of raised violet scars. Its huge muscles strained against its soaked shirt as it lifted the pale-faced man off the ground. His shrieks were so loud that they pierced the din of the storm, but they did nothing to stop the creature. Holding the man aloft in the blasting wind like a rag doll, its fingers crushed his throat with a sickening snap. Then, it tossed the broken body into the churning black oblivion below.

Place: Psychiatry Office, Boston, Massachusetts

Date: April 6th, 2018

Time: 12:22pm

Wolstone's mouth was open as he looked quietly upon the boy. Adam wiped a bit of sweat from his brow. He had repeated the dream so many times, but it didn't matter. Every time he did so, he felt the fear. Reliving the terror of it all. For her part, Catherine just tapped nervously upon her purse.

"Adam, do you watch much television?" asked Wolstone.

"Hardly, we don't even own a TV" replied Catherine.

"What about movies?" he asked.

"Sure, sometimes. But nothing violent like this" replied Catherine.

Nodding slowly, Wolstone picked up a pen and a pad of paper. He glanced quickly at the clock on the end of his desk. Whatever this dream was about, it probably was related to a trauma that took place before Adam had been adopted by Catherine. She would not be of further use. Indeed, thought Wolstone, was likely locking Adam down into a state that blocked him from accessing early memories. There were clearly tensions between the two of them.

"Catherine, would it be alright for Adam and I to spend a while in private working through his dream? Adam, would this be okay with you?" asked Wolstone.

The mother and son both nodded.

"How long do you think you two will be?" asked Catherine.

Wolstone looked towards the boy once more.

"Adam, do you have just the one dream or are there many?" asked the psychiatrist.

"Oh, there are a lot" Adam answered.

"Are they all so vivid?" asked the doctor.

"It varies. I remember some better than others. Sometimes I wake up terrified, but can't even remember what I was dreaming about" replied Adam.

"Why don't you come back at two" advised Wolstone

"Two hours? Are you sure? When I called the receptionist I only booked thirty minutes!" asked Catherine.

"Dr Hermann advised that this case would capture my interest. It has. And at my age, one comes to the office on weekends for a love of the work. If you are happy to leave me to it, I am happy to take on the challenge" said Wolstone.

The doctor's interest took Adam by surprise. He was used to confusion followed by quick prescriptions of sedatives. He had really hated those drugs. They made him feel out of control. If anything, they made things worse. Never before had he sat with someone who actually wanted to spend   so much time with him.

Standing unsteadily, Catherine gave her son a kiss on the forehead. "I'll see you in a bit sweetheart" she said. Moments later, she slipped out the door.

Wolstone took a moment to look over his notes again. He really wanted to get more out of the boy if he could.

"Adam, I know telling me about the other nightmares will not be easy on you, clearly they are stressful, but it would be helpful for me to know about them. Would you mind telling me another one?" asked the doctor.

"Sure. There's one with a lot of snow" said the boy.

"Snow… okay, anything else" prodded Wolstone.

"Yeah, a woman, or a girl I think. A girl with just one arm" added Adam.

"And you are in the snow?" asked Wolstone.

"How do you feel in the dream?" asked the doctor.

"Scared" replied Adam.

"What do you think you are scared of?" asked Wolstone.

"I think I'm scared of a lot of things, but there is definitely a fear of dying" answered Adam.

"Is it the cold from the snow that is threatening to kill you?" asked Wolstone.

Adam closed his eyes for a moment to reflect upon the snowy dream. There were bodies, bodies everywhere. Their blood was spilling out and covering the pure white.

The images, as much as he dreaded them, came flooding back.

Place: Finland

Date: 1918

Time: day

A man nearby stuck his head up from the trench in the snow and fired a shot into the distance with his rifle. Another, just behind him, prepared to do the same and suddenly went flying backwards as a bullet sliced through the top of his skull. Gore splashed out everywhere, some of it landing upon a blond girl next to Adam. He reached out to put his arm on hers, to comfort her in the face of the horror, but his hand landed on nothing. As he looked down, he realised her right arm was missing below the elbow. Just a few fragments of bone remained; the rest had been blown right off.

The soldier in front peered over the snowy trench and fired again. Bullets came flying back. The girl pulled a pin out of grenade with her teeth and threw it with her good arm towards the enemy. A deafening explosion followed. Adam gagged upon the smell of blood and smoke. Coughing uncontrollably, he found himself being expelled from the dream.

Place: Psychiatry Office, Boston, Massachusetts

Date: April 6th, 2018

Time: 12:29pm

The child's coughing continued.

"Would you like some water?" asked the psychiatrist.

The boy nodded and Wolstone ventured over to a water cooler in the corner.

Handing Adam a paper cup of cool water, he patted him gently on the back.

"Feel's pretty real huh?" asked Wolstone.

"Yeah, it's very scary. I don't like it at all" replied Adam.

Wolstone had to admit. Even by the standards of the dreams told to him by soldiers who had fought in Iraq, this was gruesome stuff. He hated to dwell on it with a child of Adam's age. At least not until he was certain such discussions were absolutely necessary. It led him to wonder if there might be more useful information hiding in less terrible dreams.

"Adam, are all of the dreams that you are having this violent?" asked the doctor.

"No, some are more sad than they are scary, but I still don't like them much. They wake me too" the boy replied.

"Okay. Can you tell me one of those" asked the doctor.

Place: Finland

Date: 1872

Time: Evening

A chorus of crickets filled the air as a full moon floated high in the starlit sky. Adam lifted a pile of farming equipment into a shed. Soaked with sweat from a hard day of working in the field and exhausted from the exertion, he turned his attention to a patio in front of a nearby wooden cabin. A rest was exactly what he needed and, as with so many of his dreams, his legs took him to where he both yearned and feared to go.

Sitting down heavily on the steps of the porch he slowly caught his breath. It was peaceful here. Where "here" was exactly remained something of a mystery. Adam knew without any doubt that this was Finland. How he knew that, he was not so sure and he really had no idea exactly where in Finland he was.

He heard indistinct mutterings from children inside the cabin that sounded vaguely like complaints about going to bed. Turning towards the window to listen more closely, a woman's voice became clear. "Hush now, try to settle down." Gentle candle light gleamed from behind a crudely fashioned curtain and in the shadows he could make out a female form moving around. The voice always came across as both familiar and eerily alien at the same time and aroused confusing feelings.

As the room grew quiet, his eyes drifted to his hands. He consciously marvelled at their strength and then found himself wondering about their youth. These were the hands of a young man in his prime. True, they were worn from daily labour in the fields, but the presence of youthful vitality was undeniable. That somehow felt wrong to him.

His attention suddenly broke from his hands as the door to the cabin opened. What a fool he was to be startled. The door always opened at the same moment in this dream and there was never any real danger here only, what was it, misery?

"Staring out at the stars again" asked the woman from behind as she slid her fingers over his shoulders.

"I'm just, I don't know, lost in thought I suppose" replied Adam.

"You've been working too hard. The children were asking about you at bed again. They miss your stories." She sat down next to him, caressing his stiff muscles.

First her fingers worked at his shoulder, soothing the tension that they discovered there. Then they worked down his spine and slowly migrated towards his thigh. Thunder rumbled in the distance.

Her raven-black hair and sapphire eyes drew him in. Those lips were so close. The honey-sweet smell of her hair… it was intoxicating. Birds called in the distance. Were they seagulls? As their lips touched, a shock struck that was as powerful as it was awful. Adam fell away. The look of anguish on the woman's young face was almost as horrible as the pain he felt.

"I am so sorry" he said.

"No. Don't be. It is me. I am being too forward" she said.

Driven by sadness, he came forward a second time and the shock jolted him once more, creating a reflex that he could not resist. He found himself scrambling away in fear.

"I...uh... excuse me" he said as he got to his feet and went inside.

Walking past a simple wooden table and chairs in a dimly lit central room, Adam moved with purpose to a bed chamber that he felt he had visited many times before. The salt of his tears formed a bitter taste as they ran down his cheeks to his lips. He wanted to stay. He yearned to make things work with this woman, but the wrongness of it all dictated otherwise. It could not be.

With a burst of fury he slammed his fist into the wall, nearly splintering the wood. He stood there for minutes in the silence breathing heavily and regaining his composure. A lone wolf's howl broke him from his reverie and slowly his eyes fell upon a floorboard in the corner. There was something there, something important.

Stepping closer he gently nudged the wood and found it to be loose. Working with muscle memory, Adam slid the board out of place, revealing a compartment carved out of the earth and lined with a thin layer of roughly cut stone. Lying on the stone were an old leather-bound book, a small bronze box and a folded bit of lavender cloth. He reached out for the cloth, tenderly lifting it up to his cheek for a moment. A tear slid down his face as the smell of the cloth brought emotions flooding back. Without a second thought he stuffed the contents of the compartment in a knapsack with an armload of clothes and headed for the front door.

With each step forward he found it harder to move, as if he was slogging his way through mud. He hated what was to come almost as much as he hated any nightmare. Indeed, in some ways this was worse. His hand reached out for the door. His soul screamed for him to stop, to pull away and avoid the suffering, but his hand opened it anyway.

Moonlight poured across the knapsack slung over his shoulder and there she was, exactly where he had left her just minutes earlier. Eyes red with tears and lips trembling with despair, she gave a deep sigh. He yearned to put his hand on her shoulder, to comfort her, to confess how much he loved her. But it never happened.

His long legs quickly carried him far out into the fields and, with the farm far behind, just barely visible in the moonlight, he reached the road he was looking for. As he stepped out upon it, the woman's sobs floated to his ears on the wind. Somehow he knew that, whether he wanted to or not, he would always hear them echoing in his mind.

Place: Psychiatry Office, Boston, Massachusetts

Date: April 6th, 2018

Time: 12:46pm

Dr Wolstone's notepad was covered in scrawled writing. He looked up with both an expression of awe and confusion.

"You said 1872?" asked the doctor.

"Yes" replied the boy.

"And before that, in the snow, you said 1918, right?" continued the psychiatrist.

Adam nodded.

"Is there anything specific in the dream telling you that date?" asked Wolstone.

"I just know" answered Adam.

That was intriguing, thought Wolstone. It was rather normal for patients to not see someone's face in a dream but still know who the person was. It was even common for them to not see much of a location, but know precisely where they were. Dates were another matter entirely. In all his years, Wolstone had never worked with a patient who had dates fixed to their dreams like this.

With such remarkable details being recalled, Wolstone wondered if Adam might even have an awareness of self. Knowing what one's self looked like in a dream was also rather rare. Occasionally interactions with mirrors and reflective surfaces granted such awareness, but under some occasions it even happened without such visual aids.

"Can you tell me what you look like in the dream?" asked Wolstone.

"Well, I'm wearing dark trousers, worn-out boots and a light shirt" said Adam.

Wolstone's eyes went to his notes. The boy had specifically mentioned looking at his hands and marvelling at their youth. That gave him an idea.

"Adam, are you an adult or a child in this dream?" he asked.

"I'm definitely a young man" the boy replied.

The doctor looked down at his notepad and weighed his next question carefully.

"I know this question may be a difficult one for you to answer, but why do you think you are so conflicted about kissing the woman?" the doctor asked.

"I don't know. The feelings are confusing. Maybe it's because she seems too familiar" replied Adam without even pausing to consider the matter.

Too familiar? Wolstone pondered it for a moment. What could that possibly mean to an eleven year old?

"Do you mean she feels like a close friend?" the doctor asked cautiously.

"No, not really. I think she feels more like a daughter. Definitely not like a girlfriend or a wife" Adam answered calmly.

Wolstone's eyebrows raised themselves. How on Earth could a boy of his age have any sense of what having a daughter felt like? This was all as intriguing as it was strange. He would have to delve deeper.

"What does it feel like to have a daughter?" asked Wolstone, briefly thinking about having not called his own daughter for far too long.

"Oh, you know, you feel that need to guide and protect. Elsa is definitely beautiful. Attractive..."

Adam stopped abruptly. Feelings were awakening within him that were desperately confusing. He just did not know how to communicate an answer to what the doctor was asking.

"I just, well, the feelings I have for her get all messed up because I feel like I need to protect her. Does that make sense?" asked Adam.

Wolstone nodded as he processed the information. Where was the boy getting all this? He noted the child's comments down as best he could and suddenly found himself perplexed by a name his own hand was writing rather mechanically.

"Did you say Elsa?" asked the doctor.

"Yeah, Elsa is her name" said the boy.

"Do you know anybody by that name?" asked Wolstone.

"How do you mean?" asked Adam.

"Somebody at school, friends, relatives" explained the psychiatrist.

"Uh, no" said Adam.

Again the doctor's eyebrows rose up. Adam's gaze met Wolstone's and there was a moment of uncomfortable silence as the boy read the psychiatrist like a book. Wolstone, for his part, was aware of it and unnerved by the fact that the child was so sharp.

"Is it bad for me to know her name Dr Wolstone?" Adam asked with genuine sincerity.

"Bad? No, not at all. We sometimes associate the names of people who we know with characters in our dreams" answered Wolstone.

"Then why do you look so concerned?" asked Adam.

"I'm not so much concerned as I am surprised. It is somewhat unusual for the names of total strangers to surface in dreams" explained the psychiatrist.

Adam pondered that statement for a moment. Did he actually know anyone by the name of Elsa? Something on the periphery of his thoughts hinted that he might, but as his mind strived to access the relevant information, it slipped away like sand flowing between his fingers.

Wolstone could sense that something was troubling the child.

"Is something bothering you?"

"Yes, your question. It is making me wonder if I might actually know somebody by that name. I have this vague suspicion that I somehow actually do" explained Adam.

This was precisely what Wolstone was looking for. He quickly mulled over the possibility that someone from the boy's earliest years, pre-adoption, had gone by that name.

"Is Elsa in any other dreams?" asked Wolstone.

"Yes, many" said the boy.

Wolstone's interest grew.

"Good, can you tell me about one of them?" asked the doctor.

Place: Southern Prussia

Date: 1867

Time: Day

The chickens scrambled to get out of the way as children came running by. A few of their little feet dropped carelessly on the tenderly tilled soil of a garden.

"Mind where you step" came a voice coarse with age.

It took Adam a moment to realise that the voice was actually his. He'd heard it before, but even so, he still found it disconcerting. Where was he exactly? He looked around and saw an old stone church behind him. There was a barn not far off behind a few oak trees and there were children playing next to a pond. His eyes fell upon the garden that a few of the kids had just trampled and his legs started to carry him to the damaged area.

Adam always found the garden odd. While half of it looked ordinary enough, with tomatoes, runner beans and citrus bushes soaking up the sun in neatly arranged rows, the rest was downright bizarre. Long tubs filled with crops resting on logs such that they were raised a few feet off the ground took up an area the size of the church itself. Alongside the tubs were large pots lush with carrot-like plants growing in them. Some were utterly flooded with water and others relatively dry.

He kneeled and, as Adam's wrinkled hands pushed the dispersed soil back into place, a shadow spread across the vegetables. A cane poked at one of the soaked pots.

"I would not think that parsnips would ever be able to grow in mud like that. Is this another one of your experiments?"

"Yes. These are the great great grandchildren of that one plant that managed to survive those heavy rains that wiped out most of our crops three years ago" explained Adam.

"You saved some of the tubers?"

"And used the pollen from their flowers to fertilise two of the most productive plants that we had last year" said Adam.

"No doubt these are more of the ideas that you picked up while visiting that Czech abbot in Brno?"

"Indeed. All of Gregor's suggestions made sense but I had no idea they would work so well." Adam paused and looked from his work, "Father, are you not supposed to be teaching Latin right now" he asked.

"I am, but I gave the students a short break so I could speak with Elsa as you requested" said the priest.

Pausing from his work, Adam turned to look the priest in the eye.

"Have you talked her out of it" Adam asked, switching from German to Latin as two younger children wandered near.

"I'm afraid not" the priest sighed. "She wants to go where people need help and after all I have taught her, I am hardly in a position to suggest that her heart is giving her poor guidance" he said.

"But the Russian Duchy? This isn't a mercy mission. For a girl as young as her it might as well be suicide. She will not survive one year up there" said Adam.

"I know" whispered the priest.

"The last northern merchants to come through were reporting mass starvation. The Russians are providing the Finns with nothing. There is plague, banditry and..." Adam's voice trailed off, his mind was lost in a sea of fragmented thoughts.

Slowly, barely regaining his composure he gave the priest a severe look.

"We gave her these ideas! We are responsible for this. We cannot just stand idly by as she wanders off into that, that, hell!" Adam seethed.

The priest studied Adam closely.

"And you regret what we taught her?" he asked quietly.

Adam shrugged with exasperation. "Not when the teachings remained in the classroom. Not when they didn't involve putting children in harm's way. You are letting her go to her death!"

The priest knelt down next to him. "I am doing nothing of the sort, she is making a choice to go. Just as you make a choice to stay and till my land" he explained.

"What? You think I should go with her?" Adam asked.

"I never said that, I only said you make a choice to stay here. If you were to break from that choice, I would never stand in your way, especially if you were helping one of our devoted to perform the Lord's will" replied the priest quietly.

"But the Duchy is hundreds of miles from here! Look at me! I'm an old man! I cannot possibly have the stamina to even get there" said Adam.

"I think, Adam, you will find that there is a great deal more strength inside you then you give yourself credit for" advised the priest.

He leaned on his cane as he stood up and then gave a sharp whistle to the children playing nearby. Adam's eyes met those of the priest a second time and it was then that he knew, without any doubt, that he would be going.

Moments later he found himself walking up to the barn alongside the church. Knapsack in hand, he swung the door of the old wooden building open. Inside, he immediately caught sight of Elsa. The raven-haired girl was so busy stocking the church's wagon that she did not even notice him. He stepped in slowly.

She moved with such a determination and focus. He felt an overwhelming sense of admiration and the feeling sent him reeling. He started thinking about Dr Wolstone's queries.

For the first time, he found himself questioning the dream. Why, he wondered, would he feel this way? If he did not actually know this young woman, and if he really did not know anybody with her name, why would this dream of her bring such powerful emotions? He paused for a moment to concentrate and found something buried deep within his mind. It felt like a dream within a dream.

There was a child's bed and a little girl under the covers. She was crying in the middle of the night and, stranger still, he had been there... soothing her.

The half-formed thought tugged at Adam's heart and his emotions grew stronger. He looked up at the young woman again. She was clearly doing well. Some chickens were already stowed on top of the wagon in crates and a number of goats were in a cart that, Adam presumed, would be towed from behind, but numerous barrels of seeds and boxes of tools remained on the ground, waiting to be loaded. Elsa leaned forward to lift one of the boxes up and strained to get it off the ground. Adam swiftly stepped in to help her carry the load.

"Don't you have tomatoes to be tending?" she asked.

"I do, but when I heard you wouldn't be changing your mind about this little mission of yours..." he trailed off.

They dropped the box onto the back of the wagon with a thud and Elsa turned towards him warily.

"The scriptures say 'love they neighbour.' I always assumed that this was the sort of thing they were presumably talking about. There are people there. People in need. It is our responsibility!"

"It is an awfully long way" Adam replied gently, trying his best to calm the situation.

She looked down at the ground, unsure of how to respond.

"Not to mention dangerous" he added.

"I know" she responded.

"The Finns are viewed as an underclass by their rulers. The Russians do not care if they starve to death. You will have few resources and very little help out there" advised Adam.

"God will grant me the strength" she replied.

That comment stung. Adam was not sure what about it bothered him so much. He didn't think he had any major issues with believing in a god, even so, it left him feeling uneasy.

"I am coming with you" he said, throwing his knapsack onto the back seat to hammer the point home.

Elsa's face suddenly went red. "What? No you are not!" she shouted.

"And why not?" asked Adam.

"Well, you, you are so... old" she stammered.

"Thanks for the sentiment, but I feel fine" he replied.

"I have to do this!" she seethed.

"Alone?" he asked.

"Yes" she responded, taking a step closer, staring him in the eye.

"Because of your parents??" he asked.

'Because of your parents' thought Adam as he continued to try and come to grips with the phrase. He had made the statement to her over and over. It always surfaced in the dream and he had never spent any time considering it, but, upon reflection, he found himself wondering where the notion had actually come from. He had no recollection of Elsa having parents. At least none that ever featured in one of his dreams.

"This has nothing to do with them" she bit back.

"I would hope not, because if you think you need to show them that they were wrong, I promise, this is not the way to do it" he shouted.

Elsa glared at him angrily as she bent down to lift another box.

Adam knew he was pushing her hard. He could tell from her response, but he could not for the life of him recall what it was about her parents that was so acutely painful for her.

"I'm sorry. That was uncalled for" Adam muttered.

She lifted the box up and over to the wagon on her own, dropping it down in place with a satisfying thud. Wiping the sweat from her brow she looked towards him once more.

"I can do this on my own. I really can, but, if you want to come..." she said.

"You are the closest thing I have in this world to a daughter. I want to keep you safe and if going to help the Finns serves that purpose, then, well, I guess the answer is 'yes', I want to come " he replied quietly.

With tears starting to trickle down her cheeks she stepped forward and embraced him with her delicate arms. In the silence of the barn, he wrapped his old wrinkled hands around her too.

Place: Psychiatry Office, Boston, Massachusetts

Date: April 6th, 2018

Time: 12:58pm

"Adam, I'm sorry to interrupt, but I have a question. I noticed you pausing quite a lot during that dream, particularly when you were arguing with her. You said you told her that if she wanted to show her parents that they were wrong, that going on this dangerous mercy mission was not a way to do it. What exactly did you mean by that?"

"I don't know. I've never really given it much thought because the dreams just repeat so often, I've come to just accept them for what they are. However, this time I was hesitating because, as I was relating the dream to you, I did start to think about what some of the things in it actually meant" he answered honestly.

"Well, what do you think about your bringing up her parents in the way that you did?" the doctor asked.

As Adam processed the question, an image of a basket emerged in his mind. A basket with a baby inside. It was in a garden, the garden he had been working in at the start of the dream. The pieces suddenly started to come together and, Adam had to admit, it was coming as something of a relief to finally understand more of what this dream was about.

"She was abandoned" he said.

"At the church?" asked the doctor.

Adam nodded.

"And the priest raised her there?" asked Wolstone.

"No. Well... not entirely. I think I was the one who raised her" explained the boy, feeling quite satisfied to have finally recalled that important detail.

Fascinating and highly appropriate, thought Wolstone. An adopted child having anxiety dreams about being left with an abandoned baby to raise on his own. It made Wolstone wonder how exactly Adam had ended up with Catherine. For a moment he considered asking, but quickly decided otherwise. It just wasn't reasonable to ask such a question. The boy would be unlikely to remember and, if he did, his memories would be heavily coloured by descriptions of his adoption by his family. Even so, Wolstone very much wanted to hear more about this fictional adoptive relationship Adam had invented.

"I apologise for cutting you off. What happens next in the dream" asked the psychiatrist.

Place: The Baltic

Date: 1867

Time: Day

Adam turned his head away from the ocean as the next wave came smashing into the ship's hull, spraying the deck with its freezing salty mist. Thick as his wool cloak, leather gloves and boots were, the cold was seeping deep into his bones. It was agonising. A bitter wind suddenly blasted him against the railing, nearly knocking his fur cap from his head. Pushing it back into place and standing upright once more he blinked a few times and, amidst the thick clouds and storm surge, he saw land.

He had long thought that the Russian Duchy of Finland would be something akin to the eighth layer of hell, covered in ice and filled with souls tormented by disease and starvation. The sight of the distant coast did little to alter his expectations.

As the land came into view in the morning light he could see Helsinki's harbour. The buildings around it were all covered with snow and surrounded by an ethereal aura of freezing spindrift. The docks themselves stood in front of the buildings in stark defiance of the conditions. The ferry lurched to the side as yet another large wave slammed into it. A bell rang loudly from the crow's nest. Crewmen from high above began shouting commands.

Adam had experienced enough of the upper deck. And besides, he thought, they were nearly there. It was time to wake Elsa.

Gripping the railing tightly, he descended into the bowels of the ferry. Everyone aboard had heard the bell and was readying themselves for departure, making it difficult for Adam to make his way through the chaotic masses, but eventually he found his way to the corner where he had left her. She was wrapped up in a heavy coat and buried under a layer of blankets. He stepped closer and nudged her gently.

"We are almost there" he whispered.

She stirred slightly but made no further response. He nudged her again, a bit more insistently.

"Elsa, they rang the landing bell, we need to get ourselves ready" he said reasonably loudly while shaking her shoulder.

Her slender arms emerged from hiding within her warm cocoon of wool and furs. They slid around Adam's arm and fastened themselves tightly. Utterly unhindered by his age, he leaned back and hoisted Elsa to her feet. She looked tired but healthy. That was better than many others on the ferry. He knew there had been an outbreak of cholera at the docks in Riga and it seemed clear that several passengers on the lower decks were suffering badly.

Elsa threw on her travelling clothes and fastened a heavy cloak over herself. Looking ready to withstand a blizzard she glanced at the crates of supplies that she and Adam had tied down in the corner of the ship the night before.

"I'm concerned about your decision to replace so much of the flour with parsnips" she said as her brow creased.

"Why the worry?" he asked.

"Well, a generous scoop of flour can make enough bread to keep a whole family on their feet for a day while a parsnip of the same weight is barely enough food for one" Elsa replied.

"Yes, but you can put one parsnip in the ground and grow a plant that yields ten more. You cannot do that with flour" he said.

"But the Finns are starving right now" she complained.

"And the reason is because they just experienced their wettest summer in over a century. All of the root vegetables that they depend upon to make it through the winter rotted in the ground. If that happens again this summer we will still be able to grow parsnips which we can both give to other people to eat and give to others to plant in their own fields" explained Adam.

"Oh Lord, these are those stupid parsnips from that mud experiment that you started after we visited that Czech monk." Elsa sighed with exasperation.

"He's an abbot, not a monk. And listen, Brother Mendel is on to something, his work might just..."

Suddenly, a wave forced the boat sideways and they were both thrown down into the pile of blankets and hay that Elsa had been lying in. The fierce howl of the arctic storm echoed down the staircase.

"If this is the Finnish spring I'd hate to see their winter" Adam laughed.

Elsa smiled grimly. "And you were all worried about famine being the problem. See, we aren't going to die of starvation. We'll freeze to death long before that" she laughed.

"Lovely thought, but I have no plans to freeze to death either" he stated flatly. He nimbly got to his feet and pulled a map out of his coat.

"So while you were asleep I was looking at our route through Helsinki, the one that we were planning on making. Realistically, given this weather, it has crossed my mind that, short as the distance is, we might not make it to the countryside near the village of Espoo by nightfall" he said.

Elsa's hand reached out of its hiding place inside her cloak and gently squeezed his own. Her soft blue eyes gently met his.

By God was she beautiful. If only he had been born into the same generation as her. Feelings of warmth stirred within him. The thoughts and sensations caught Adam off guard and he immediately started reflecting upon them.

Were these experiences new? He did not think so. He had experienced them before and they had, like now, sometimes been tinged with a sense of conflict, but there was something more to it all that he could not quite figure out.

Elsa leaned close and whispered into his ear "The Lord is walking with us this day. We will make it."

The smell of honey on her hair and the feel of her breath on his ear proved intensely distracting as he realised how great   his longing actually was.

Place: Psychiatry Office, Boston, Massachusetts

Date: April 6th, 2018

Time: 1:05pm

"I'm sorry" apologised Adam, aware that he had fallen into a long pause.

"It isn't a problem" advised Wolstone, quickly realising that he was moving into an area that was hardly one he was experienced in dealing with.

Sex was certainly not something he was uncomfortable with. It came up frequently with his adult patients who had either seen rape during tours of duty or, worse, experienced it first hand in detention centres and prisons. However, dealing with the matter of sexual awareness in children was hardly his forte. He knew enough to be honest and direct on the subject though.

"Adam, do you know how babies are made?" asked the psychiatrist.

"You mean... biologically?" asked the boy.

"Sure" replied Wolstone, uncertain as to what sort of answer he was going to get from an eleven-year old.

"Well, a sperm cell fertilises an egg cell, doesn't it? That's what they've taught us at school" offered Adam.

It was certainly a more scientific response than Wolstone had anticipated, but he wanted to hear more.

"And the sperm cell meets the egg cell how?" asked the doctor.

Adam sensed that he should feel uncomfortable answering the question, but found that he didn't at all.

"It happens when a woman and a man have sex" replied Adam in a matter of fact manner.

"Is it wrong that I am attracted to Elsa in the dream?" asked Adam bluntly.

There it was, the question that Wolstone himself was pondering, set out in the open.

"What do you think?" asked the psychiatrist.

"I do think it is wrong" offered the boy, feeling mildly unsettled making such a bold statement while still not entirely sure that it was actually wrong.

"Why?" asked Wolstone.

"Well, probably because of my age I guess" offered Adam, shrugging his shoulders.

"Because you are so much older than her?" asked Wolstone.

"Yes and no. I am definitely much older than her and that does create a sense of wrongness, but if anything it is our relationship that makes it wrong" replied the child.

"Do you mean the parental feeling that you mentioned earlier" asked Wolstone.

"Yes, that's exactly it. Really, it is as if age is meaningless and all of the discomfort comes from the type of relationship we have" answered Adam.

Wolstone considered the statement carefully and tried to figure out how it might, in some way, relate to pre-teen sexual development. Conflicted sexual feelings towards mature women, like aunts and teachers, were common enough for the age of eleven. At least, that was what he thought. It had been ages since he had properly studied the matter in a university setting or read up on the latest in the academic literature. However, little boys having conflicted feelings towards young women while visualising themselves as older was way beyond anything Wolstone had ever learned. He made a note to make sure to talk to the child at a later time about his interactions with girls in his daily life and decided to move on.

"So what happens when you and Elsa reach Helsinki?" asked the doctor.

Place: Helsinki

Date: 1867

Time: Day

The high street of Helsinki was like something out of a nightmare. To Adam, it seemed as if the snow was trying its best to cover over the atrocities of the famine, but it was not falling heavily enough to entirely block from view the corpses littering the sides of the road.

Covered in their heaviest coats and blankets, Adam and Elsa drove the horses onwards, but it was no easy task. They had seen dozens of emaciated people on their way into the city and, due to the foul conditions; they had been forced to move on without stopping to help.

The situation was rapidly growing increasingly alarming. More and more desperate souls were emerging on the streets and, noticing that Adam and Elsa had a wagon loaded with supplies, came to them petitioning for aid in great numbers. There were far too many for them to help and they were not stocked to arrive and immediately deliver large amounts of food. They were carrying the tools necessary to bake bread and aid farmers but handouts in Helsinki had never been part of the plan.

They turned a corner into a square with a dramatic white cathedral capped with three dark green copper domes encrusted with thick icicles.

"This is Senate Square" advised Adam as he took a quick look at his map. "We are right on course." It was then that disaster   struck.

Adam and Elsa were suddenly engulfed by a sea of skeletal hands. The throng of starved people was so thick that the horses struggled to move through without trampling any of them. Elsa's eyes went wide with fear as the starving citizens of Helsinki descended.

"Forward" Adam said gently.

She did not move the reins. The hands were beginning to claw at his cloak. He could hear them trying to force the lock on the back door of the wagon.

"Elsa, forward" he said more sternly.

Still nothing. He reached over to shake her. Elsa had gone rigid, frozen with fear. Trying to take the reins proved pointless, in her panic, she was gripping them too tightly. The sea of desperation was growing overwhelming. Adam cringed as he heard the sound of wood splintering behind him. The back door of the wagon was literally about to be ripped off its hinges.

Pushing aside a gaunt man climbing his way onto the wagon, Adam leaned dangerously far forward over the end of the wagon and slapped the horses hard with the back of his hand. They immediately broke into a run. The burst of speed forced the crowd to scatter but also caused Adam to lose his footing. As the wagon raced out of Senate Square, he found himself falling towards the icy cobblestones.

With nearly electric reflexes, he instinctively grabbed hold of the bridling, but it was not enough to save him. His legs struck the frozen ground hard and were swiftly dragged into the deadly gap below the wagon. The pull was immense.

Adam could taste the bitter adrenaline in his mouth and, in the moment, spotted the nail beds on his fingers turning bluish-purple under the strain. His muscles ached with fatigue but, in spite of the exhaustion, they surged with an energy that prevented him from falling further. He knew he should have died in that moment but found the strength nonetheless to pull himself up.

Exhausted from the exertion, Adam dropped heavily into the seat atop the wagon. He threw a quick glance at Elsa, she was breathing, but still in a state of shock from the troubling experience.

The dirt and ice encrusted cobblestones of Helsinki gave way to roads of powdery snow as they travelled deeper into the countryside. Pastures dotted with icicle-covered cottages transformed into pine covered plains and, bitter as their initial travels had been, Adam's heart was warmed as the arctic clouds gave way to sunnier skies.

"That looks pretty good" Adam said pointing at a field as they crested a small hill.

"What looks pretty good?" asked Elsa.

"That patch of land between those two hills over there" he said pointing to the east.

She looked more closely and could see a meadow where the snows had retreated. A dilapidated shack sat nearby.

"You don't think someone has already claimed it do you" Elsa asked while pointing to the shack.

"If the land was claimed, it was claimed a long time ago. For all we know they may not even be alive any more" Adam said.

They drove the wagon up and over a lonely road surrounded by pines as they neared the meadow. The closer they got, the more Adam was sure that this would be an ideal place to settle. Considering the terrible state that it was, Adam realised the shack could not have recently been abandoned. There was no doubt the ramshackle little building had experienced several serious winters without seeing any repair.

Adam pulled the wagon to a halt. Elsa eagerly hopped down and, as she did so, she heard something snap. At first Adam thought it was just a branch, but as he looked over the edge of the wagon, he realised it was the forelimb of a wolf attached to an emaciated canid corpse. Instinctively, Elsa pulled her cloak closer around herself. Adam stepped down next to her and started to tether up the horses.

"I'm curious. Of all the places you could have picked to go and help people, why here?" he asked.

Elsa paused to look at him aghast. "There's a famine Adam" she said.

"Yes, I know that. But people are suffering in places that are both safer and closer to home" he said.

"They are suffering far more here though and I think this is where God would want us to go" Elsa said pointedly.

Adam carried down another crate from the wagon, pondering the concept of God wanting him to go anywhere. "Do you think God judges us based upon the amount of suffering we alleviate?" he asked.

Elsa looked down for a moment. "I… I'm not sure" she said. He handed her a sack of parsnips to carry down.

"Neither am I. So why set yourself such a dangerous task" he pressed.

"I don't know. After being raised at the church and always being provided for…" she trailed off.

"You felt indebted?" Adam asked.

"Yes. I think so" she replied.

"You know, you didn't ask to be abandoned any more than you asked to be cared for. There is no debt…" he said.

Adam briefly recoiled at his own words. This was an old bit of the dream. It was one that he had not experienced for some time. Why was he suddenly able to recall it now? Rather than risk losing it, he simply allowed the dream to flow.

"It's different when you grow up knowing you had parents who didn't care" she said quietly.

"You don't know that. They could have been ill" he advised.

"I suppose" she said.

"Or worse, they might have been in some sort of danger that forced them to give you up" he added.

"What were yours like?" she asked, eager to change the direction of the conversation.

"Who? My parents?" Adam asked.

"Yes. You must have had some" she enquired.

"Well, yes, I did" he stammered.

"They have passed away?" she asked.

"Yes…" he replied, growing withdrawn.

Adam himself winced at his own response. His words with Elsa were flowing with the dream, happening almost automatically. Even so, there was something about them that was foreign. There was also, what was it? Anguish?

"If it is hard for you to talk about them…" she said.

"No, no. They have been gone for so many years… It isn't that" he said.

It was a lie, or at least a partial one, he knew that much, but he wasn't sure where the pain was coming from.

"Then what is it?" she asked.

"I don't think we got on particularly well" he said.

"Why?" Elsa asked.

"Honestly, I don't think I ever met my father's expectations" Adam replied.

"He wanted you to be something you were not?" she asked.

"Hmm. I never thought about it in that way but, yes, actually" he said.

"You know, I saw that all the time with the children from the town in Latin class" Elsa said in a matter of fact tone as she started pitching their simple cloth tent.

"Really? How so?" asked Adam.

"Oh, there were some who tried to continue the family trade and just could not do it well. There were others who aimed to make money and failed. There were many who tried to be people who they simply were not" Elsa said, sighing briefly as she looked him in the eye.

"Yes, do not think for a moment that your burden is one that only you carry. There are many who struggle because they do not think their fathers approve of who they are" she explained.

Now keenly focused on the conversation, Adam stopped lifting crates and looked at Elsa with both a sense of curiosity and hope.

"You think it is not a matter of choice but a matter of who you are at birth?" he asked.

"If you mean, do I think God makes us who we are, then yes. I think so" she replied.

"But we can change over time... with enough time..." he queried.

"Are you asking can a man born good go bad?" she asked.

"Yes, or vice versa. Can a child born a monster turn to a life of virtue" Adam asked.

Even though it was just a dream, Adam could feel considerable emotion invested in the question.

Elsa paused for a moment, looking at the expression on his face carefully. She was sensing something; of that much Adam was sure. He could feel it too, but he couldn't quite work out what it was. A sense of desperation perhaps? Elsa exhaled slowly as she made up her mind.

"It must have been horrible" she said, reaching out to stroke his cheek.

"You have no idea" he replied, eyes drifting towards the melting snow bank as an uncomfortable silence drifted over them.

"Never mind that. It was a long time ago. Come, let us build a farm, grow some food and feed people" he said with a weak smile.

Place: Psychiatry Office, Boston, Massachusetts

Date: April 6th, 2018

Time: 1:12pm

"Forgive me for interrupting again, but I am curious Adam, what do you think about that question?" asked the doctor.

The boy looked at him with curiosity. "Which question?" he asked.

"Whether we are born to be the way we are?" asked Wolstone.

"Do you mean like, if you were born to be a psychiatrist and if my dad was born to be an engineer?" asked Adam.

"Well, not exactly, but sure, answer that question first if you like" replied Wolstone.

"I guess I think our abilities determine a lot. Like my dad for instance, he's really good with numbers and so all the engineering comes easily to him" said Adam.

"What about with regards to how we behave towards one another?" asked Wolstone.

Adam pondered the question for a moment before answering.

"That's more of a choice I think" he answered tentatively.

"You mean, bad people choose to be bad and good people choose to be   good?" asked the doctor.

"Mostly yes, but I don't think it's always true" answered the boy.

"How so?" asked Wolstone.

"Well, think about the situation in Syria right now" said Adam.

Wolstone was impressed by the child's awareness of current events and paused in surprise for a moment.

Adam looked at the doctor and found himself amazed that perhaps this learned man might not actually know about the Syrian civil war.

"You do know about their civil war, right?" asked Adam.

"Yes, yes, of course. Sorry, go on" said the psychiatrist.

"Okay, well think about what a kid my age would have to go through to survive over there. He'd have to steal food, steal clothing, and possibly even kill people to get by" explained the child.

Wolstone nodded and motioned Adam to continue while feeling genuinely stunned by both the boy's knowledge and the depth with which he was processing the dire humanitarian situation.

"So... stealing and murder. We classify both those things as bad behaviours and people who engage in them are called bad people, but are they really?" asked Adam.

"What do you think?" enquired the doctor.

"I've thought about it a lot, and I don't think it's fair. If a situation that you are in forces you to do these things

69

that we label as bad, I am not sure they really are" said the boy.

"What role do personal feelings play in all of this? Does it matter if a person forced to do bad things by his or her situation actually enjoys or hates doing the bad things?" asked Wolstone.

"I don't think so. At least, I do not think it matters at the specific moment when they are forced to do the stealing or killing. But I do think it matters if liking doing these things leads people to continue doing them even when their situation no longer requires them to. Does that make sense?" replied Adam.

It was wisdom that was well beyond the years of any eleven year old Wolstone had ever met. In fairness, it was wisdom that rivalled that of many adults he knew. It left him wondering why a child, who could not possibly have ever known the horrors of Syria, Iraq or Afghanistan, would even spend time contemplating such matters.

"Adam, how do you think you behave in general?" asked the doctor.

"What? In my life every day?" asked Adam.

Wolstone nodded.

"I think I am good" answered the boy.

"What do you think drives you to be good?" asked Wolstone.

"Well, I guess it is because I often feel dirty. As if I have done bad things" replied Adam.

The psychiatrist was transfixed by the response. Behaving as a beacon of virtue to compensate for having once behaved badly was common enough in adults who felt overwhelming guilt over past events, but it seemed odd to see such a psychological situation in a child.

"Have you done bad things?" asked the psychiatrist.

Adam paused for a moment to consider the matter.

"No" he answered carefully.

"You don't sound certain. Why do you think you feel dirty?" asked Wolstone.

"I don't know. Might it be because of the dreams? I mean, they are very violent" said Adam with an unsettling look of sobriety.

"Maybe. Would you mind telling me more about your experience with Elsa?" asked Wolstone.

"Sure, but the next piece of the dream that I can actually remember is later, after the snow and ice were gone" replied the boy.

"That's fine, tell me about it" encouraged the psychiatrist.

Place: Finland

Date: 1867

Time: Day

Adam looked forward from the back of their wagon. Elsa was upfront and handling the large line of desperate people who were waiting for any help that they could offer. He glanced down at the barrel of grain that he was shovelling into burlap bags. It wasn't much, but for people with nothing it would help.

"Please wait just a moment" Elsa called out in halting Finnish to the people in the line. There were at least three dozen of them, all clearly hungry, many worryingly thin. Elsa turned away from the crowd, stepped over a large hound sleeping behind her and hopped over a box of parsnips to get to Adam.

"We are going to need at least ten more, many of them completely full" she said, breathing heavily.

"Ten more? How many people are out there?" asked Adam.

"At least thirty, many with small children" she replied.

He passed her an armload of bags. "Here, give them these, but keep in mind, if we get this number next week, we won't even last the summer before we run out" he advised.

"And our crops?" Elsa asked.

"I already told you, they won't be ready until early autumn. Hand out the parsnips too but make sure they know that they are for planting not eating. We can't have another calamity like last week" he answered sharply.

Elsa returned to the front and handed out the grain to one needy family after the other. Adam came forward with a few more bags in his arms and helped her for the next few minutes as the line thinned.

"What do we have left back there?" Elsa asked.

"Some wheat, some barley, those broccoli leaves that you cut earlier and some cabbage. We are going to have to start seriously cutting back on what we give out until we replenish our supplies" he explained.

Elsa was about to respond when a shape at the end of the road caught her eye. It was an old woman slowly limping along followed by a number of children.

Adam wrinkled his brow, "Is that…"

The same lady with all the kids from the past four weeks… yes, I think so" Elsa replied.

"I keep forgetting, what was her name, Lissa? Nissa?" he asked.

"Keisa" said Elsa with a warm smile.

"Same bags as last time?" he asked.

"Do you have the heart to give any less?"

In response Adam turned around, went back to the supply space inside the wagon and brought forward the few bags that they had left. When he got back, Keisa was close, leaning heaving on her cane.

"Is there nothing left?" the old lady asked.

"We do not have much, but we knew you'd get here so we set a little aside" Elsa answered in her crude Finnish.

Adam handed over two bags.

"Bless you both" Keisa said as the oldest of the children, a little boy of no more than twelve years in age, looked over at the hound sleeping on the wagon next to Elsa's feet.

"And may The Lord bless you" replied Elsa automatically to the old woman as she watched the boy's interaction with the dog.

Elsa marvelled at the fact that the little boy's hands were shaking.

"He is fearful of the dog? He was not this way three weeks ago" Elsa said.

"Pekka has changed much since his father died. Now, even the donkey scares him" explained Keisa with a small chuckle. Pekka, for his part, seemed unamused.

Elsa walked over to the boy and knelt down on the ground next to him. "She's really very friendly." The boy looked at her nervously. Adam smiled at the interaction; Elsa was always good with children.

"Would you like to pet her?" Elsa asked.

Pekka shook his head and pulled back a bit.

"And why not?" she asked.

"I'm scared" replied the boy.

"But why? You were not scared of her before" Elsa said.

The boy's eyes grew large and glassy. His hands went limp as the colour drained from his face. Elsa reached over and stroked Pekka's shoulder gingerly to try and relax him a bit.

"You know… I don't even remember my father, he left so early in my life, but things turned out okay" Elsa whispered in her rudimentary Finnish.

"Will you be here every week?" the boy asked.

"Every week. Yes. And you know our farm is right there over the hill from yours if you ever want to visit" she said.

Keisa cleared her throat and the children rapidly gathered around her as she prepared to hobble back up the road.

"Again, thank you" said the old lady.

"Of course Keisa, and as before, if you ever need any help…" said Elsa.

"Yes, I am still thinking it over" the old woman replied.

And with that, Keisa went back up the road with the children following behind. As they left, Adam and Elsa turned their attention towards putting the remaining supplies away. They worked in silence for many minutes as the summer sun started to slip behind the hills. Then, when the evening came, so too did the howls of the wolves. The hound sprang to her feet and looked every which way with sudden attention as the sounds reached her ears. But Adam and Elsa had grown used to it. Hopping back on top of the wagon, they slowly started to ride along the road to their cabin.

"You are encouraging her to pass along a few of the children to us" Adam asked.

Elsa nodded solemnly.

"Seven children would be a burden on a farm with healthy parents. For a single grandmother, I can scarcely think how she survives" he said.

Place: Psychiatry Office, Boston, Massachusetts

Date: April 6th, 2018

Time: 1:19pm

Adam stopped speaking and looked at how fast Dr Wolstone was writing. Never before had anyone asked for him to recall so many of his dreams nor had anyone ever been so interested in the details within them. While he still doubted this psychiatrist was really going to be able to help him banish the nightmares, he had to admit, he was beginning to have a sense of hope.

Wolstone looked up at Adam. "And?" asked the doctor.

"What?" asked Adam.

"Well, it doesn't stop there does it?" asked Wolstone with interest.

"No. There is more, but it is very fragmented" said the boy.

"What happens to Keisa? What about the children" asked the psychiatrist, keen to find out if the topics of adoption or orphaned children would again find their way into one of Adam's dreams.

"I think there are tools..." said Adam.

"Tools? What kinds of tools?" asked Wolstone.

"Stuff for use on the farm. I think I am looking for them" said Adam.

"Where?" asked Wolstone.

"In the field. There was a hoe and a shovel and..." the boy trailed off.

"Had they been taken by someone?" asked the doctor, trying to help.

"No" replied Adam, mildly frustrated by the interruption. "And there is a sound in the air. It is evening. I am afraid of something" said the boy.

Wolstone scanned his notes and saw the mention of a sound earlier that might prove frightening but decided against helping just yet. It might boost Adam's confidence if he could pull the dream together on his own, he thought.

"An axe. That's the tool that I find. It's lying near bushes by the edge of the field. And the reason I particularly want the axe is because I can hear wolves howling" said Adam, rather pleased that he was reassembling the dream.

"Very good" said Wolstone, "do you want to carry on?"

Place: Finland

Date: 1867

Time: Night

The wolves howled a macabre chorus in the distance that raised the hairs on the back of Adam's neck. As he shuffled around the field in the pale shadows of the night he first discovered a hoe, then a shovel and finally an axe. As he picked the last tool up, he found himself rather reassured to have the weapon in hand. It was, admittedly, just a dream, but there seemed more to it than that...

As always, his legs walked him over to the simple storage shed that he had built behind the cabin. When he opened the door of the shed and started putting the various tools away he was brought to immediate attention by a rustling coming from bushes not more than a few feet away. Quietly he put down the hoe and held up the axe. Adam stalked up to the bushes. Stepping closer and chilled with fear, he swept aside the branches expecting the worst. But the worst was not what he found.

There, shivering in the darkness and looking up at him with filthy tear-streaked eyes, was Pekka.

The wolf howls were growing louder and, on instinct, Adam scooped the boy up with his left arm and went inside.

As soon as Elsa saw the child, she grabbed a thick wool blanket and wrapped it around him.

"What has happened?" she asked, clearly nervous.

"Grandmamma has become very ill, her breathing, it is bad. She is coughing and there is blood. We have no more food..." he said, shivering under the blanket.

Elsa picked up a kettle from the top of the stove and poured a cup of mint tea for the child.

"Drink this, it should warm you" she said.

"What did you tell the others to do?" Adam asked the boy in the best remedial Finnish he could manage.

"I told them to stay with grandmamma" the boy replied.

Adam looked over at Elsa. They exchanged bleak expressions. Watching them, the boy's eyes grew wider.

"Was that the wrong thing to do?" he asked.

"No, no. You have done a good thing" consoled Adam.

He reassuringly put his hands on Pekka's shoulders, turned towards Elsa, and switched into German.

"We will have to go to Keisa's. Tonight" he said.

"You think she will still be alive?" Elsa replied, also in German.

"I doubt it" he said sadly.

"Then why rush out now? The wolves..." she asked with apprehension.

"Because I am worried about the children being near her sickness" replied Adam sternly.

"Oh God, you think it will move to them?" she said with a knowing look.

"Many people have been dying lately from a cough that causes blood to come out of the lungs. Everything I have read makes me think the longer the children stay near her the higher their chances of developing the same disease are" he said.

Elsa nodded in understanding, already reaching for her coat and boots.

In moments they were out the door and on the wagon. Adam cracked the whip hard to drive the horses into a near gallop. Next to him, bathed in the moon's cool light, Elsa held Pekka close and translated for Adam as Pekka gave her directions.

The roads leading to Keisa's farm were in a dire state. Overgrown with vines and partially flooded, Adam was forced to bring the horses to a halt short of her property by a few hundred meters. He jumped down from the wagon, lantern in hand, with Elsa and Pekka close behind.

Stepping over numerous creepers and holes filled with stagnant water, they made their way ever nearer. Insects buzzed around them and then, as they passed a copse of trees, they caught their first glimpse of the house. It was in total disrepair with paint peeling off all the walls, wooden beams falling loose, cracked stones along the foundation, and broken hinges on the windows. It looked nearly uninhabitable.

Suddenly, an inhuman screech pierced the silence of the night. Elsa jumped and held Pekka tightly. Adam stopped in his tracks. He knew it was only an owl but a quick look at Elsa and the boy revealed them both to be pale as ghosts. They would not be of more help. Indeed, the chances were high that the boy would both a liability if there was any real danger.

"This will only stress him more. He showed us the way, that is enough." Adam whispered to Elsa in German.

"Yes" she said through pale lips.

"Go back to the wagon and close yourself inside. I will be as fast I can" he told her.

"But Adam, if there is danger..." she said, reaching out to him defiantly.

He turned towards her with impenetrable severity.

"The grandmother is ill or dead, I can handle either while collecting the children. Go back and wait for me" he said, leaving no room for negotiation in his voice.

Elsa gave him a grim look but turned back just the same.

The door to the house was badly rotted and the hinges rusted to the point of being nearly broken. As his lantern light poured in, it glinted off piles of worn and rotted equipment on the floor of the front room. He noted a cabinet in the corner on its side with junk strewn over and around it. A foul smell assaulted his nose. Garbage. A mix of food waste and what he thought might be human waste was thrown about everywhere.

As he looked a bit closer, his eye caught a glimpse of something red mixed in amongst the piles of junk. Blood. Fresh blood. He drew his hunting knife, threw his cloak over his shoulder and stepped carefully further into the shambles.

If the front room was bad, the kitchen was worse. Supplies were strewn everywhere, seemingly tossed about with heaps of rotten waste and mixed, ominously, with more of the blood. A sudden creaking sound to his side startled him. A door, out the back of the kitchen, was blowing ever so slightly in the night-time breeze. And then he heard it, the sound of nervous breathing.

At first Adam was sure the breathing was coming from beyond the creaking door, but as he listened more carefully, he realised it was much nearer. Somewhere inside. Was it inside the kitchen? He rotated his lantern around the space to get a better look at the mess. There were a few cabinets, but the sound was not coming from any of them. Then he spotted a ladder, attached to the corner wall and going up to a tiny loft.

Adam swiftly stepped over the refuse, tucked his knife away into his boots, put the lantern on the ground and started climbing. At the top, the sound of the breathing was much louder. He swung open the flat panel door in the ceiling and was met by the faces of five intensely terrified children.

"All is okay. Come. Come" he said as calmly as he could in his broken Finnish.

"Sussihukka! Sussihukka!" the children stammered in fear.

Adam had heard that word before, but he was at a loss for what it was.

Sussihukka… Help? Danger? Both made perfect sense under the current circumstances, but he really wasn't sure and, frankly, it didn't matter. He had to get them out.

"Come" he said more firmly, reaching out his old arm to encourage them to climb down.

He did his best to show them that, at least, he was not afraid. It worked. One by one they slowly started making their way down, huddling in the corner beneath the ladder.

"This way" he said, pointing towards the front room and eager to get them out of the hovel. They started to walk and it was then that he saw more. Out of the corner of his eye he caught sight of a bit of movement, just beyond the blowing kitchen door in the back garden. Without even thinking about it, he leaned out the door ever so slightly to get a better look at whatever it was that he saw. Horrified, he realised the moving thing was a gnawed human limb jiggling about below a shrub and lying in a pool of intestines. He only had a split second to question why the limb, clearly dead, had been moving around amidst the pool of gore when a mouth full of fangs came lunging out at him from the dense vegetation.

Sussihukka… wolf. That was it.

The children screamed and scattered. The wolf knocked Adam to the ground as it slashed and bit at him. He struggled but his old muscles were no match for the powerful animal. He rolled to the side to try and get the predator off, but he was not fast enough to avoid its jaws as they ripped into his shoulder. Blood poured out of him. The pain was intense, but not intense enough for him to forget his knife. With the beast latched onto his shoulder

Adam swiftly took the opportunity to stab the creature in the throat. Shaking wildly and shrieking in pain, the wounded wolf ran for the bushes, taking Adam's deeply inserted knife with it.

Adam quickly scrambled to his feet only to see several sets of green eyes flickering at him in the darkness. As he looked at the ground in the moonlight, he realised, there was blood everywhere outside, and along with it were bits of muscle, bone and organs. This was the remaining gore of a full adult body that the animals were feeding upon. These wolves were not actually hunting him; they were fighting to protect their already claimed prey.

In an instant, the rest of the beasts were lunging. He dodged the first two and watched as they landed on a pile of garbage in the kitchen. The third came towards his leg, biting into his boot and forcing him to fight to maintain his balance. He struggled to break from its grasp but was simply not strong enough. It pulled him down, bit hard into his other shoulder and pinned him.

The two wolves, now inside, turned their attention towards easier prey. The children's' screaming was intense as they ran to hide behind dilapidated pieces of furniture. Adam wanted to help. Indeed, his soul was crying to have the strength to break free from the vice-like jaws of the wolf that had him on the ground. As he strained to fight it, he heard thunder in the distance and started to feel a surge of strength flow through his veins.

His hand, deathly pale from the loss of blood, clenched into a fist and guided by muscles that he hardly knew he had, came crashing down on the wolf's head. With a crack, the bones in the animal's skull splintered as it dropped lifeless.

In seconds, Adam was in the kitchen. The wolves paced back and forth as they lunged at the children. Two of the kids were already wounded with bites. Guided by fury and seemingly unhindered by his injuries, Adam interposed himself between the beasts and the children. The wolves wasted no time in attacking. One lashed out at his throat, but his arm, now the colour of a fresh bruise and crisscrossed with scars, struck the creature in mid-air with tremendous force. The wolf sailed across the room and snapped its spine as it smashed into the wall. The second beast went for his leg. It managed a solid bite but did not live long enough to dig its teeth deep into Adam's flesh as his fingers quickly wrapped themselves around the predator's neck and, with nail beds as blue as ice, crushed the very life out of the animal.

The children raced to the wagon and, ushered by Elsa, climbed inside next to Pekka. Adam followed, covered in gashes and cuts.

"My God. What happened to you" Elsa asked.

"Wolves. Lots of them" he replied as collapsed into the passenger seat and Elsa grabbed a hold of the reins.

"What? Inside the house?" she asked.

"And the back garden" he added.

"Keisa?" she asked.

"You don't want to know."

"Yah!" Elsa cried as she cracked the reins and the wagon shot into the darkness of the forest road.

Place: Psychiatry Office, Boston, Massachusetts

Date: April 6th, 2018

Time: 1:29pm

"Adam, I'd like to talk to you for a moment about this transformation you keep describing" said Wolstone.

"What transformation?" the boy asked.

"You know, the one where you see your arms become covered in scars. You described it happening when you fell off the wagon in Helsinki and just now when you were fighting with the wolves" the doctor explained.

"I just fought off the wolves with my fists" Adam answered.

"Yes, I know, but you said that your arms became covered with scars and that your nail beds turned blue" Wolstone enquired.

"I'm not sure I understand what you are asking" Adam replied, looking at Wolstone with an honest sense of confusion.

As much as Adam's situation perplexed him, this was something that Wolstone had seen before. It was not uncommon for the war veterans suffering from post traumatic stress disorder to tell him their stories in great detail and then be utterly incapable of recalling certain horrific specifics when asked about them later. It was, admittedly, an annoying aspect of the condition, but it was also entirely normal.

Some psychiatrists felt that this was a conscious decision being made by patients to avoid talking about isolated moments that were particularly hard for them to cope with, but many argued it was an unconscious defence mechanism that the brain used to protect itself from becoming unhinged when exposed to truly unsettling events. Regardless of which theory was correct, Wolstone was certain this was what he was seeing in the boy and bewildered by why it was there at all. What could the child possibly be protecting himself from? He hadn't been to war or ever been attacked. What pre-adoption experiences could he possibly be reacting to? It was, undeniably, as mysterious as it was challenging.

Wolstone let out a long, slow breath.

Adam could tell that he was frustrating the psychiatrist and immediately felt badly about it. Dr Wolstone was clearly trying hard to help him, harder than anyone he had ever met before, and it bothered him that he wasn't giving the doctor the information that he really needed to hear. Adam tried again, as desperately as he could, to focus on this idea of transformation that the psychiatrist was asking him about, but again, he came up with nothing.

"I'm sorry if I'm not telling you what you want to hear. I really am trying to be helpful" said Adam genuinely.

Wolstone felt for the boy. His eyes looked exhausted. It was clear that the nightmares were exacting a terrible toll.

"Not a worry. You are telling me what you can and, honestly, the more you explore these dreams, the more the both of us will discover" said Wolstone.

"You mean that by describing the dreams you think I will remember pieces of them that I normally have not noticed before?" asked Adam.

"That and more. I suspect there are dreams you are having that you are not even aware of when you wake up" explained the psychiatrist.

"Do you think making me aware of these dreams will help me to get rid of the bad ones?" asked Adam.

"I think it is a first step, a big first step, into working out why you are having such trouble making it through the night" said Wolstone.

"I hope you're right" said Adam.

"Trust me, we'll get there" Wolstone replied encouragingly.

Adam smiled faintly.

"Do you think you can manage for twenty or so more minutes?" asked the doctor.

The boy nodded and continued.

Place: Finland

Date: 1867

Time: Day

Adam emerged from a thicket of pines with an armload of firewood. He felt some pain in his shoulder and when he looked down upon it, he saw a bandage. He found some others on various bits of his body and immediately realised these had been left over from the wolf attack. While his skin was wrinkled with age, his wounds seemed to be healing well.

The voices of children pulled him back to attention and suddenly Pekka, along with two of the other children, emerged from the forest, each carrying small bundles of wood. Together they walked back to the cabin and, as Adam glanced over at the henhouse, he felt words start trickling out of his mouth in much improved Finnish.

"Pekka, after we drop this off, can you check the hens again for eggs?" he asked.

Pekka nodded and scampered off as the group set the wood down next to an already large pile adjacent to the stable. Adam hopped up the steps onto a newly built porch and opened the front door. The fire in the hearth provided instant relief from the chill outside. Indeed, the difference in temperature forced a grim realisation into Adam's mind, winter was not far off.

He saw Elsa busy in the kitchen cleaning root vegetables and handing them off to one of Pekka's siblings to place in a cellar dug out beneath the floorboards. Then, as Adam looked around the room, his gaze drifted to one of the children, a little girl wrapped in blankets by the fire and lying very still. Elsa looked up at him with concern.

"How is she?" Adam asked.

"Not good. I think she is getting warmer, but I don't have the feel for it that you do" Elsa replied in German.

"Hmm. Let's see" he said as he stepped over to the girl and felt her forehead. She did not move much, barely tracking him with her eyes. Adam sighed deeply, pulled the blanket down and put his ear to her chest.

Adam never understood this bit of the dream. He wasn't entirely sure what he was doing, but he always had a sense of sadness. He seemed to just know that she was dying.

"Johan did not show up to trade for barley yesterday" Elsa added.

Johan... thought Adam. A neighbour perhaps?

"He is ill too?" he asked.

"From his wife's description, I think so" said Elsa.

Pekka entered with a basket of eggs, pausing for a moment to look at his sister in the blankets before handing them to Elsa.

"Bless you sweetheart" she said, kissing him tenderly on the forehead.

"Just put them over there" she added, pointing to a spot in the corner of the kitchen.

The fire in the hearth was beginning to burn down.

"Adam, do you mind giving it some more wood and fanning it a bit?" asked Elsa.

Adam did as he was asked. He threw in the wood and gave it a good, full breath of air. The flames flared upwards and with them, came smoke, ash and a dream of death.

Place: Finland

Date: 1868

Time: Night

Adam wiped away a layer of frost from the inside of the window and, with eyes that felt heavy with sleep-deprivation, he stared out at a grim landscape of soulless white.

He'd been here before. He knew this nightmare, it was one that had haunted him from early on. A shiver went down his spine as he sensed the horrors ahead.

The farm was blanketed in snow. He could still just about see the ground where the wagon had left tracks on the way out to the road perhaps a day or two earlier. It was also visible beneath a canopy that was sticking out in front of the porch. And then there were the graves.

Beyond the trail carved by the wagon was a smaller one running just fifteen feet over to two piles of stones. Looking upon them brought pain... and phantoms.

A memory within the dream stirred and he could see Elsa dragging her feet in agony as she sobbed on her way back along the snowy trail to the cabin.

Adam realised that, given the weather, the path to the graves would normally have vanished beneath the flakes within days, but Elsa was routinely visiting them. She refused to let go.

Turning away from the window he looked to the hearth in the grey light of the winter afternoon. Three of the children were already asleep, curled together under a blanket by the fire with the dog breathing gently next to them.

Adam knew that it was best for them to stay separated from those who were ill. Quarantined. That was the term. He did not know how he knew it, but he did. He had read it somewhere, at some point in a book. Was it in the church in Prussia? With the priest? No. He was certain that wasn't it. It was irritating to not be able to remember. Like having a splinter, stubbornly stuck just beneath the skin. Frustrated, Adam pushed the thought away and, for the sake of gaining Dr Wolstone's insight, allowed the nightmare to unfold.

He lifted a candle from the table, walked down the narrow hall and opened the door at the end knowing what was behind it. On the single bed in the small space was Pekka in a nearly comatose state. Adam felt an urge to pull away but his arm, guided by the dream, brought the dim light of the candle ever closer. The boy was wasting away. His breathing, even in sleep, was ragged. With an expertise that he barely understood, Adam unconsciously reached for Pekka's carotid artery. The pulse was so weak. Lifting the child's gaunt hand, he pinched the ends of his fingers gently while watching his face. He knew there was supposed to be a response, what it would look like, he was not quite sure, but something inside him told him that it would be obvious. Nothing. With skin as grey as ash, the boy was falling fast into Death's grasp. It was then that Adam noticed himself gazing upon his own hands holding the boy's. He was so old now. So old and here was a boy who had barely begun to live. Tears welled in Adam's eyes. It was an unbearable tragedy.

Adam sighed deeply as he lifted himself up from Pekka's bedside and made his way to his own room. There, he found Elsa. She was as pale as he had ever seen her, sitting upright in her bed, reading the scriptures. She had become a ghost of her former self. Gone was the indomitable will and courage he had seen in the eighteen-year old when they had left Prussia only a year earlier. He wanted to hide his sadness, but as she put down her book and gazed at him, he knew immediately that his feelings were being read.

"Maybe if we took him to Helsinki..." she offered.

"No. It is too far and too cold. Look what happened when we took Tanja and Aamu" he said sadly.

The words flowed out of his mouth automatically. Adam was not even sure what he was talking about, but there were strong emotions connected to what he was saying and he felt the misery gnaw at him as he spoke the names of the dead children.

"But if he does not eat soon..." she trailed off.

"I know" he replied, looking down at the floor.

The conversation was like having a knife dug into his gut and yet, he knew that it was never here when he awoke from the nightmare.

She stood up weakly and wobbled on her feet.

"And what about you? Have you eaten tonight?" he asked.

"Does it matter?" Elsa asked.

"It does" he said.

"I don't feel for food" she replied, throwing a blanket over her shoulder as she stumbled towards the door.

"You have to eat" he said.

"I cannot" she whispered.

"Elsa" he said more forcefully.

"We are doing nothing! Nothing!" she gasped.

"We are not doing nothing! We are doing the best that we can" he said, with as much emotional support as he could throw into his voice.

She turned towards him and clutched his shirt as if she was clinging on for life.

"Then why do they keep dying?" she asked desperately.

"Because there was a famine Elsa and because plagues follow famines. That is the way the world works!" he replied.

He knew what he was saying to be true, but even so, the words were agony.

"But children... Oh God!" she cried, letting go of his shirt and collapsing to the floor in ever increasing sobs. Adam knelt down and embraced her as warmly as he could.

"Elsa, you must have courage, you must be strong" he said.

"I can't. I can't watch him die. No! Please! No!" she whimpered.

"It is going to be okay my love, it is going to be okay" he said as she wept. He stroked her back, whispering calming words in her ear and, slowly, her sobbing calmed and she drifted into the peace that only sleep could grant.

He lifted her limp body to the bed and looked upon her in the moonlight that spilled through the small window in the corner. She was both cold and white. In fact, to look upon her in this state was not much different from looking upon a fresh corpse. Slowly, a terrible realisation settled upon him like a heavy covering of snow... if the boy dies he will take her to the grave with him.

As he set Elsa down, Adam felt something drawing him to the corner of the room. He walked over and put his hands down to the wooden floor. There, his fingers found a false wooden panel covering a small compartment. The panel opened silently and, in the bleak shadows of the night, Adam found the small bronze box and worn leather-bound book he was searching for.

He gazed towards Elsa again, this time with feelings of determination and fear replacing his sorrow. He reached for the box, lifted it up, strode towards the door and walked out into the darkness of the hall.

Place: Psychiatry Office, Boston, Massachusetts

Date: April 6th, 2018

Time: 1:52pm

"You jumped from one dream to another in the middle" said Wolstone.

"I know. The images and environment of the first dream made me realise there was actually a related nightmare that I had been ignoring. It was like walking through a familiar building and suddenly noticing a door that I'd not opened in a long time" explained Adam.

"And how did it feel to enter that long abandoned space?" asked the doctor.

"I'm not going to lie, it was unpleasant. Actually, it really scared me" said the boy.

"Why?" asked Wolstone.

"Well, I guess I'm fearful that accessing the nightmare somehow makes it more real. That it increases the chances of it haunting me more often in the night" explained Adam.

Dr Wolstone let out a long sigh and ventured a brief glance at the afternoon sun as it pierced through the blinds in his office. It was nearly two. They would have to wrap up soon. Adam looked at the psychiatrist expectantly.

"Your worries are not unfounded. In the short term, you might have more vivid nightmares" explained

Wolstone. "But, by relating the worst of your dreams, you are giving me the opportunity to sift through the information found within them so I can help you to grapple with the deeply buried matters that are so bothering you. Hopefully, that will help us bring these nightmares to a decisive end" said the doctor.

"Do you think you can really do that?" asked Adam hopefully.

"Yes I do" said Wolstone with confidence, even though he was feeling a bit overwhelmed by the boy's situation at the moment.

A knock came at the door.

"Come in Catherine" said Wolstone.

Catherine opened the door slowly and poked her head in as unobtrusively as she could manage.

"I hope I am not interrupting?" she asked.

"No, not at all. We were just finishing up" replied Wolstone, waving her in.

"Adam, does the dream that you were telling me about just now, the one where you collect that box from beneath the floor and walk out into the hall, sometimes continue or does it always end right there" asked Wolstone.

"Always there" responded Adam.

"Have you ever thought about how the dream might end?" asked the doctor.

"You mean, when I am not sleeping during the day" asked Adam.

"Yes. Do you ever think about it when you are awake" said Wolstone.

"Hmm, sometimes I imagine Elsa starting to eat again" said Adam.

"Because the ill child... what's his name?" asked Wolstone.

"Pekka" replied Adam quietly.

"That's right, because Pekka starts getting better?" asked Wolstone.

Adam felt a pang in his gut as the doctor mentioned that name. Wolstone watched as the child's eyes grew sad.

"No, I cannot shake the feeling that he actually dies" said Adam.

A shadow of concern crept across Catherine's face as the dark words were spoken by her son.

"It's okay sweetheart, it's okay. Remember, it's just a dream. None of this is real" advised his mother as she moved in to smother him with a hug.

Embraced in her arms, Adam glanced towards Wolstone with a mixed look of frustration and discomfort.

Wolstone had to admit, he was frustrated by the woman's interference as well. He audibly cleared his throat and seemed to swiftly get the message across as Catherine let go and sat back down.

"So, if the boy does in fact die, how do you rationalise Elsa's survival?" asked the doctor.

"Because I kept the child alive" answered Adam.

The words made no sense to Adam as he spoke them, but he knew them to be true.

"What did you say?" asked Wolstone.

"I kept Pekka alive" said the boy quietly.

"But, I thought you said he did not get better?" asked Wolstone.

"I know. I don't think he does" Adam replied, feeling deep confusion about the matter.

Still baffled but also aware of the time, Wolstone made some last few notes and closed his book.

"Right, well, we've made some real progress today I think" said the doctor.

"It sounds it! You are certainly getting a lot more out of him about these dreams than I ever have" said Catherine.

"Adam, would you like to continue in a week or so" asked the doctor.

Adam did not have to think about it for long and nodded his head in response. He wasn't entirely sure whether this doctor's techniques were actually going to work, but there was no doubt in his mind that during their two hours together he had become aware of much that he had entirely forgotten about over the years.

"Okay, when would like to see him again?" asked Catherine.

Wolstone looked over his calendar.

"In around a week would be ideal, perhaps Saturday April 13th, I have a slot that day at two in the afternoon" he suggested.

"That should be fine" said Catherine, noting it in her phone as she stood up.

"Actually, Catherine, would you mind staying for a moment and having word?" asked Wolstone.

Catherine nodded.

"Adam it has been a pleasure meeting you" said the psychiatrist.

"You too" said Adam hopping out of his chair and offering his hand to the psychiatrist. He hadn't intended to do it. The action had happened nearly automatically, but, even so, it felt like the right thing to do.

Wolstone clasped the boy's offered hand with both of his.

Catherine smiled and laughed ever so slightly as the boy left the room

"He can be overly formal at times" she said.

"I can see that. Really, he is remarkable in many ways" said Wolstone.

"Are you thinking he is going to need medication" asked the mother, suddenly airing concerns that Wolstone fully expected to hear.

"Possibly, but not yet. Certainly not now while we are still exploring the basics of these dreams that he is having" explained the   doctor.

"They are disturbing aren't they" said Catherine.

"Yes, but they are also littered with details that could prove extremely useful in the long run" advised Wolstone.

"I always tell him to just try and remember that they are only dreams" continued Catherine, not really listening.

Wolstone paused for a moment upon hearing those words again and questioned whether it was worth it to correct her at this point at the risk of possibly making her even more nervous. Considering the state of his patient, it did not take him long to decide to take the risk.

"You know Catherine, for the moment, I'd actually like you to stop saying that to him" said Wolstone.

"What?" asked the mother.

"That they are just dreams" said the doctor.

"But they are. I mean, listen to them. They are ridiculous!" said Catherine with an uncomfortable smile.

"I'm not saying that they are anything other than dreams, but to Adam, they are much more. While they might seem like total fantasy to you, it could be harmful to disregard them so blatantly" explained the psychiatrist.

"Even if I am just trying to make him feel less scared?" asked the mother.

"Even if you are trying to make him less scared, yes" advised Wolstone.

"Okay, I will try" replied Catherine, lifting her handbag off the adjacent chair as she started to stand.

"Oh, actually, there is one more thing. Would you mind telling me what the circumstances were under which you adopted Adam" asked the doctor.

"Circumstances?" asked Catherine.

"Yes, was he adopted from out of the country, from a single mother who simply couldn't look after him any more, from an orphanage, that sort of thing?" asked Wolstone.

"Huh, I'm surprised he didn't tell you himself. He's already told all the kids at school. He was abandoned at the local hospital" said Catherine.

"I beg your pardon?" asked Wolstone, genuinely amazed.

"He was brought in by his parents with a very high fever. The hospital staff did all they could to try and bring it down, but it wasn't enough and he ended up in a coma. He wasn't stable enough to be discharged so the staff kept him and the medical bills just kept climbing. After a month his parents vanished" she explained.

"They what? People can't just vanish!" said Wolstone.

"They can when they are using fraudulent credit cards. I think the costs got too frighteningly high so they dumped their child at the hospital and fled, possibly out of the country, where the insurance companies couldn't find them. They owed hundreds of thousand in the end" explained Catherine.

"And Adam?" asked the psychiatrist.

"After two months of loud debate over whether he should just be disconnected from life support, he just got better" explained the mother.

"Did the doctors do anything that caused his improvement?" asked Wolstone.

"Well that's just it, they didn't. The only thing related to his awakening from the coma was a break-in at the hospital that took place a few days before" she explained.

"They think someone broke in and gave him some sort of medication?" asked Wolstone.

"Your guess is as good as mine. The media was wild with mad-scientist stories. You know, with titles like 'crazy doctor breaks in to hospital and trials drug that saves child in coma!' I've never bought into any of that, I think it was just God's will, but either way he fully recovered in a matter of weeks."

"And that was when he came into your life" asked Wolstone.

"Yes. We had been searching for adoption options after I had my fourth miscarriage at the same hospital here in Boston that he was at... I guess you could say fate just brought us together. He really is very sweet if you can get past all the dark war stories he is always rattling on about" she said.

Wolstone nodded as he considered it all.

"Thank you Catherine. Thank you very much. I look forward to seeing you both again in a week" said the psychiatrist.

And with that, the mother exited, leaving Wolstone alone with his thoughts.

He leaned back in his chair and paged through his notes. Where the hell to begin? There was just so much. Okay, well, best to start breaking things down, he thought as he pulled out a fresh pad of paper and got writing.

The issue of adoption was, unquestionably arising over and over again. Adam was adopting the girl Elsa and then adopting the children in Finland. At first, it seemed to be a repetitive element of the dreams, but as Wolstone pondered it, he realised it was not nearly as repetitive as it at first seemed. Elsa was adopted, loved and lived. The Finnish children were adopted, loved and died. Or least Wolstone thought he had that right.

Flipping back to his notes Wolstone nodded to himself as he double-checked the details. Died was perhaps not entirely accurate. Two of the children died, but the fate of the eldest, Pekka, was unclear. Even Adam did not seem to understand whether the little boy lived or died. Either way, here were two distinct fictional adoptive scenarios that ended quite differently. Undoubtedly Adam was struggling to understand his own adoption and that made perfect sense considering the traumatic story surrounding the hospital, his severe illness and subsequent abandonment when he was only two years old. Even so, from the information he had collected Wolstone knew there had to be much more to the case than just issues of adoption.

In spite of the fact that Adam was able to describe so much about the dreams, which on its own raised numerous questions in the psychiatrist's mind, the boy was coming up blank and unaware when asked directly about many key moments. Wolstone flipped through the pages and looked for his tell-tale marks that indicated Adam had blanked out. Yes, precisely as he had thought, both took place during moments in the dream where his body was changing into something horrific, one where he was saving himself from falling under the wagon and another when the wolves were attacking. There was clearly something to these moments that was important.

In most patients Adam's age, Wolstone would link such fear of physical change with a fear of puberty. He'd never seen it before, not personally anyway given that he almost never worked with kids, but he had read about it in the journals on occasion. It wasn't all that common, but when male children had father figures who were particularly cruel or aggressive, they sometimes developed a phobia of becoming adults themselves. While Wolstone was used to reading about this phobia manifesting in the form of increased infantile behaviour or shirking of responsibilities to fend off taking on an adult role in society, he had read about at least a few cases where the fear took the form of transformation nightmares where the pre-teen had nocturnal panics over becoming something physically powerful, frightening and aggressive. They, in effect, were terrified of becoming the male monster they lived with. The male monster... there was something about that phrase that seemed to ring a bell.

Wolstone again went searching and quickly found what he was looking for. The boy had specifically asked the question in his dream 'if a child born a monster could turn to a life of virtue.' The psychiatrist smiled. Damn he was good. There, right on the page, was pre-puberty anxiety. Yet, as he considered the sentence, he started to realise it was not as clear as he had at first thought. The cruel father/puberty anxiety phenomenon involved children worrying about transitioning from a life of virtue to the life of a monster, not the other way around. If anything, Adam's words were entirely backwards for the condition Wolstone had been considering. He was going to have to mine for more information and try to get a better understanding of how the boy was viewing himself in the dreams. With that in mind, he made one last note on Adam's file 'ask about self perceptions again' before moving on.

He had another patient in an hour, one of his veterans. It was classic stuff, the man was suffering from memories of terrible events, acting out violently against his wife, unable to be an effective father for his kids and barely sleeping through the night. Wolstone let out a long sigh, he didn't need to prepare for the session. Unlike Adam's situation, it was a textbook case, best to get on with his pile paperwork.

It was incredibly annoying. Every time he felt like he was cutting the pile down in some significant way, it seemed to grow back again. He picked up the first few files. Lord, not more applicants to study psychiatry at Harvard. He liked teaching his one class per term at the medical school, it kept him sharp and he got to meet some bright young people but he hated the selection process almost as much as he hated grading papers. When were these things due? July, excellent! Wolstone tossed them aside and opened up the next folder in the pile.

Ethics committee applications. He quickly counted them. God, there were seventeen and he had to get through them by May 14th. Wolstone looked up at the calendar again. That date was too close for comfort, particularly with the schedule he had. Best to get started...

Part 2

Place: Imperial College, London

Date: February 7th, 2015

Time: 4:14pm

"Any progress?" asked Dixon.

Ida jumped up from her microscope at his unexpected entry.

"Yes, but not on any of the things that I am supposed to be working on" she replied acidly.

Dixon gave her a quizzical look.

"Your special project has got a bit out of hand" Ida explained.

"What, the stuff that I left with you a couple weeks ago?" he asked.

"Yeah, take a look at this" she said, moving aside to let him look down her light microscope.

He shrugged his shoulders and looked up at her.

"So what? They're replicating. Cells are supposed to do that Ida" said Dixon with his characteristic sarcasm.

"I know, but they aren't supposed to do it for a hundred generations. I'm pretty sure bacteria can replicate over and over again for eternity, but I thought all mammal cells were supposed to go quiet after replicating around sixty times" she said.

"They are. That's the Hayflick Limit" he said, putting his eyes back down to the microscope, "Huh, I'll admit, that is unusual. Are you certain they've really bypassed the limit? Not miscounted or anything" he queried.

"A hundred percent certain. In fact, I've replicated dishes of these little guys four times!"

"What did the label on the sample these came from say" asked Dixon.

"There was just a cryo shelf number, nothing else" she said.

"And you took them all out of cryo?" he enquired.

"Nope, only about a quarter" replied Ida.

"Wow, they've replicated fast" he whispered looking more closely.

"I know" she said.

Dixon lifted his head up from the microscope as an idea dawned on him.

"I'll bet I know what these are. They have got to be HeLa cells" he said.

"Say that again?" asked Ida, not quite sure what he'd said.

"You know, those mutant cells that came from a patient who died in the US in the 1950's" he said.

"Oh HeLa! Yeah, yeah, we worked with those last year in cellular biology" she replied.

"Yes, those cells can be stored at -70 and brought back to life easily enough. As long as they are given good conditions and plenty of nutrients, they will replicate forever" Dixon explained.

"My prof last year called them the immortal cells. If I remember correctly, they took them from a black lady without her consent when she was dying from cancer. Created some serious social tensions" said Ida, looking down the microscope once more.

"Indeed. Look, I wouldn't worry too much about them. The box they came in was from Charring Cross Hospital, I'm sure they have more than a few HeLa lines over there for training the medics. If you want, feel free to cultivate them but make sure to keep cracking on with the neuron transplants. We have stroke patients to treat."

Place: Psychiatry Office, Boston, Massachusetts

Date: April 13th, 2018

Time: 2:01pm

As Catherine left, Adam slumped into the chair across from Wolstone. He felt terrible. The nightmares were getting worse. His sleep was more disrupted than ever.

"You look tired" offered Wolstone.

"I am" said the boy, rubbing his eyes.

"I am very sorry about that. As I said before, things might get worse before they get better" explained the doctor.

Adam nodded. It made sense that intentionally picking apart the dreams and nightmares might cause them to arise more readily when he went to sleep at night. What he wasn't sure of was how studying them was going to help to get rid of them.

"If you don't mind, I'd like to talk about your self perceptions in the dreams you told me about last time" said Wolstone.

"How do you mean?"

"Well, I am curious about whether you know what you look like in them. For example, how old are you in the dream with the cabin in Finland and the children that you adopt?" asked the doctor.

"An old man" the boy replied without missing a beat.

"But in the other dream that you were telling me about. You know, the one where Elsa tried to kiss you and you could not bear to kiss her back. How old are you there?" Wolstone asked.

"A young man" Adam replied.

"What about the man on the warship in the storm?" asked the doctor.

"Who? The one who gets shot?" asked the boy.

"Yes, the dream where the man with the gun is killed by the creature" continued Wolstone.

"A young man" replied Adam.

"Can you determine if he is the same young man as the young man in Finland who flees from Elsa when she tries to kiss him?" asked Wolstone.

Adam paused for a moment and thought about it. He could recall the dreams clearly enough, but getting a sense of what he looked like in them was not as easy as he initially thought it would be. He concentrated, very much wanting to help the doctor if he could.

Wolstone marvelled at the child's behaviour and briefly shuddered. His intensity was definitely something to behold. It was a sort of fierce concentration the likes of which he had not seen since the days when he himself had been in medical school.

"No, I am not the same young man on the boat as I am when I run away from Elsa" Adam responded slowly with a vague sense of uncertainty.

"You seem   unsure" prodded Wolstone.

"Well, it is difficult to determine. The men are different, but I'm always them. Do you understand? So they are and are not the same" said the boy.

"I see. Your presence of mind in the dream is what draws them together?" asked Wolstone.

"Yes, that's it" agreed Adam.

"Okay. What about Elsa? Is she the same age in these dreams?" asked Wolstone.

"Yeah, I think so" the boy answered.

Interesting, thought Wolstone. Adam was seeing the same young woman in the dreams but was viewing himself at very different ages even though the dates that he was reciting were all relatively close to one another.

Wolstone's mind stuck on that thought. The dates. Might there be something to them? There were so many and all so precise. Did they form a logical order or were they just random? This was something he could explore.

"Adam, can you tell me the year of the great Finnish famine?" the doctor asked.

"1867" Adam replied instantly.

Wolstone glanced over at the blue and white flag stuffed with a bunch of pens in his coffee mug at the end of the desk and exhaled softly.

Adam could tell he had just blown the doctor away with something but he wasn't sure what. Was he not supposed to know the year of the famine? The fact just seemed so obvious to him. Indeed, the idea that anyone might not know it   seemed ludicrous.

"Is something wrong Dr Wolstone?" asked Adam, sincerely curious.

"No. You just know your history better than I do, and my mother was Finnish" Wolstone replied.

"I'm sorry" said the boy.

"Don't be. Um, do you have dreams associated with meeting that priest and starting work in the field next to the church. You know, the church where you described meeting Elsa as a little girl and looking after her" asked the doctor.

"Yes" said Adam.

"Do you have a date associated with those events?" Wolstone asked.

"Sure. 1833" replied Adam straight away.

Wolstone noted it down next to 1867 on his pad. Wow, there was a logic here. If the character in the dream had met the priest in Prussia when he was a young man in 1833 he would naturally be an old man when travelling to Finland with Elsa shortly after 1867. Fascinated, Wolstone decided to press on.

"What about... what about the year you when you first met Elsa?" pressed Wolstone.

"1853" said Adam.

Again, there was a logic here that immediately fell in line with her age in Finland as an eighteen or nineteen year old. Wolstone glanced at Adam sitting there quietly. Was he a mathematical savant and calculating these dates without showing it? Wolstone certainly didn't think so.

Savant skills like those tended to go hand in hand with autism and, while the child sitting in front of him was not neurotypical, he was definitely not autistic either. He could simply be a genius, mused Wolstone. But even if that was so, he didn't buy the idea that the boy had planned this all out in advance and memorised a bunch of dates either. What would be the point? Just keep collecting information Wolstone and you can figure it all out later, he thought to himself.

"In what year did Elsa try to kiss you?" continued the doctor.

"1872" replied Adam.

That too fit with the descriptors of Elsa's age as presented in all of the dreams. She was functioning continuously in the dreams and aging normally while Adam was not. Wolstone looked around the office, grasping for where to go next.

"Can you tell me what year is it now?" he asked.

"Sure. 2018" the boy answered.

Wolstone shook his head in confusion and looked again at all of his notes, 2018, 1940 on the warship, the kiss in 1872, the famine of 1867, Elsa's arrival in 1853, Adam's first interactions with the priest in 1833...

"You don't happen to have any dreams from 1810 do you?" he asked, immediately regretting the question as an unprofessional half-joke that he realised he should never have even verbalised.

Adam felt the pain from the question as soon as it was asked. He could sense his pulse increasing rapidly and his blood running cold. There was something there... something dark and terrible.

Wolstone watched as the boy went silent and started staring out into nothingness. His pupils dilated and his face lost its colour. The psychiatrist waited patiently, keeping track of the water clock in the corner, counting the drops to make sure he was giving the boy a reasonable amount of time to break from his reverie. Thirty seconds.

"Adam? Are you okay?" Wolstone asked quietly.

Feeling a mix of fury and fear, Adam turned to look out at the sky for a moment to calm himself down. It was not easy. He found himself longing for unspeakable things... bloodshed... violence.

Wolstone watched the boy fix him with a deadly serious expression.

"I don't want to talk about that year" he said, slowly gripping the sides of his chair with claw-like fingers.

Wolstone looked at Adam and Adam looked right back with an ice cold severity. Wolstone did not have a lot of experience with kids but he had enough to know that this was not normal. Adam continued to stare straight at him with such startling intensity that he was driven into retreat.

"How about a drink? I'm thinking of a tea, would you like something? Water? Juice?" asked the doctor.

No. Not here, not again, thought Adam. This man's intentions are only good. He wants to help. The feelings were horrible and difficult to dismiss, but as he gazed back at the sky, he managed to come back to reality. Sighing deeply, Adam looked down at his hands. Thank goodness. They were the soft flesh of youth once more, exactly as they were supposed to be.

The boy's freezing stare melted away and the vice-like grip that he had on the chair eased.

"I'd like an orange juice please."

The doctor poured himself a tea and got Adam his juice from a mini-fridge in the corner. Sitting back down and sipping his drink, he looked down at his notes again. With Adam's reaction to the mention of 1810 he suspected that hearing about the dream tethered to that time would be crucial but he would have to tip-toe around it to get the child to speak about it in the way that he needed.

"Okay. Well, if that date is out of bounds, what about the 1820's. Do you have any dreams from then?" Wolstone asked.

Place: Austria

Date: 1822

Time: day

He had barely a moment to take in his surroundings before pain lanced into the bottom of his foot.

"Ouch!" Adam exclaimed as he fell to the muddy ground and lifted his filthy foot up towards his face to figure out what it was he had stepped on.

There, in the overcast grey light, he could see the offending thorn that had impaled itself into his flesh. He probed into his skin with his long and dirty fingernails to try and pry the intruder out. His fingers were youthful and nimble, but not nimble enough. Only drops of blood emerged, swept away quickly by the steady drizzle of the Austrian spring.

Groaning quietly to himself, Adam gingerly lifted himself off the ground and started hobbling towards a nearby shack. He was standing in the midst of a garden of sorts. It didn't look to be a particularly well-tended garden. Indeed, there seemed to be more weeds than edible plants present, but as poorly looked after as the garden was, he found himself stepping carefully to avoid causing any damage.

As he got to the shack he wiped off as much of the dirt as he could manage from his tattered and soaked clothes. A wagon rolled down a dirt road nearby. He could see the wagon master staring at him and felt a half impulse to say something in greeting but then found that the words were absent. Was he too shy to speak? Too scared? Or were the right words somehow unknown to him? He shivered, more from fear than from the damp cold, and opened the door.

Inside the shack he could see a small bed of hay with an old worn blanket in the corner. Next to the bed, there were books piled on the ground. Was he a farmer? It certainly looked like it but yet, he instinctively knew that there were far too many books for a poor farmer to have. Indeed, he sensed that most farmers in the area were illiterate. Even so, the presence of the reading material somehow comforted him. On a table in the corner of the shack he spotted a basket with some bread, a knife and a few stunted root vegetables sitting next to a vaguely familiar book bound in leather and a quill pen.

Adam quickly went to the table, sat on an adjacent stool, grabbed the knife and got to work on the thorn. In moments, he had it out. He rubbed at the wound with a bit of cloth and found himself gazing at the book. Driven by the force of the dream, his hands opened it up.

There, on the first page, the words "I Victor…" met his eyes. There was more, but his fingers swiftly flipped through the book, searching.

The pages were covered in precise handwriting and intricate diagrams. The material present on these pages always baffled him. The drawings and notes could only have been produced by someone who had been blessed with years of high quality schooling, possibly even a university education, and yet his place in life was clearly nothing more than that of an impoverished farmer. His fingers continued on relentlessly, ultimately finding a page with a roughly drawn field on it, littered with crude notes scribbled in French. While these notes were in the same book as the immaculate and precise works found on the earlier pages, the writing here carried no resemblance to them at all.

Adam studied the notes next to the drawing of the field for several minutes and flipped through a few more crudely written pages before he found what he was looking for. 'Plant de tomate seulement à la fin du printemps par temps doux.' Ah, that was the problem; he had planted them too soon. Damn! The seeds had probably rotted while sitting in the soil as it had been drenched with all the recent rain. At least he had the good sense to have only used half of the seeds he had bought earlier in the month, but he was going to need more. With that, he closed the book, gave his bloody foot one last wipe with the cloth and went out the door.

Place: Psychiatry Office, Boston, Massachusetts

Date: April 13th, 2018

Time: 2:13pm

"I have a quick question" interrupted the psychiatrist.

"What is it?" asked the boy.

"How old are you here?" asked Wolstone.

"I'm a young man, maybe in my twenties" replied Adam.

"But you are different from the young men we meet in your other dreams?" asked the doctor.

"Yes, but... How did you know?" asked Adam.

"Well, the dreams are all very logical. You have rules associated with them and one of those rules seems to be that characters do not repeat over time without aging or being replaced" explained Wolstone.

"I hadn't thought about it like that before" said Adam as he mulled over the concept of his dreams having rules.

"I'm curious, are you always alone on this rustic farm of yours?" asked Wolstone.

"What? In Austria" asked Adam.

Wolstone nodded, noting "Austria" in his notes next to "1822."

"No. There are other people nearby" replied Adam.

"Can you tell me about them?" asked the psychiatrist.

Place: Austria

Date: 1822

Time: day

The summer heat was intense, baking the ground and making the dirt road almost unbearable to walk on. Even with his heavily calloused feet he could feel the searing heat and the sharp pebbles. This was rough going. As Adam grimaced from the pain, a group of men rode by on horseback looking down on him with their bearded faces. One muttered a mild hello.

He somehow knew that they were from the town nearby. How he knew, he was not certain, but he had definitely seen at least two of these men before. He felt that it was in his best interest to be friendly or, at the very least, polite. A greeting welled up inside him but it fell flat. The words would just not emerge from his mouth. As the men rode by, his eyes fell to the ground and he clutched the leather book in his hands ever more tightly with his sweat soaked fingers.

In minutes he arrived at a junction and turned off the road towards a grassy hill. There, he climbed up and sat down under a pear tree. It was a good spot. There was shade, a small spring nearby and, most importantly, an excellent view of what looked like a superbly run farm.

Memories started to stir as Adam reflected upon the moment. Lots dreams of coming to look at this farm surfaced. He had studied it before, possibly many times, but his visits had always been in the evening hours after he had finished work on his own land. The visits had been

126

useful and allowed him to learn much, but he needed to learn more and was now coming to see the family responsible for this farm in action during the day.

The family members, both young and old, were hard at work in the fields. Old ladies plucked berries, children tilled soil, young men carted around water. No wonder they were so successful, there was a veritable army here. But Adam realised it was not just numbers that made the farm such a success; it was also the skill of the farmers. Tricks and techniques had been passed down from generation to generation, with the young being taught by the old. Unlike him, these people knew exactly what they were doing.

Adam made notes furiously as he spotted specific plants being pruned, watered, and nurtured in various ways. Some of the techniques he had already learned from trial and error, but others were new. Entirely focused on his note taking, Adam initially made no notice of the woman hard at work at the base of the grassy hill that he was on but gradually, he found it nearly impossible not to notice her.

Sweat beaded along her delicate feminine jaw and soaked the edges of her chestnut brown hair. Drawn back into a tight ponytail, her mane bounced gently up and down as she pumped water out of the ground. The roundness of her hips, the muscles in her arms, and those eyes... they were unlike anything he had seen before. They were brilliantly golden brown, full of life and something more.

The woman briefly glanced up at him and her full lips parted into a subtle smile. Her eyes quickly looked back down again. She kept at work but one hand drifted from the pump and moved to the top of her shirt. It was wet and hanging loose. Adam assumed she was going to pull it more closely to better cover herself in front of him, but to his astonishment, she did the opposite.

Smoothly and slowly she slid one side of her shirt down from her shoulder to her upper arm. The soaked fabric started to drift further on its own, revealing the top of her delicate breast in the afternoon light. Suddenly, the woman's playful eyes shot back up at him and met his gaze.

Gush. She pumped harder, breasts bouncing, glistening with sweat. It shot out in bursts. The water from the pipe splashed both into her buckets and onto her clothes. Adam's soul was on fire, but then, as always, the dream came crashing to an end.

"Hey!" yelled a man in the field, following his shouts with German that was far too fast for the full sentence to make any sense.

The man was obviously angry. His face was red and he was pointing. But Adam was uncertain of what he had done.

The man started shouting more loudly. Raising his hoe up into the air in a fury and running closer to the hill. Adam picked out the word "daughter" from the tirade but didn't need to understand much more. He had done something wrong and was going to be hacked up by farm implements if he didn't get away. With that, he closed his book and fled back to the road.

Place: Psychiatry Office, Boston, Massachusetts

Date: April 13th, 2018

Time: 2:25pm

Oh goodness, thought Wolstone, more teenage sexual angst. He knew he was supposed to explore this based upon the kissing dream that Adam had related a week earlier but he was being cowardly and avoiding dealing with the area of psychology with which he had little practical experience. He knew this was going to be difficult be he had to address it, especially given the arousing dream that the child had just told him.

"So, Adam, let me ask, do you have any friends who are girls?" asked the doctor as steadily as he could.

"Sure, several" said Adam, realising the psychiatrist was choosing his words carefully.

Adam felt a smile forming on his lips; it was actually kind of funny watching the psychiatrist try and gear up for a conversation about sex. The man was obviously uncomfortable bringing up the topic with him.

"Do you play with any of them?" asked Wolstone, regretting the wording of his question almost as soon as it left his mouth.

Adam laughed, noticing more of Dr Wolstone's discomfort.

"Sure. There are a few on my soccer team. One of them, Alice, she's really good. She reads a lot too and likes many of the same books that I do. We talk about it sometimes at lunch" explained the boy.

"Have you ever kissed a girl?" asked Wolstone.

"What? I'm eleven!" he replied with more laughter.

Wolstone smiled. All normal, he thought, but then paused as he further digested the response. No, not quite. It almost sounded as if Adam was giving him the response that he felt he had to give for a child of his age.

"Adam, do you want to kiss a girl but feel like, because you are eleven, you are not allowed to?"

Adam had not thought about it that way before. Images of Alice's athletic body running after the soccer ball in the field appeared in his mind and with them, came feelings that he banished as soon as they surfaced. No, that was wrong, he thought. She was only a friend. He did not want anything more. That was a path that only brought pain.

"No, not really" Adam replied.

Wolstone could tell the child was lying but could not really determine if such dishonesty was all that strange. He had read that pre-teens could be this way. Confused, unsure, and quick to use deceit to shield their emerging feelings from others. That was all normal with kids of this age, right? He made a note to phone up a few of the people he knew who actually specialised in this area. For the moment, he would just have to collect as much information as possible and wing it.

"Do you have any other dreams where that woman from the farm   appears?" asked Wolstone.

Adam nodded.

Place: Austria

Date: 1822

Time: night

Candlelight gently caressed the pages as he read the words.

Naked I came from my mother's womb, and naked I will depart.

The Lord gave and the Lord hath taken away; may the name of the Lord be praised."

It never made any sense and yet, the dream always brought him to this same biblical passage.

Adam paused from his reading for a moment to listen. The sound of footfalls reached his ears. Something was definitely outside. Guided by the dream, his hands grasped the small knife and lifted the candle as he quietly got up from the table. The footfalls were close, not far beyond the door. He stepped up to it, drew in a deep breath and quickly threw it open. There, in the shadows, were those enchanting golden-brown eyes that he had seen in the early summer. In the distance, down the road, he could make out the orange light of flames. Torches, lots of them, were coming closer. Adam immediately felt his mouth go dry.

She stepped closer, looking up at him with those penetrating eyes. But they were not lit with the playful glint that they had held before; they were now filled with fear.

"You are in danger" she whispered forcefully in German.

Adam drew back confused.

"They are coming for you" she continued.

"Who?" Adam stammered.

"The villagers... If they find you..." she explained.

"What are you talking about?" Adam asked in the best broken German he could manage.

"You have to understand! They think you are cursed! They think because their crops grow badly, that it is because of you. They think you are making unmarried women pregnant. They think you are stealing. They are coming to kill!" she said with great urgency in her voice.

"But I have done nothing!" he replied.

"Listen, it doesn't matter. They are not going to discuss any of this with you. I tried to talk them out of it, it was no use. They don't care if you are innocent or not. They are coming. Now! You must leave or you are going to die!"

He looked into her eyes, those eyes that had such a power to pull him in. The voices from the approaching mob started to fill the air. Thoughts came shooting through his mind unbidden. He had done nothing more than try to learn how to grow food. Nobody had laid claim to the land he had settled upon. He was a good and innocent man. This wasn't right. He broke from the woman's gaze and found himself staring at the biblical text on the table. With a sigh, he turned back to her.

"Where do I   go?"

"Follow the road. Follow it until the people no longer speak German" she said.

"And take this" she added, handing him a small folded piece of lavender cloth.

He looked at her curiously and her serious lips creased into the same smile he had seen before. It set his soul on fire.

"To remember me" she replied with every bit of warmth she could muster.

Quietly, she leaned forward and kissed him on the lips.

"Now, you must go!" she added urgently.

With that, Adam stuffed a bronze box tucked away under his table along with a number of books into a knapsack and ran out the door.

Light from the mob's torches was making the branches of the trees glow a dim yellow. They were close. Too close. With fear in his heart, he sprinted into the darkness of the woods.

Place: Psychiatry Office, Boston, Massachusetts

Date: April 13th, 2018

Time: 2:35pm

The psychiatrist's pad was covered in notes. He finished adding a few sentences and looked up at the boy.

"Have you read the book of Job?" asked the doctor.

"No, I don't think so. What is it?" asked Adam.

"A biblical tale, about a kind and faithful man who God tests" explained Wolstone.

"How is he tested?" asked Adam.

"By commanding Satan to destroy his home, wipe out all the animals on his farm and slay his family. The man, Job, is left with nothing and yet, in spite of all the horrors, he never curses God. That is where the passage you mentioned comes from" said Wolstone.

"The Lord gave and the Lord has taken away" whispered the boy without thinking.

"Yes, that's it" added Wolstone.

Adam sat quietly in the chair pondering the words.

"God gave him his life and then took everything to test his faith" the boy said quietly.

"You haven't had any biblical study have you?" asked the doctor as he made a few notes.

135

"What? Oh... just a little in school" answered Adam.

And yet, thought Adam, he felt like he knew the bible quite well. He couldn't quote any of the text off the top of his head, but he felt like if someone were to get him started reciting a passage that he would be able to continue flawlessly.

"Have been asked to read Job at all?" asked the doctor.

"Um, no... Not that I remember" replied Adam.

This was hardly surprising, thought Wolstone. Job wasn't exactly elementary school material. Yet the boy had to be collecting his information from somewhere. The warship during World War II, the Finnish history, the biblical text... There had to be some sort of exposure that he was unaware of. But how to find the source?

"What are the books that you and your soccer friend, what's her name...?"

"Alice" replied Adam.

"Yes, Alice, what books do you both like so much?"

"Oh, we love Jules Verne's books. *Journey to the Centre of the Earth*, *Twenty Thousand Leagues Under the Sea*, that sort of stuff. But I think our favourite is *Jurassic Park*" replied Adam, grinning broadly.

"I love that book too" smiled Wolstone, "What is it specifically about that book that makes it your favourite?"

"I think we both really like the dinosaurs, but on a broader level, we find the questions that the book asks to be much more interesting than the recent movies with Chris Pratt"   explained Adam.

"How so?" asked Wolstone.

"Well, the first book asks whether we always have the right intentions when we develop scientific experiments. Like, if we do develop the ability to bring dinosaurs back from the dead, is that something that we really ought to do? Even if it would be cool to have a dinosaur park... you know?" explained Adam.

Wolstone nodded as he took further notes.

"I mean, practically, genetically, Alice and I both know the book is way off. They used frog DNA to fill in gaps in the dinosaur genome. I mean, that's just ridiculous. Dinosaurs were reptiles so the DNA of crocodiles would have made more sense or, even better, the DNA of some bird species. But I guess being that scientifically accurate would have ruined a key element of the book" Adam rambled.

"Really, and what would that have been?" asked the doctor, transfixed.

"Well, the dinosaurs in the park are able to spontaneously swap their genders. That is an ability that they gain from the frog DNA that they have inside of them. This gender changing is what allows them to start breeding even though the scientists who designed the park figured they had genetically engineered the dinosaurs to all be female and unable to breed. While the science is flawed, I find the key message fascinating. Life will always find a way" said the boy with an electric enthusiasm.

Wolstone had to admit it, he was keen to keep exploring just how well read the child was and speculated that all of his reading was what made it possible for him to have such remarkable historical awareness, but he feared pressing too hard. He had the boy's trust. Adam was opening up and readily speaking of his dreams and Wolstone did not want to jeopardize that. Rather than further explore his current readings and studies, it seemed best, he thought, to let the child relate more of his dreams and see if he could find any other leads in them. With that in mind, the doctor changed direction.

"So, let me ask, what year did you flee from the Austrian mob?" enquired Wolstone

"1822" replied Adam.

"Does the dream ever continue? Or does it always end there?" asked the doctor.

"Always there" answered Adam.

"And you are a young man in this dream?" asked the doctor.

"That's right" replied the boy.

Wolstone considered his notes for a moment. 1833, a young man in Austria. 1867, an old man in Prussia. Was this a continuation of a single life?

"Adam, are the man who cared for Elsa and the man in this Austrian countryside dream the same?" asked Wolstone.

The boy looked at him in confusion.

"I know that they all feel the same because you are always seeing the world through their eyes, but beyond that similarity?" asked Wolstone.

"Well one is young, dirty and poor and one is older and clean" explained Adam.

"I know that, but are they physically the same individual?" pressed Wolstone.

"Do you mean, are they the same body?" asked Adam.

"Yes, that is precisely what I am asking" the said doctor with considerable eagerness.

Adam found himself having to focus again. It was not an easy question and he had to look carefully back into the dreams.

"Well, now that I think about it, yes. Yes, they are the same. But different ages" answered the boy.

It was extraordinary, thought Wolstone; this was a continuation of a single life in a dream. Were the other dreams also fragmented pieces of whole lives? And why would such elaborate narratives emerge at all?

Adam looked at the psychiatrist quizzically as he sat in silence behind his desk making notes. There was no question that the doctor was processing information he had gleaned from their discussion but Adam found himself wondering where the doctor was going with all of this. The age of his body in the dreams, the girl he played soccer with, the years associated with the various dreams he had, his personal love of *Jurassic Park*... was anything useful going to come from all of this?

Wolstone glanced up and noted the child staring at him. For a moment he felt as if he was the one being analysed by a psychiatrist. Adam just kept on staring, clearly ready to move on, so Wolstone pushed his notes aside and re-engaged with the boy.

"Right, okay. So, let me see if I have this right. One man in your dreams starts on a poor farm, is chased by a mob, ends up living in a church, meets Elsa, and then looks after the children in Finland with her. The other is a young man who is living with Elsa but does not fall in love with her and abruptly leaves one night when she tries to kiss him. Is that all correct?" asked the doctor.

Adam nodded.

"And what about on the warship during World War II? Is that the same man who flees from Elsa in the middle of the night?" asked Wolstone expectantly.

Adam pondered the question for a moment, seemingly uncertain.

"It is alright if you don't know" advised the doctor.

"No, I think I do know, it's just that I have to focus to tease the elements of the dreams apart. I think the man on board the boat is different from the other two" answered Adam.

"Okay. Interesting..." said Wolstone.

There were gaps in all of this, thought Wolstone. There was clearly something before 1820 that he wanted to get at. A story of obvious importance, but he knew he wasn't going to get there directly. And then there were the gaps between 1867 and the ship off the coast of Norway in World War II.

"Adam do you have any dreams that follow from when you left Elsa in 1867?" asked the psychiatrist.

Place: Helsinki

Date: 1873

Time: day

It was, admittedly, a beautiful location for an open air theatre, thought Adam. It was bounded by birch on one side, an exquisite nobleman's estate on the other and facing a stone rise that had the making of a perfect natural seating space. It would be hard to find a better place for such a structure. Adam sighed, put on a layer of mortar and hefted another brick into place. The work was hard, but the building of the foundation for the stage itself would soon be finished. If anything, the weather only encouraged him along. With the sunny sky, chirping birds and blossoming flowers, it was actually enjoyable.

Suddenly, he heard the side door of the estate fly open. Adam's strong, young hands kept hard at work in spite of the distraction that he knew was treading his way.

"Hello Adam" the girl's voice chimed in accented Finnish.

"Hello Helene. Done with your studies for the day already?" Adam responded in near perfect Finnish.

He managed a quick glance at her while continuing his work. There was something about the brown braids and the eleven-year-old's glimmering eyes that really threw him. She had to be the most inquisitive child he had ever met.

"No. Not my language work, but I told grandmamma that speaking with you counted as part of that" the girl replied.

"And she approves of you spending time with a brick layer?" he scoffed.

"She approves of me practicing my Finnish rather than talking to my friends in Russian" Helene replied.

"And what about your Latin?" he asked in Latin with a wry grin.

"I already told you, I don't need to speak that language, only read it" she responded in Finnish.

"Fine, but I'm telling you, some day you might find it useful" Adam replied.

A quiet silence fell between them as he continued laying bricks. Helene made to busy herself picking a few flowers but Adam could see out of the corner of his eye that she was still watching him intently.

"You obviously have something on your mind. What is it?" he asked.

She gave him one of those impish looks that he knew was going to lead to an uncomfortable question.

"Do you have a wife yet?" she asked.

"I... I beg your pardon?" Adam stammered.

"Well, I was just thinking, you are handsome, strong, and know so much about the world..."

"That you felt you needed to know my marital status?" he asked.

"Does answering my question embarrass you?" Helene asked innocently.

"No. Not at all! Does your grandmother know you think about such things?" Adam responded.

"Are you crazy? She does not think about these things. Last night when grandfather hosted some of his cantonists for dinner and we lit the candles all grandmamma could talk about was how the story of the slaves in Egypt is found in both the bible that the soldiers are using and ours and how we must never give up the fight for freedom" she said.

"Well, most of the cantonists are Jews and their bible is the basis for ours" Adam advised.

She glared at him. Adam turned back to his bricks.

"So, how often does your grandfather host them?" he asked as he tried to change the subject.

"Too often!" Helene spat.

"Try to show some sympathy. The cantonists have had it rough. Taken from their families as boys and forced to become soldiers. That your grandfather takes them in on their holidays is a kindness. It cannot be that bad" he replied calmly.

"Oh but it is! They just babble with grandfather in another language the whole time" she whined.

"That's probably Hebrew" Adam advised.

"Ah yes, And that is another useless language grandmother says I should learn one day! Tell me, were your parents so merciless?" she asked.

"Not really. I was not made to learn much of anything" Adam replied soberly.

"Lucky you" she said as she flopped down onto the grass and looked up at the sky.

"Actually, I regret it" he said sadly.

"What were they like?" she asked, as she rolled onto her belly.

"Who?" Adam asked.

"Your parents. Did they let you do what you wanted" Helene asked.

Adam fell silent for a moment. There was something to the question that cut him. He wasn't sure what it was, but deep down, he detected pain. It was like an ancient unhealed wound that was beginning to fester.

"I'm sorry, I didn't mean to hurt you" she said gently with a maturity beyond her years.

"That's alright. It's not your fault" he answered as he regained his composure.

A moment passed as they sat in silence. Then, abruptly, the side door of the mansion opened and an older woman's head poked out.

"Helene, I told you to take a few minutes, not the whole afternoon!" the elderly woman shouted in Russian.

"I thought you said I was part of your language practice?" asked Adam.

"You are. Hey, wait a minute, you speak Russian too?" Helene asked in fluent Russian.

"A little" Adam answered in the same language.

"How do you know so many languages if your parents didn't make you learn them?" she asked.

"I studied hard. You should too" he answered, still in her native tongue.

"But you are so young!" she said with astonishment breaking across her face.

"I'm a quick learner" Adam answered with a slight smile.

"I'll bet you've travelled a lot. All of father's emissaries speak loads of languages too. Where have you been?" she pressed.

"Helene!" shouted the elderly woman.

"Scat!" was Adam's only reply as he playfully swiped at her with his free hand.

Dodging him with ease, Helene scampered towards the house. Adam got back to his brick laying, still managing to watch the little girl out of the corner of his eye. He turned slightly when he noticed her stop in her tracks about halfway back to the estate and noticed as the mercurial playfulness on her face was suddenly replaced by a sincere look of thoughtfulness. Damn it, he thought, she is up to something.

146

Place: Psychiatry Office, Boston, Massachusetts

Date: April 13th, 2018

Time: 2:42pm

It was a different story with different people, but the elements were repeating themselves, thought Wolstone. Here, again, was Adam interacting with a young girl in a role that was not exactly that of a parent but that of a mentor and friend. Moreover, even the conversations they were having were similar. Just as Elsa had asked him about his relationship with his parents, so too was Helene asking this question. It made Wolstone curious if a direct line of questioning on the matter might bear fruit.

"Adam, excuse me, but I'd like to take a break from the dream for a moment and ask you some questions about your home. Is that okay?" asked Wolstone.

"Sure" replied Adam, curious as to what exactly the psychiatrist had in mind.

"Do your parents let you do the sorts of things that you want to do?" asked the psychiatrist, watching Adam carefully for an emotional response.

Adam felt a need to think about the question carefully. Just as in the dream, there was something about the enquiry that hurt. He wasn't sure what it was precisely, but deep down, he sensed the wound. He could see Dr Wolstone watching him and immediately knew the psychiatrist was gleaning information from his reaction. He initially felt a desire to hide how much pain he felt, but then reason kicked   in.

147

"I can't explain it, but the question is agonising to think about. It doesn't make any sense because my parents let me do the things that I really want to do. They take me for soccer, the library, to the forest. We play games, they offer help when I need it... it is very confusing to feel this way when they are nothing but good to me" explained Adam cautiously.

Wolstone appreciated the child's candour. The response fell in line with what he had long assumed. There had to be quite negative parental interactions that Adam was exposed to during the two years before he was adopted. He decided to continue along the direct route.

"Can you remember anything of your days before being adopted? Perhaps what your previous parents were like?" asked the psychiatrist.

It was a question that Adam had been asked many times before and had never been able to answer. Even so, he wanted to give it a try again. If anyone was going to be able to help, it was going to be Dr Wolstone and he wanted to support him as much as he could.

Wolstone watched as the boy stared at his desk and went into that same intense state of focus once more. A minute passed before the boy looked up at him.

"I'm really sorry. I try to find memories of my early days but all I get are the dreams" said Adam sadly.

"That's okay" advised Wolstone, "Then let's just stick to the dreams for the moment. Do you have any dreams where you actually have any of your parents present?" asked Wolstone.

Adam thought about it for a moment and suddenly a dark dream stirred, releasing a whirlwind of pain. He tried his best to focus on the dream, to reconstruct it for the doctor, but the hurt quickly became too great and he was forced to let go.

Wolstone could see the frustration and anguish on Adam's face, as if he was struggling with some sort of demon.

"I want you to know I think it is admirable how hard you are working at this" said this psychiatrist.

"I just couldn't. I couldn't get at it" said Adam, breathing hard and feeling the weight of the effort on his shoulders.

"It's okay. Let's try something else. What about parental figures. Are you close to anyone who feels motherly to you?" asked Wolstone.

Adam considered it for several minutes, scanning his dreams for any such relationship. Wolstone watched the water clock to keep an eye on the time as he didn't want to disrupt the boy prematurely.

"I honestly cannot think of any dreams where I have that sort of relationship" answered Adam.

Fascinating, thought Wolstone. No maternal figures at all in a young boy's dreams. That was almost unheard of. Even so, he did his best to shrug the matter off and move on.

"That's alright. What about fatherly figures?" asked the psychiatrist.

149

Again, Adam pondered the question. There was the priest who taught him Latin and employed him to look after the grounds of the church, but he didn't really feel a father-son relationship with him. He kept thinking and then his mind settled on someone. Nikolay.

"Yes, there is one" said Adam.

"Excellent. Tell me about him" replied Wolstone.

Place: Helsinki

Date: 1873

Time: day

Adam was suddenly back at the foundation of the open air theatre that he had been building in the dream where Helene had come out to bother him. Yet the foundation was now not more than a few days away from being finished. He felt a sense of pride at the structure that he somehow knew he had completed all on his own. As he marvelled at his work, he noticed a shadow approach from behind.

"My granddaughter tells me you speak Russian" said a strong and noble male voice speaking in clear, aristocratic Russian.

"I do. Some" replied Adam in the best Russian he could manage as he continued laying bricks.

"And German?" continued the voice.

"Yes, I know it" Adam responded, turning to face the black-bearded man in the military uniform standing behind him.

Adam's blood went cold. This was not just any Russian, this was Nikolay Adlerberg, the man appointed by the tsar to manage all of Finland. The realisation hit him hard. He knew somebody important lived in the estate next to the outdoor theatre, but he had no idea it was the governor general. Oh no, Adam thought, Helene had to be his daughter. What trouble had that girl gotten him into?

"And you speak French, Swedish, Latin, and Polish too?" asked Nikolay.

"I do sir" Adam replied, trying his best to remain formal and not make eye contact with someone so much more powerful than himself.

"And yet, here you are, laying bricks for the stage in my garden" said the governor general, switching politely into Finnish.

"I suppose" Adam responded, still wary, but uncertain of where this conversation was going. Was he to be punished in some way?

"Only the wealthiest of aristocracy and oldest of clergy can boast such skills, yet my staff tell me you come to us from a farm near Espoo" said the governor general.

Adam's stomach tightened into a knot. They thought he was a spy. His thoughts went racing back to the moments when he had revealed his language skills to Helene. He should never have done it.

"I guess I have an ability with languages" replied Adam, trying to make nothing of the skills that he feared he might now be executed for having while performing such mundane labour.

"I'll say! But I don't understand, why are you here laying bricks for my stage?" asked Nikolay.

"I guess I have a soft spot in my heart for the arts" answered Adam cautiously.

"As do I. Indeed, I simply cannot get enough of them, but honest people with your skills are rare. Have you ever thought of pursuing any other occupations more suited to someone with your talents?" Nikolay enquired.

"Sir, you do understand that I am a Finn, yes? Only Russians can get the sorts of occupations that you are speaking of. For whom could I possibly work" asked Adam as he started to feel vaguely reassured that he wasn't about to be put in the hangman's noose.

"Well, perhaps for me? The Russian administration here in Helsinki has need of people like you" Nikolay explained.

"What would I be doing?" asked Adam.

"Exactly what you seem to do so naturally, speaking with people in their various languages and translating" said Nikolay.

"And the stage?" asked Adam.

"Masons in Helsinki are easy enough to find, linguists like yourself... not so much. Here, come inside and at least discuss it with me over a pot of tea" offered Nikolay, extending his hand out to Adam.

The sun was setting upon the horizon and, with hindsight, Adam realised, so too were his days of manual labour.

He reached out, grasped Nikolay's hand and suddenly felt himself flashing forward to another dream.

Adam found himself in a formal looking stone building. The rain was pelting itself hard against the ornate windows. Outside, the dismal grey clouds appeared almost as depressing as the grim gargoyles spitting forth water from their mouths in the storm.

"Thank you for taking the time to speak with me" said a pudgy and balding man with bushy white eyebrows and a wide moustache in perfect German.

The man turned to look at Adam expectantly and Adam's mouth started translating into Russian all on its own.

He knew this place. He could swear that he had been here before, but when?

Place: Psychiatry Office, Boston, Massachusetts

Date: April 13th, 2018

Time: 2:51pm

"Is something wrong?" asked Wolstone.

"Um... not really. It's just, this dream. I don't know how I am telling it" explained the boy.

"Why?" queried the doctor.

"I haven't had it before" explained Adam.

"What? Ever?" asked Wolstone.

"Well, that's just the thing. I have this weird feeling that I actually have had it before but I cannot remember when that was" said Adam.

"That is actually quite normal with dreams" said Wolstone.

Adam sat there staring at Wolstone's shelf of books for a few moments, trying to figure out when he had last had the dream. It was infuriating that he could not place it.

"You do realise you are in the minority with your ability to keep track of the details in your dreams the way that you do. It's okay if you cannot remember exactly when you had it" advised Wolstone.

"That isn't the problem. It just feels different to me from the others. It is much more foggy. Does that make any sense?" asked the boy.

"Somewhat. I must admit, I am very interested in hearing more. Does it bother you to continue?" asked the psychiatrist.

"Not at all" responded Adam quietly.

"Then please do" said Wolstone encouragingly.

Place: Berlin

Date: ????

Time: evening

"Yes, the proscenium arch that they craft is extraordinary. I am very much looking forward to performances commencing there next year" replied Nikolay with polished diplomacy.

That was it. This was the Palais Beauvryé, the French embassy in Berlin where the German chancellor, what was his name... Otto von Bismarck and Nikolay Adlerberg met in person for the first time at a reception hosted by the French ambassador. The two men had a long standing spat over payment of several German artisans who Nikolay had hired for design work in the theatre he was building in Helsinki. Nikolay swore he had paid the agreed fee and Bismarck begged to differ. Worse, Bismarck ultimately made the decision to share some unfavourable words about Nikolay to Tsar Alexander.

Adam knew that Nikolay was furious but was unwilling to let the personal slight damage relations with the chancellor. Instead, their cordial and hollow banter continued. For his part, Adam felt just a bit bored since Bismarck spoke Russian and, after Adam's initial introduction, was speaking directly to Nikolay with remarkable fluency.

"Yes, their work is truly second to none and even more impressive when you consider that two of them are actually Poles. How such skill found its way into such a lowly lineage I really do not know!" laughed Bismarck.

As Nikolay laughed along with the chancellor, Adam managed a quick look at himself in the reflective glass of the rain spattered window. He was dressed in the formal attire of a diplomat. Adam glanced at Nikolay. He had much more grey in his black beard than he had when Adam had been laying bricks. What year was this? Why couldn't he recall?

The two men shook hands and Adam's legs led him down the hall with the governor general.

"That man makes me want to vomit" said Nikolay.

Adam nodded. He couldn't remember the full conversation but he did recall something bothersome about it. Nikolay looked at him with a bit of concern.

"What is it?" he asked.

"What?" replied Adam.

"I've known you long enough to know when something is on your mind" said Nikolay in a matter of fact manner.

There was something, but what was it? And then, the issue sprang into his mind. The Polish. Bismarck was treating the Poles poorly. Not because they were inherently bad people but because he viewed them as second class citizens.

Relieved to finally have the dream coming clear, Adam gave Nikolay a half smile.

"You know me too well" Adam said.

"It comes from seven years of constant travel by your side" replied Nikolay.

Seven years! Had it been seven years since he had been building the foundation for the theatre? Was it now really 1880? Adam was astonished by how he could not know this. He always knew where and when he was. How was this happening? Where was this dream coming from?

"What is it?" asked Nikolay, sensing unease in his friend.

"Every time I hear him talk about the Polish like they are rats beneath his feet, it makes me shudder" explained Adam.

"Are they not a lesser race?" asked Nikolay.

"What? Like the Finns?" inquired Adam.

"That is different" replied Nikolay defensively.

"Why? Because you and I are friends?" asked Adam, feeling the conversation start to flow more naturally.

"Adam, you bring great honour and integrity to your people, but you are not like the rest of them" responded Nikolay calmly.

"Do you ever wonder if that is only because you gave me a chance that other Finns usually do not have?" Adam pressed.

"Now you are starting to sound like my daughter" Nikolay replied, "The little rebel…" he added quietly under his breath.

"You make rebel sound like a bad word" prodded Adam.

"It is when she argues with me about Finnish rights at the dinner table in front of my lieutenants" stated Nikolay flatly.

Suddenly that dream stirred too. They had been eating with the cantonists again. It had been the Sabbath and the candles that Nikolay always lit for the men were out on the table. It was a sacred night, one that the governor general usually only reserved for the top ranking cantonists but Adam had still been there. Nikolay had welcomed him into his home as one of his own. The vision revealed Helene too. She was older now, a girl in her late teens, and arguing with her father with a will of steel. There had been shouting, a lot of it.

"It was just you, me, Helene and your most trusted officers" cautioned Adam, "nobody was present who would ever report her to St Petersburg."

"And her dating behaviour! God! Kissing Finns in public! The girl is trying to get herself killed" Nikolay muttered.

More elements of the dream came flooding back. The tensions between Finland and Russia were rapidly moving towards a boiling point. The Russian government was forcing Finns to become second class citizens in their own country. Adam recalled that a rebellion was in the air at the time and that the danger for Russians who were viewed as sympathising with the Finns was greater than ever.

There was no getting around it, thought Adam, Helene was indeed playing a dangerous game but the last thing he wanted was Nikolay coming down on her with an iron fist. That would only exacerbate matters.

"There is not a soul here who would dare hang your daughter" advised Adam, putting a reassuring hand on the older man's shoulder.

"But if I do not get a tighter grip on her, she could get us all in a great deal of trouble. Remember, I am much more lenient with the Finns then St Petersburg would like me to be. There is a great deal that I do not ever tell them" said Nikolay soberly.

"Have you ever thought it might be best to trust the teenager to actually know what she is doing?" asked Adam.

"Hah! You speak like you actually know what it is to be a father Adam! Trust me; the hell I am going through with her is unlike anything you could possibly imagine!" Nikolay laughed.

There was something about the statement that sent his mind whirling. Adam was certain that Nikolay hadn't meant anything by it, but still, the way he was so casually dismissing Adam's ability to understand the raising of a child, bothered him. He could do it if he wanted to.

The thought hung in his mind for a moment and he tried to take a few seconds to reflect upon the dreams that he had previously related to Wolstone. He had raised children, hadn't he? The more he thought about it, the less certain he became, eventually feeling mired in confusion.

As he broke from his own contemplation of fatherhood, Adam dared a glance over at the bearded governor general and found that he too was lost in thought. Adam was not sure how he knew but he could tell that the older man was pondering what to do with Helene. What to do with Helene indeed... thoughts of her eyes emerged in Adam's mind as the carriage rode off into the rainy darkness and as they struck his soul they sent his mind spinning.

Place: Helsinki

Date: 1881?

Time: evening

In an instant, those glimmering brown eyes were right in front of him.

"But I can't really tell if he likes me too" said Helene, looking up at him with the enthusiasm of youth.

What? Where? Adam quickly looked from side to side. He was in the foyer of the Alexander Theatre that Nikolay had built in the tsar's honour. Something big was obviously about to happen because the place was decked out and everyone was dashing about in formal attire. His eyes suddenly came back to Helene. She looked beautiful in her gown of white silk. He looked at her eyes again. Those eyes... he could not help but sink into them.

"What do you think? Do you think he likes me?" she asked eagerly.

"Who?" Adam asked in genuine confusion.

"Hannu of course!" she said in a sharp whisper.

Something about that name seemed out of place. He remembered her dating someone else but couldn't quite recall who it was. Prying eyes from people in the foyer were looking their way. He was certain others were listening in and that just seemed bad for both of them.

"Let's talk about this somewhere else shall we" he said, walking into an   alcove.

Then the name he was searching for jumped back into his mind.

"I thought you were seeing Eino" said Adam out of the corner of his mouth as Helene trailed right behind him.

Glancing towards the front doors he could see that, in spite of heavy snow, a clear path had been perfectly shovelled from the road up to the entrance of the theatre. Swedish flags were in place flying next to large Russian ones.

He immediately remembered everything. The night before had been one of the state dinners with the Swedish king that Nikolay had arranged just before he retired and the king had shown considerable interest in the new theatre. So this had to be what, 1881? Adam wasn't entirely certain but glad to finally have at least a mild idea of where and when he was.

"No, don't be ridiculous! Eino and I broke up weeks ago" said Helene not without a bit of mischievous glee in her voice.

Adam turned his back to the door so he could speak to her while keeping a close eye on the hustle and bustle in the foyer.

"I don't understand" he said, switching into Latin for the sake of keeping the conversation as secret as possible. "Are you intentionally trying to piss your father off by dating only Finns?" he asked.

Helene rolled her eyes as the Latin found its way into their conversation.

"Do we have to do this again?" she replied in the same language.

"It is good practice for you and don't try to change the subject" he said with a smile.

"No, I am dating them because I like them!" she said with a defiant glare.

By God was she impossible. Adam glared back as best he could but in moments the ice between them melted. Smiling softly, Helene reached close and pulled a stray bit of lint off of his jacket.

"Yes... I do it to annoy him a little" she replied in Latin. "But it is wrong to give them so few rights. This is their country" she added.

"Yes" agreed Adam.

"See you agree with me" she said with a beaming smile.

"You know I agree with you, but look at the position I am in. What can I do? I am just a translator!" he said.

"Nonsense! You are my father's most trusted advisor and your position will be one of considerable influence when he retires next month" she pressed.

Adam saw the governor general turn the corner. Standing tall and regally dressed, he looked sternly towards his daughter.

"Not here and not now" Adam whispered to her as Nikolay walked over.

"I see you had the decency to at least dress yourself like a lady of our house today" he said sourly.

Before Helene could find time to make an equally sharp reply, the Swedish entourage started to pour in.

"I feel completely disrespected" Helene whispered into Adam's ear.

The Swedish king entered. Surrounded by guards and dressed in flowing robes of white, blue and gold he was a sight to see. Walking just behind him was a young man in his twenties dressed in robes similar to those of the king. There was something awfully familiar about him. Adam had dreamt about this younger man before, but he couldn't pull things together well enough to remember a name.

"Disrespect? You haven't seen disrespect until you've seen this His Majesty at work" Adam replied with quiet sarcasm.

The king ceremoniously stepped towards Nikolay as a page shouted "King Oscar the second of Sweden and Norway!"

Helene playfully poked Adam in the side of his gut.

"Governor General" said the king in well practiced Russian.

"Your majesty. It is an honour as always. Shall we?" Nikolay asked in thickly accented Swedish as he calmly gestured for the king to enter the open doors of the theatre. The king started to walk forward but took a moment to turn and look down his nose at Adam.

"Yes, of course, but we have no need of servants to be by our side during these entertainments" said the king.

Nodding with quiet understanding and just a hint of exasperation, Nikolay led the king into the theatre while subtly gesturing Adam to depart.

Place: Psychiatry Office, Boston, Massachusetts

Date: April 13th, 2018

Time: 3:07pm

"You look distressed, what is it?" asked Wolstone.

"Do you know that feeling of knowing you know something but not being able to remember just what it is?" Adam asked.

"All the time. Trust me, as you get older it happens more often" smiled Wolstone.

"Are you experiencing that feeling now?"

"Yes" said the boy.

"The younger man in the robes. I am sure I know who he is. I have had dreams about him before" said Adam.

"Do you mind if I help?" asked Wolstone.

"Sure, but how can you? It is my dream, not yours" said Adam.

"Well, if he was in robes like the king but younger might he be the king's son" speculated Wolstone.

"Yes, I already know that!" snapped Adam in frustration. "He is the prince, but the name, it is on the tip of my tongue, as if I once knew it" said the boy.

Wolstone turned towards his computer and pulled up Google. He'd wanted to do this for a while but had not yet had the chance. Given the boy's near photographic awareness of historic events, he figured the internet would be able to provide an answer quickly enough and simultaneously test just how accurate the details in these dreams actually were.

"You said the king's name was Oscar, right" asked Wolstone.

The boy nodded.

"Well, if the king at that time was Oscar, it looks like his son's name started with the letter 'G'" said Wolstone.

"Gustaf" answered Adam immediately.

Wolstone smiled quietly.

"I want to tell you a memory I have of Gustaf from that night at the grand hall before I forget it again" said Adam with a hint of enthusiasm in his voice.

A memory thought Wolstone. Now there was a new word…

Place: Reception Room, Alexander Theatre, Helsinki

Date: 1882

Time: evening

Adam found himself approaching Gustaf with a pot of tea. The young prince was sitting in a decidedly unprince-like manner across two chairs he had pulled together. His cape was released and hanging askew across a nearby sofa. Adam glanced down at himself. He was at least still properly dressed and looking as if he belonged in the formal space.

"Care for some more tea?" The words trickled out of his mouth in near fluent Swedish all on their own.

"What? Yes, don't mind if I do" replied Gustaf.

"And the tennis? How has it been?" asked Adam.

"Simply splendid! Have you had a chance to try the sport out yet?" asked the prince.

Adam shook his head. He couldn't remember ever even having played tennis.

"Yes, I know. The affairs of state are relentless, but they can have their benefits in the flesh" smirked Gustaf.

"How do you mean?" asked Adam, genuinely confused.

"Come now my friend. I see the way she looks at you…" said the smiling prince.

"Who? Helene? Hah! You must be drunk" replied Adam, feeling ever so slightly uncomfortable with the topic.

"You laugh?" asked Gustaf.

"I do. It is preposterous. She is Nikolay's daughter" exclaimed Adam, looking sideways briefly to make sure that the reception room doors were still closed.

"Adam. After so many of our meetings, I think I know you well enough to say you have feelings for her" chided the prince.

Adam could feel his face growing warm. It was horrible.

"Ah. See, I can sense these things. When will you ask her?"

"Gustaf, I cannot" replied Adam sharply.

"But you must. You clearly fancy her" continued the prince undeterred.

"It is impossible" said Adam, growing impatient with the badgering.

"Why? Because you think you are too old for her?" asked Gustaf.

"What? Too old? No!"

"Then don't be a coward" teased the prince.

"I am not a coward. Her marriage is being politically arranged" he whispered harshly,

"I'm sorry my friend. I really am. I did not mean to push you on this. But if I may ask, why an arranged marriage?"

Adam paused, uncertain of how to reply.

"She is not royal is she?" asked Gustaf.

"Orders from Count Heiden. He is to be the next governor general and is coming in with instructions to 'Russianise' the Finns" said Adam coolly.

"Nonsense. It will never work. We tried that with the Norwegians... what a mess" commented Gustaf.

"Regardless, St Petersburg is serious. There is a wealthy and powerful Finnish nobleman in the northeast who is sympathetic to Russian rule. He recently lost his wife and..." Adam trailed off.

"And she is to marry him?" asked Gustaf.

"Yes" replied Adam with a tinge of sorrow in his voice.

"Willingly" the prince asked.

"Oh, lord no! She doesn't even know yet, but when she does, trust me, you will hear the screams all the way in Stockholm" Adam responded casually, glad to finally be off the topic of his own feelings for the girl.

"Have you had any thoughts of interceding on her behalf? Arguing, perhaps, that a marriage to a senior advisor of Finnish heritage would be even better?" asked Gustaf with a wolf-like grin on his face.

"You are terrible. You know that don't you?" commented Adam.

Gustaf laughed heartily.

"No point in evading the question" said the prince with a smile.

"Of course, I dream of such things" said Adam with a sigh, sitting down into the chair across from the prince, glad to have the feelings off his chest.

"But you are fearful of St Petersburg?" asked Gustaf.

"No actually. That isn't it at all" replied Adam sincerely.

"What then?" asked the prince.

"I'm not sure. I think I am fearful of Nikolay" said Adam.

"But why? He is so good to you. I would think he'd be pleased to have you as a son-in-law. Really, you are already almost part of the family" commented Gustaf.

"Well that's just it. I don't want to damage what I have. He is like a father to me and that feels important" Adam replied quietly, looking into his empty tea cup as if he might find some answers there.

"But that is nonsense! You already have a father who I am sure is very proud of all you have achieved" said Gustaf.

Thoughts suddenly bolted through Adam's mind. Thunder, wind, lightening...

The seconds ticked by.

"Adam?" asked Gustaf quietly.

Adam broke from the nightmare with a start, gasping in air as if he had been deep underwater. There was something awful down there. Something he truly hoped he would never have to face.

"That's the disturbing thing Gustaf" said Adam suddenly feeling very tired. "I've been having trouble remembering my childhood in recent years. I see children holding their parents' hands, I see them playing with their parents, having picnics and I think, I must have had that, but then I try to remember and everything is obscured... as if I am trying to look out on a landscape during a blizzard. I sometimes have these disturbing dreams..." continued Adam.

The sounds of pomp and ceremony started to echo from beyond the doors. Gustaf stood up to leave but paused for a moment, looking towards Adam with concern.

"Will you be alright?" asked the prince gently.

"Yes, yes. Of course" answered Adam calmly, knowing the lie for what it was.

"It might not be a bad thing you know. Sometimes it is better to not remember. Maybe you are forgetting on purpose" commented the prince as he strolled towards the door.

"Do you think so?" asked Adam.

"Oh yes! Sometimes after getting really drunk I wake up next to ugly people with no memory of how I made it to their bed. I consider the drink to have done me a great favour by wiping my memory" laughed Gustaf as he swept his cape sideways with a flourish and went out the door.

Adam laughed at the joke but found the idea sticking. Forgetting things on purpose, now there was something to ponder.

Place: Psychiatry Office, Boston, Massachusetts

Date: April 13th, 2018

Time: 3:22pm

"Dr Wolstone, is it possible for people's minds to intentionally forget things that they do not want to remember?" Adam asked.

The question caught the psychiatrist off guard. Wolstone was not opposed to explaining psychological principles to his patients. He had, on more than a few occasions, explained to veterans of the wars in Afghanistan and Iraq that they likely had memories of horrid things buried within their minds that they did not consciously know they had there. Sometimes being honest about this proved counter-productive by creating states of denial in patients who liked to believe they were in full control of their own faculties when they were not, but sometimes it worked the other way around. Sometimes patients who learned that their minds were hiding secrets became more adept at tracking them down.

It was a gamble to be sure, but Wolstone suspected that it would be more useful to be open with Adam since he seemed to have little ego and appeared willing enough to question his own fallibility. And besides, the kid was so sharp and resourceful, there was a good chance he would find out all on his own whether Wolstone told him the truth or not.

"Yes, it is possible for the mind to hide things from us" answered the doctor.

"Why does it happen?" asked the boy.

"Well, we do not entirely know, but research psychologists speculate that it is a self-defence mechanism in the brain" explained Wolstone.

"Do you mean to help it forget things that would cause harm if the brain kept thinking about them all the time?" asked Adam.

"Yes, precisely" replied the psychiatrist.

"Like burning bodies and stuff?" asked the boy morbidly.

"Well, yes, but it is not always physical horror that triggers the effect, sometimes lost memories can simply be triggered by very upsetting circumstances" explained the doctor.

"Is that what you think is wrong with me?" asked Adam sincerely.

Adam watched the psychiatrist carefully; he very much wanted to know the therapist's hypothesis about why he was having the dreams and was not keen to be misled, even for his own good.

Wolstone could feel himself being studied and brooded over the matter in silence. This needed to be dealt with delicately, he thought. To go deeper he was going to need Adam's help but he did not want to risk the boy becoming fearful of what he might find buried deep within himself. If that happened, the child might construct barriers. Barriers that Wolstone worried he might never breach. He needed more information and more time.

The psychiatrist looked over at Adam and immediately knew he would not be able to get away with a direct lie, not with this patient at any rate. The only option that he had was to be partially honest.

"I'm really not sure yet" Wolstone said with as much warmth as he could muster.

Adam, for his part could not read the doctor's face and, given that he usually found that he could, he immediately realised the psychiatrist was hiding something.

"Adam, you paused for quite a while when you were recalling the bit of the dream where Gustaf asked you about why you felt so concerned about damaging your relationship with Nikolay by possibly pursuing a relationship with Helene. Can you elaborate upon that a bit?" asked Wolstone.

"Sure. I feel a really wonderful friendship with him. He respects me. He trusts me. He celebrates my accomplishments" explained Adam.

"And when Gustaf asks about you already having a father who is likely proud of you, I noticed you went silent for a while. Can you tell me what you were thinking about at that point in the dream" asked the psychiatrist.

"No" replied Adam simply.

"I don't understand. Are you saying 'no' because you can't recall why you paused for so long or 'no' because you don't want to talk about it?" asked Wolstone.

Adam felt cornered. The truth was he was starting to remember dreams that he wished he could forget forever. Moreover, as he realised just what the dreams were, he feared that talking about them would only make matters worse. He looked up and caught the doctor studying him. There was nothing he could do, the psychiatrist's expert eyes were fast and reading him like a book.

Well, they were certainly getting somewhere, thought Wolstone. The mixed sense of realisation and fear that he was seeing in the child's eyes was the same look that he had seen in hundreds of post traumatic stress patients just as they were rediscovering information buried deep within their minds. He knew from experience that the road ahead would be rough, but was pleased to have got to this point with the boy.

"Adam, I know how much fear and pain you are feeling. Please, let me help you" said Wolstone

"I just... can't" replied Adam, feeling his chest tighten up and his hands grow cold.

The boy's breaths were becoming shallow and his hands were quickly getting that claw-like look as they grasped the side of his chair. Wolstone badly wanted to press on but didn't want to cause a panic attack in the process.

"Okay. Let's skip those questions for a while and talk about Helene. Can you tell me a bit more about what happened with her? Did she really end up getting married to the Finnish loyalist in the north that you mentioned" asked the doctor.

Adam's breathing slowed down as they veered away from the dreams that held such horror for him. Even so, the associated darkness was still lurking in his mind and he feared the ways in which it might taint the rest of his thoughts.

"What do you think? Can you tell me a bit more about what happened to Helene?" asked Wolstone again.

The child nodded, sank deeply into the chair and let the memories come swirling back to life. Wolstone let out a gentle sigh of relief that his redirection had worked and, as the boy started telling more of his tale, the doctor made certain to underline a single word in his recent notes. Father. Much as Adam did not want to discuss it, they would have to get back to that topic soon.

Place: Adlerberg Estate, Helsinki

Date: 1883

Time: night

What was that? Adam sat up with a start. Had he been sleeping? A single candle flickered on the table next to his bed. Sleep, that seemed the likely explanation. He looked down and found a scattering of political documents on his bed next to his pillow. He must have been reading and nodded off. He glanced at the full moon hanging behind the lightly clouded sky. It was late. Why had he suddenly woken up? What did this have to do with Helene?

A gentle knocking came again. He suddenly realised, it was her.

"Yes" he whispered quietly, anxiously.

The door opened slowly, revealing Helene in the shadows of the hall dressed in clothes that looked as if they had been dragged through a barn. Her hair was tucked away beneath a boy's hat. Slung over her shoulder was a knapsack. Her eyes were rimmed with red. Adam leapt out of bed.

"What are you doing?" he whispered with intensity as he hastily pulled his dressing gown together.

"Leaving" she replied sternly.

"I can see that, but tomorrow…" he reminded her forcefully, the words beginning to flow again with a life of their own.

181

"I don't care. I won't marry him" she answered defiantly.

With hands trembling, she pulled a map out of her knapsack and spread it across the bed.

"I have been to these woods and know my way through them, but I need you to tell me where I can find safe passage beyond. Does my father have many soldiers stationed in either of these towns?" she asked.

"Helene" Adam whispered with concern.

"I know you know. Tell me" she ordered with a force of will as strong as Adam's.

"Why? So you don't have to see them hang your father for treason" Adam responded quietly.

Helene threw him a defiant glare.

"Because that is what they will do to him for losing you" he added.

Her eyes started to fill with tears as she plunged her face into his chest. Her quiet cries filled his room. He put a gentle arm around her.

"I do not want that" she sobbed quietly.

"Then let us think this through rationally. Is this nobleman in the north, Constantin Linder, a bad enough person to marry to warrant sending your father to the gallows?" he asked.

"Probably not" she sniffled.

"Constantin is Finnish?" Adam asked.

"Yes, but he is a traitorous dog. Taking bribes from St Petersburg and acting as their puppet" she spat.

"Have you considered the alternative?" Adam probed.

"What?" asked Helene.

"Extermination" he said quietly.

"I don't understand" she replied.

"I see it happening with the Poles. Bismarck is setting up policies to eliminate them" he explained.

"You had not told me" she gasped.

"Listen, I am not saying that 'Russification' of the Finns is something that I approve of but it could be so much worse. And, if you build a good relationship with Constantin, you may be able to influence him. You could possibly even hinder St Petersburg in the long run" said Adam.

A flash of light flickered across the window and the rumble of thunder softly shook the room.

Adam suddenly felt a chill run down his spine. Had there actually been thunder that night? He wasn't so sure. Was something darker leaking in?

Realising he was starting to lose his grip on this particular dream, he turned his attention back to Helene as she quietly processed what he had been saying.

"But I do not love him" she replied simply.

"I know" Adam answered soberly.

They fell into a long and uncomfortable silence. Her gaze drifted up to meet his. More thunder echoed in the distance. Her hand reached out for his. Tenderly, their fingers came together. She leaned forward and gently kissed him on the neck. The moment was electric.

In seconds he was lifting her in an embrace. The room quickly grew shadowy and a gust of wind, thick with the scent of rain and ozone, filled the room. Their lips met in fiery passion, oblivious to the distraction.

The hairs on their arms lifted with the charge of static as their clothes fell to the floor and their bodies entwined. The cries of gulls mixed with thunder echoed in the distance. Yet another bolt of lightning flashed in the turbulent sky, illuminating Adam's hands as they clutched the milky white flesh of her back. Another gust blasted them as they laid across the bed. More flashes. The bolts were perilously close. Windows shaking and ground trembling...

And then it struck. A burst of blue and white fiery light so overwhelming that it pierced wood, glass, flesh and bone. A crushing, smothering darkness, fear made corporeal... It poured over them both. Adam gasped in terror as it swamped him.

"Adam" Helene cried as the darkness threatened to consume her.

"Adam" she cried again, now in a more forceful voice.

It was not Helene's voice, but still, it was one he knew.

"Adam. Breathe. Don't let the fear overtake you. Try to hold on to the memory" said the voice.

Wolstone! Like a noise occurring during a deep sleep and weaving itself into a dream, the psychiatrist's voice was finding a way in.

"I'm here, nothing bad is going to happen. Come on kid, stick with it!" said the doctor.

With the doctor's urging, Adam realised his instincts had been correct. This storm did not belong here. Where it belonged, he dared not think, but Wolstone was right, concentrating on the current dream was the best way forward. Adam closed his eyes and, as he exhaled, the darkness started to recede.

The candle light flickered gently over the bed as she brushed his lips with yet another tender kiss.

"Nobody needs to know" Helene whispered as she pulled the sheets up and over them both. Beneath their soft warmth Adam experienced pleasure beyond anything he had ever felt before and suddenly went hurtling into another dream.

Place: Finland?

Date: 1883

Time: day

The white of the sheets gave way to the white of winter and Adam found himself standing in a corridor looking out a manor house window onto a snowy town square. He was absolutely certain that this was not the Adlerberg estate. He was pretty sure it wasn't even Helsinki. Where was he?

He blinked his eyes a couple of times to get used to the brightness of the snow and started to make out the signs of the stores along the edge of the square. There was a bakery, a forge, a meat monger... the names were all in Finnish, so he had to still be in Finland.

Out of the corner of his eye he noticed a man on horseback trot down a road and into the square. The man was fast approaching and he had a package of sorts in his arms. Adam wasn't sure what it was but he sensed it was something that he needed to see.

Moving of their own accord, Adam's legs took him down the brightly lit hall to the front door. By the time he got there a servant had already received the package and, as Adam neared, she immediately handed it over to him. He untied the cord holding it together. The package was filled with envelopes, there had to be three or four dozen of them. One placed at the front of the stack instantly caught his eye.

TO: Constantin   Linder

CARE OF: Adam Korhonen

FROM: Vasilli Tovalev

Things started to get a lot clearer. His instincts had been correct, this wasn't Helsinki but it was Finland. This was the northeast, the town of Joensuu, and he was working as an advisor to the regent here, the man named Constantin who had married Helene. It was peculiar, but somehow the thought of her marrying Constantin did not seem as troubling as he expected it to.

In moments Adam's arms were quietly sliding open the ornately decorated door at the end of the hall. The vast room ahead was filled from wall to wall with books. In the centre of the space, at a desk piled with documents and well-oiled texts, was a bearded man in his mid forties with his back to Adam. Just beyond the man, part way up a ladder and perusing books, was the unmistakable figure of Helene.

Adam waited for a moment in silence as they seemed to be engaged in conversation and he did not wish to interrupt.

"But this is English!" said Helene as she pulled a book from the shelf.

"Yes" said Constantin in a matter of fact tone of voice as he signed one of the documents on the desk and pushed it aside.

"Wait. You read English?" she queried.

"And speak it too" he replied, scribbling on another paper.

"How?" asked Helene.

Constantin turned from his papers and picked up a cup a tea as he looked over at her, his eyes caught sight of Adam. The bearded regent gave a quick wave of his hand, urging Adam to come in.

"My grandfather created the family wealth by making chronometers that helped crews at sea to keep the time" he explained.

"But how did that teach him English?" she asked.

"The British Royal Navy hired him and..." he trailed off as he caught sight of the letter in Adam's hand. His eyes quickly drifted from the paper to Adam's grim expression. He put his head in his hands and sighed.

"More orders from St Petersburg?" Constantin asked with exhaustion in his voice.

"I'm afraid so" replied Adam.

"What is it this time? Further tax increases?" asked the regent.

"That and worse. We are to ensure that all business in Joensuu is conducted in Russian" answered Adam.

An angry expression drifted across Helene's face as she exhaled quietly. Constantin's head turned ever so slightly, watching her from the corner of his eye.

"When must it begin?" asked Constantin.

"In a month's time they are sending observers to consider our progress" explained Adam.

"It is a bold move... Don't you think?" said Constantin.

Adam nodded carefully.

"Does St Petersburg give any indication of how I am supposed to enforce this when they know full well that I hardly have a spy in every place of business in Joensuu?" he asked.

"No sir, they do not" replied Adam.

Constantin leaned back across his desk chair and looked up at the ceiling, seemingly thinking matters over.

"Adam, what did Nikolay do when St Petersburg sent these sorts of messages?" asked the regent.

"He always followed orders" answered Adam, immediately recognising the lie for what it was.

The bearded man arched an eyebrow and Adam somehow felt compelled to say more.

"He followed orders based upon how practical they were to enforce and how much he felt high command actually cared" replied Adam, astonished by his own admission.

Constantin smiled faintly.

"So, do you think St Petersburg is sending this because some official on their end needs to be mollified or because St Petersburg really wants this to happen?" asked the regent.

"Honestly, I think they sent this because they have a penchant for paperwork" answered Adam, doing his best to stifle a small   smile of his own.

"And what do you think Count Heiden is going to do with these orders now that he is governor general?" asked Constantin.

"I'd assume that, like Nikolay, he will apply them to the best of his ability" replied Adam carefully.

Constantin pushed aside the papers and leaned forward on the desk with his hands clasped together.

"But what does that mean exactly? Will he just make a show of enforcing them or will he actually come up with some sort of ludicrous plan to get the Finns who all hate the Russian language to start conducting all of their business in it?" he asked.

"Constantin, my father was always loyal to the tsar" said Helene, descending from the ladder with a note of concern in her voice.

"You misunderstand me my love. I am not interested in gaining political points with high command by outing the great Nikolay Adlerberg for having been soft on the Finns" said Constantin.

Helene looked at Constantin in confusion, her facing growing red with concern as his beard broke into a sly grin.

Come now, both of you. Helene, it has been eight weeks since we married and, Adam, it has been six weeks since Nikolay sent you out here to help us get Joensuu's affairs in order. I think we can end the deceptions. There's no need for lies" he said.

Helene's gaze drifted towards Adam's with concern, her hand slipping down to her belly.

"We all are here because we believe that we can do more for Finland by working with Russia than by fighting against her. Yes?" said Constantin with a glimmer of mischief in his eyes.

A smile started to creep onto Helene's lips. Adam too felt the joy. He remembered now. Constantin was not the Russian lapdog that many believed him to be but rather a moderate who was playing his hand with St Petersburg very carefully to ensure the best for his people.

Then Adam's thoughts started drifting to Helene's reaction. Her hand... It had moved to her stomach. Memories stirred and realisation started to set in.

Minutes later, Adam was walking down the corridor away from the library and towards the stairs. He passed the guards, passed the servants and climbed to the top floor. There, his legs brought him to a small room with a window looking out over the snow-covered town. Closing the door behind him, he pressed his face up against the cold glass as he drew in a long, ragged breath.

"That was awful" he said to himself.

"What?" asked a distant voice that he knew well, but not from this place.

"I thought he knew" answered Adam, staring out the window.

"Knew what?" asked Wolstone from his office in Boston. Adam's imagination rapidly incorporated the psychiatrist's visage into the fabric of the dream to help explain its presence, carving it into the glass of the window as a vague reflection of the doctor.

191

"That, that… she…" Adam's voice started to break with emotion.

"Was pregnant with a child?" asked Wolstone.

Adam exhaled again deeply. He looked out over the town through the reflected image of the psychiatrist. The snow on the buildings was heavy. The land was deep within winter's grasp. He could feel the brutal cold emanating through the window in spite of there being three layers of glass but the chill it brought was nothing compared to the chill that ran through him as he spoke a name he had not spoken for what felt like decades.

"His name was Aulis" Adam whispered.

"And what of Constantin? How did he react to this?" asked Wolstone.

"I don't think he ever knew. If he did, he had the good grace to never show it" Adam answered.

"Were there others?" asked the psychiatrist.

"Yes. There was a second boy, Erno, and then a little girl" replied Adam.

Tears started to stream down his face as their memories came crashing upon him.

"Mandi. She was very dear" murmured Adam.

"And these children, what was your relationship to them?" asked Wolstone, knowing the answer full well but wanting Adam to say it himself.

"I was their father" Adam replied quietly.

"What can you remember of your experiences with these children?" asked the psychiatrist.

Beyond the window, winter rapidly melted into spring and spring gave way to summer and then autumn. Months flew by and, as Adam looked down upon the tops of his hands, he watched them wrinkle with age. He drew in another deep breath and, in the blink of an eye, he plunged into another dream.

Place: Joensuu

Date: 1895

Time: day

The appearance of a snake skeleton's fanged mouth directly in front of his face caused Adam to instinctively lurch backward. A mix of other skeletons sat on the table next to it.

"I don't understand, you say they are closely related but how can that be. This one has legs and this one does not. Surely they cannot have such differences and still be relatives?" asked a golden-haired boy sitting next to him.

"But I want to go outside!" squealed a little girl from the other side of the room.

Adam blinked his eyes several times, taking it all in. He was in Constantin's library again, of that he was certain, but when was this? The boy... the boy sitting next to him was his first child with Helene, Aulis. He seemed to be about eleven years old. Adam glanced over to his side and found a little brown-haired boy of about four building a jigsaw puzzle on the floor next to a tiny blond girl of about two who was drawing with a coloured pencil while distractedly gazing at the windows down the hall. Recognition struck and he quickly realised these were Erno and Mandi. Yes, that was it, Dr Wolstone had encouraged him to reflect upon his memories of the children and here he was with them.

There was a tugging at his shirt sleeve and Adam turned to give Aulis his attention. By God, it was like looking in a mirror. The boy had so many of his features.

"Adam?" asked Aulis, looking at him expectantly.

Yes, thought Adam, the question about the snake. Adam looked at the mounted skeletons. There was a viper, an iguana, a badger, a monkey and a turtle. He wasn't sure how he knew, but he definitely knew what these skeletons were. Moreover he knew that the viper and the iguana were, in fact, closely related. He wanted to tell Aulis that 'they just were' related, but his mouth said otherwise.

"With life, things are not always what they seem. Just because the iguana has legs and the viper has none, says very little about their relationship to one another. When the viper's ancient relatives came to live in certain environments, like holes in the ground where legs impeded their ability to move around, their relatives that had the smallest of legs did best" explained Adam.

"But they still had legs?" said Aulis with a fox-like smirk on his face.

"Yes, but their offspring had a range of leg sizes, with some having bigger legs than their parents and some having smaller legs. And since they were still living in holes, the ones that did best and bred the most were, again, the offspring with the smallest legs. So you have a situation where, over time, the animals that kept doing well and breeding most often were the ones with the smallest legs and so, legs just got smaller and smaller over the years" said Adam.

"That's impossible" said Aulis, with a dismissive wave of his hand, "legs can't just vanish like that, there would be traces left behind" added the boy.

Why this memory? Why had he come here? This was just one of the many science lessons he had given the child. What was it about this day that had made the memory stick so completely, Adam wondered?

Aulis' words caught his attention once more. Yes, there would be traces left behind. He looked over at the viper's tiny, vestigial leg bones and something deep inside his mind awakened. Vestigial... That word was important.

"Don't underestimate the power of time Aulis. A lot can change with the passing of the years and you are right, there are indeed clues that are often left behind. Even after major changes have set in we can still see evidence of old relationships. Look closely here" Adam said, pointing at the shrunken bones near the snake's pelvis.

"These were once the viper's leg bones" he explained.

Initially, Aulis looked at the bones in awe but in moments his expression changed to one of scepticism.

"So what? Are you now going to tell me that we have a tiny tail revealing a relationship to monkeys?" asked the boy as he pulled the skeleton of the monkey closer and started examining it.

"Yes, exactly" answered Adam.

Aulis pushed the monkey skeleton aside and gazed up at Adam with his intense, icy blue eyes.

"Show me!" the boy commanded.

Guided by the memory, Adam got up and went to a pile of books on a nearby table. He paged through one after another, not finding what he was looking for until his hand suddenly fell upon an old and familiar leather-bound text. Reluctantly, he lifted it up. Aulis looked up at him with a fierce curiosity.

"What is it? What do you have there?" asked the boy.

"Just wait a moment" replied Adam quietly.

As Adam opened the text, the words "I Victor..." scripted in precise letters, briefly caught his eye before his fingers flipped past and made their way to pages deeper within. They stopped on a page with an intricately drawn human skeleton and an exploded sketch of the human tail bone. He lowered the drawing to the table and Aulis came close to study every detail.

Victor... he knew that name from somewhere.

Place: Psychiatry Office, Boston, Massachusetts

Date: April 13th, 2018

Time: 3:53pm

The boy's eyes drifted to the water clock on the doctor's desk. He just stared at the relentless droplets as they cascaded through the device. Wolstone could see the child was tired. It was understandable. He had been through a lot. The panic attack he entered while describing the sexual encounter with Helene had clearly been particularly taxing. He worried about letting Adam leave in the vulnerable state that he was. Indeed, the child's case was getting stranger and stranger by the minute, but there was no point in pushing the boy needlessly.

A knock came at the door. Wolstone looked at the clock and immediately realised the time. By God had the session flown by.

"Yes, come in" he said.

Catherine cautiously opened the door.

"I'm not disturbing you I hope?" she asked.

"No. Not at all. We were just finishing actually" said Wolstone.

Wolstone briefly considered asking to speak with Catherine privately about Adam's social interactions with others, particularly girls, but quickly dropped the idea. He had the boy's trust and that, at this stage, was everything. He did not want to risk losing it by speaking with his mother about private matters behind closed doors. Even if it was normal for child psychiatrists to speak with parents about their kids in private, and he knew it was, Wolstone was neither used to such things nor keen to do it with this particular patient.

Adam came to shake his hand once again, and after Wolstone set another appointment with Catherine, the boy and his mother left.

With the office finally to himself, Wolstone turned to his notes and got thinking.

The boy had just mentioned the name 'Victor' and the psychiatrist sensed he had heard it mentioned before. He flipped through his pages and found it. Yes, the boy had said the name when he had been describing a dream of living in poverty and trying to grow vegetables somewhere in pastoral Austria. The name had been in a book he had kept in his shack.

Wait a minute, thought Wolstone, it was also in a book in this dream with Aulis. He looked closer at his notes and realised, in surprise, that the boy had described the book in both cases as being worn and leather-bound. What an intriguing thing, the child seemed to be importing the same book into both stories. Wolstone made a note to make sure to follow up on that next time.

Leaning back in his chair and looking out at the afternoon sky, he pondered the case carefully. The child was suffering from post-traumatic stress, of that Wolstone was certain, but he found it exceedingly difficult to believe that harmful experiences endured before his adoption could alone translate into such a rich fabric of tales with historically accurate elements present throughout them.

Curious, Wolstone hopped up and opened a few reference texts from his book shelf. He paced a bit as he paged through the different articles. Gradually, he came to realise that the only theory he could even begin to consider for this case was that Adam had suffered early on in some way and had an exceptional memory that allowed him to recall with great accuracy a mix of material read in obscure history books over the years. If that was so, it would account for the remarkable factual aspects of the dreams that were being described. Even so, Wolstone was at a total loss for what the child could have possibly endured to get into the state that he was.

He returned to his desk and looked over his pages of notes. He had several underlined words that seemed to keep being associated with stress: father, kissing, and thunder. That gave him an idea.

Wolstone quickly stood up and collected a box from the top of his shelf. He opened it and started sorting through a stack of cards with pictures on them packed within. After a few minutes, he had the twenty or so that he would use during their next session.

Two weeks until he would see Adam again… it was a shame he would have to wait so long before working with the boy. He looked at his watch and then glanced up at the calendar.

It was 4:10 in the afternoon and he had no more patients on the schedule. The choice between going home early to his lonely house and staying at the office proved an easy one. Colleagues sometimes had joked that he was more closely married to his work than he was to his wife. He had laughed along with them all those many years but, when he eventually lost her, it bothered him all the more to realise they had been speaking the truth.

Wolstone frowned deeply as the memories washed over him. He always made the argument that he was changing lives, making the world better by throwing everything he had into his work. Whether it was authoring academic papers on new psychiatric techniques, working with PhD students to complete their theses or helping traumatised patients to recover, he always had an excuse for not keeping up with old friends or, worse, not giving his wife the affection that she deserved.

A tear slid down his cheek as he remembered coming home and finding the note that she had called the paramedics and asked them to take her to the hospital. He'd not been taking calls because he'd been with a patient and she had no way of getting in touch. She hadn't even bothered to tell him that she had been experiencing pelvic pain months earlier. If she had, he thought, he might have seen the cancer for what it was early on and got her some help before it spread so widely. She might have even lived...

The minutes went by and slowly the misery of his failings slipped away with the afternoon sun. He had work to get on with. Wolstone swivelled over to face his pile of paperwork and suddenly found himself wondering where had he left off.

Medical school applications, no, he wasn't working on those yet. A few new patient files were scatted at the side, but again, they were hardly urgent and not nearly as interesting as Adam's case. Then his eyes fell upon the folder. Ah yes, ethics committee applications. Wolstone had to admit, he was making good progress. He'd already read through six requests and most were rather easy to approve, but one had given him a lot to think about and he'd ended up leaving it to ponder for a while.

A Harvard biochemistry lab was asking permission to chop off the front right limbs of salamanders. At first glance, it seemed barbaric, but as he read through the proposal, he found that the experiment was not as unethical as it seemed. The researchers were attaching green glowing proteins to certain cells in the arms of the salamanders and, since the amphibians had the ability to regenerate lost limbs, the team was tracking the glowing proteins to literally watch which cells were doing what during the regeneration process. The whole point was so the lab could develop better ideas on how to help people with missing arms and legs potentially regenerate their limbs. It had tremendous potential and, quite frankly, sounded fascinating.

Wolstone's pen hovered over the approval check box for several moments before he put an 'X' in it. Yes, he thought, it was the right thing to do. And besides, the salamanders weren't losing their limbs permanently; they'd grow them back quickly with the high quality food the lab team was planning on feeding them. He put his thoughts down into the comments box and picked up yet another ethics file.

He opened the document and read, 'Request to transplant a .2 gram subventricular tissue sample into a comatose patient.' Oh boy, that was going to be too heavy to deal with this late in the afternoon... best to leave it for a morning when he had a strong black coffee on hand. And with that, he moved   on to something simpler.

Part 3

Place: Imperial College, London

Date: June 26th, 2015

Time: 3:41pm

Ida's hand knocked on the frame of Dr Dixon's open door as she stood in the starkly decorated university hallway.

"I know it probably isn't particularly conducive to my progress as a PhD student to come into my supervisor's office and say you were wrong..." said Ida with a grin.

"But you're going to do so anyway, aren't you? Come on in" replied Dixon from his desk.

He leaned back in his chair.

"So, tell me the error of my ways" he said.

"Well, you remember that box of random samples you gave me to sift through back in January..." she asked.

"Oh Lord, not more about your pet HeLa cells" he said, rolling his eyes in amused exasperation.

"Well that's just the thing, they're not HeLa cells. They can't be" she said as directly as she could without sounding rude.

"What do you mean they aren't HeLa cells?"

"It isn't possible. First, take a look at the colonies they are creating and compare them to these from my textbook showing what HeLa colonies look like" she said as she handed over a printout and her book.

Dixon grabbed his spectacles to take a closer look at the images.

"Well, it is possible that these particular HeLa cells were genetically altered to behave differently" he mused.

"I don't think so. I got a reply from Charring Cross Hospital on the shelf number that was attached to the sample. They don't have any details on why the cells were collected and stored, but they do have a date for when they came into the collection" explained Ida.

"Yeah, and what's that? 1970 or something?" asked her supervisor.

"Try 1947" she answered smugly, crossing her arms in satisfaction.

Dixon whistled in surprise.

"And check this out" she said, pulling a paper from her bag, "HeLa cells were collected from an American named Henrietta Lacks just before death in 1951 and didn't start getting widely used in medical research until 1954 when Salk used them to figure out how to make the polio vaccine. That means the cells that we've got here cannot be from that patient. They're from somebody else" she said rather exuberantly.

"Are you telling me you think we've got a different strain of immortal mutant cells?" asked Dixon, starting to show some genuine interest.

"I do" replied Ida.

"Any idea who they were collected from?" he asked.

"I'm working on that. The folks at Charring Cross are searching their archives for information but, as I am sure you can imagine, the files from the 1940's are pretty messy" said Ida.

"I would imagine... Golly, wouldn't that be interesting if there was a Lacks family relative who somehow ended up in London" speculated Dixon.

"It would be, but I don't think that's very likely. Look here" said Ida, pointing at the third page of the paper she'd laid on his desk.

"Henrietta's cells replicated lots but didn't actually ever form anything. The ones that I've got in the lab are behaving differently. A lot of them are staying connected after replicating. Take a gander at this" explained Ida as she produced another two images from her folder.

"What am I looking at?" asked Dixon as he started examining it.

"That's a close up of the cells that are replicating in the culture. Look familiar?" she asked.

"This is nerve tissue" replied Dixon.

"I actually think the stuff you gave me was a sample of subventricular tissue suspended in cerebro spinal fluid

"What?" asked Dixon, genuinely confused.

"Subventricular cells, you know, the ones that were proved twenty years ago to spawn new neurons throughout our lives" she explained.

"Thank you. I know what subventricular cells are. Being old, I actually remember when their discovery turned our field upside down and proved that we do keep producing new brain cells throughout our lives. But wait a minute, if these really are subventricular cells, are they behaving normally?" he queried.

"If by behaving normally you mean, 'Are they producing baby neurons?' Then the answer is yes" she replied.

Dixon's snowy eyebrows raised themselves far above the rims of his glasses in surprise as he let out a long slow whistle.

"Now that is something. Okay. I don't want you to let your other work slide too much, but let's give these cells a bit more attention, shall we" suggested her supervisor.

"Sure. What should be our next step?" she asked.

"Try to raise the neurons in a few different cultures and see how they develop. Oh, and get David Gibbs from microbiology over here to have a look. I'd be quite keen to get his take on all of this" said Dixon.

Place: Psychiatry Office, Boston, Massachusetts

Date: April 27th, 2018

Time: 12:06pm

Wolstone felt terrible. The child looked more exhausted than he had when they had met at the beginning of their first visit. He knew that leading the boy to explore the haunting dreams would be the best way to identify the real world events behind his nightmares, but even so, it was upsetting to see the child suffer so.

"Your sleep is getting worse?" asked Wolstone.

Adam nodded. He was barely making it through the night. The dreams were more powerful than ever. Like never-ending cinema being fed directly into his brain. He was finding it impossible to get any peace.

"It... it is getting harder" said Adam.

"I understand. Would it be okay to take a break from the dreams for a moment to play a small game?" asked the doctor.

"Sure."

"Okay, I am going to show you a number of pictures and, as you see them, I want you to tell me the first thing that pops into your mind. Can you do that?" asked Wolstone.

Adam nodded.

"Fine, here we go" he said.

The psychiatrist flipped over the first card revealing a pink rose.

"Flower" said Adam.

Normal, thought Wolstone. The doctor flipped over another.

"Telephone" said Adam.

"Dog" answered the boy as another card was revealed.

Then came the responses that Wolstone had been waiting for.

"Creation" replied the boy as he responded to the card depicting a young couple kissing.

"Life" the child spoke as the card with the lightning bolt was revealed.

Wolstone wished, for all the world, that he had a card with an image of a man clearly identified as a father, but even so, the responses that he got spoke volumes. Not a single patient of his had ever replied to the kissing card with the word 'creation.' Love, romance, and passion were common. Occasionally, he got warmth or happiness, but creation? That was just weird. And using the word 'life' in response to the lightning bolt card? That too was a first. Destruction and danger were the common ones. Sometimes storm and thunder cropped up, but life? The only reason why a child would have that idea would be if he knew about...

"Adam, are you familiar with the Miller-Urey experiment?" asked Wolstone.

"You mean the one conducted in 1952?" replied the boy.

"Um, I think so. I'm not as good with dates are you are. Can you tell me more?" enquired the psychiatrist.

"Well, there were two scientists, biochemists I think, who used electrodes and sparks to transform inorganic chemicals into the building blocks of life, right?" said Adam.

"Precisely... and what was the argument that they made based upon their results?" asked Wolstone.

"They argued that lightning strikes on ancient pools of water containing the proper chemicals were likely responsible for setting the stage for the evolution of simple life" answered Adam.

Well, thought Wolstone, there it was. The child was obviously having his answers to the test shaped by his scientific understanding. Wolstone briefly flirted with the idea of heading over to the Harvard and MIT biochemistry departments to see if he would get similar responses from the researchers who had spent their entire lives studying this stuff.

Thus, while unusual, the responses were not illogical. Kissing was a first step that people took towards the creation of a child and the boy's knowledge made it clear that he viewed electricity as an essential ingredient for life. Nevertheless, Wolstone found it difficult to understand why a child would enter into panic attacks when presented with the concepts of creation and life? He certainly knew of adult patients who had such issues. They had often been abused as kids and held considerable anxiety over the idea of becoming parents themselves, but he had never heard of any cases where this anxiety had manifested in children.

Wolstone leaned back into his chair as he looked at the boy. To hell with it, he thought. Never mind that cases like this had never been documented before. Here was a highly gifted paediatric patient with a combination of post traumatic stress and a form of parental anxiety. It was utterly crazy to see such a mix, but Wolstone had nothing more to go on. The only way to resolve these matters was to find their root and that meant digging deeper. He decided to pursue the name that Adam had mentioned at the end of their last session.

"Adam, you mentioned the name Victor in the dream you were describing at the end of our last session, do you have any dreams with anyone of that name?" asked the doctor.

The exhausted boy looked confused.

"You said the words 'I Victor' were written in the front of the book you showed Aulis when you were studying in the library together" explained the doctor.

More confusion; Adam had no idea what he was talking about.

Damn was this frustrating, thought Wolstone. This had to be another post-traumatic block. Something the boy was able to describe from the dream but not something he was actually aware of. The doctor decided to try a different tack.

"You mentioned a leather book with a human skeleton drawn in it when you were trying to show Aulis the human tail bone" explained the psychiatrist.

Adam nodded; he remembered describing that book in the dream.

"Can you tell me anything more about that book? Does it appear in any other dreams?" asked the doctor.

Adam looked down at the ground with sadness. He knew where the doctor was going with his line of questioning. He feared where they were headed. Even so, he trusted that the psychiatrist had his best interests at heart. With that in mind, he concentrated on thoughts of the book and let the dreams emerge.

Place: Constantin Linder Estate

Date: 1900

Time: night

"These authors are such cowards with their explanations" exclaimed Aulis as he slammed his fist into the table with the pile of medical and biology books on it.

The anger in his voice jolted Adam out of his focus on a pile of diplomatic documents lying on the desk in front of him. He looked around; this was Constantin's library again. Aulis was definitely older, perhaps sixteen now and, as Adam saw his own reflection in a polished brass lamp next him, he realised that he too was aging. With nearly grey hair and a fair few wrinkles under his eyes he realised he had to be in his forties.

"What is the matter?" Adam asked, hearing the age in his voice.

"They are obsessed with descriptions but don't ever ask the questions of how or why" hissed Aulis.

"What have we spoken about?" said Adam sternly.

"Yes, yes. Sorry. I know. Patience" replied Aulis.

"That is alright. Now what is the trouble?" he said, stepping over to the teenager and putting a reassuring hand on his shoulder.

"It says that the nerves are connected to the brain and that the brain uses them to send signals to muscles, but it does not specify how any of this is actually done" explained Aulis with frustration in his voice.

Adam took off his glasses, rubbed his eyes and thought the matter over for a moment. He had to admit, he did not know exactly how signals were sent via neurons to muscles either. Not off the top of his head at any rate. But he knew where he could find the information and it wasn't going to be in any of the books that Aulis had available in the library.

"Let me think this one over and get back to you in a while" advised Adam.

The sound of a bell ringing emanated from beyond the library doors. Adam realised he could faintly smell food. He started to walk towards the doors and turned back to Aulis.

"Are you coming?"

"I just want to finish this" replied Aulis, not bothering to even look up from his medical texts.

"You know how much your mother hates it when you miss meals" Adam admonished.

"Just one more minute" said the teen.

"And she always blames me" Adam muttered under his breath.

He stood by the doors for a minute longer waiting but Aulis did not budge.

"Be along as soon as you can" he said, as he stepped out.

Adam walked down the brightly lit hall as the bell rang again. The smell of the food was growing stronger and he was hungry, but something tugged at him as he passed by one particular door. Without thinking he stopped and his hand reached out for the door knob. He twisted it and the door creaked open revealing a space that was immediately familiar.

It was a small and comfortable room with a bed, a desk, and closet all huddled together. Adam stepped in leaving the door to the hall ajar while taking off his glasses and laying them down on the desk. This had been his bed chambers for years. And yet, for some reason he had not had dreams of being here for a very long time.

Instinctively, he turned around to leave, as if there was something to this space that made him uneasy but the desk beckoned him to come closer. He sighed briefly and ran his hands down the side of it. He found that his fingers brushed up against a small peg and that, as they did so, a finely crafted concealed panel opened. When he looked at what was inside, he discovered a bronze box and a leather-bound book.

With trepidation, he put his glasses back on and lifted the book out of its hiding place. His fingers readily flipped past sections on "formation of stomach acid" and "tissue regeneration" before finding "control of the nerves." The faded French text was technical but understandable.

Suddenly, the door to the room creaked ever so slightly and Adam glanced over his shoulder. Aulis was standing in the doorway, his gaze directed towards the book in Adam's hands. The bell rang again.

"Are you coming for dinner?" asked Aulis.

"Yes, yes" stammered Adam, "I will be right there."

As soon as Aulis left, Adam put the book back in its hiding place and slid the panel shut.

Place: Psychiatry Office, Boston, Massachusetts

Date: April 27th, 2018

Time: 12:14pm

Wolstone felt he was going around in circles. He looked over at the boy and found him just staring out the window again.

Wolstone let out a long deep breath. Okay, just asking about the book wasn't getting him anywhere. Asking about Victor was pointless as the kid would not even recognise the name. But perhaps this Aulis character might give him a way in. The boy had commented that Aulis was gazing at the book from the hallway. Earlier he had said that Aulis seemed hungry to learn anything and everything the book had to offer. And yet, Wolstone mused, it was always clear from the stories that the book was never simply handed over to Aulis. It was as if there was something to hide. Indeed, thought the psychiatrist, the book itself was often described as being hidden in the dreams. Wolstone scratched his head. It certainly seemed worth a try.

"Adam, do you recall ever having a dream where you give Aulis the book to read on his own?" asked Wolstone.

Adam felt a pang of fear hit his gut as the doctor asked the question.

"No" answered the boy sharply, surprised by his own forceful response.

Wolstone studied Adam's face carefully. The child wasn't lying, but at the same time, the psychiatrist could tell that there was more that he was holding back. That was a new element to their interactions. Adam had proved unable to recall certain aspects of dreams and on one occasion had blatantly refused to discuss a dream associated with the year 1810, but until now, Wolstone had not encountered anything like intentional concealment or deception from the boy at any time. He decided to pry further.

"Did Aulis ever take the book from you?" asked the doctor directly.

Again, Adam felt wrenching pain hit his gut.

"He never got a hold of the book" Adam lied, almost as a reflex.

Wolstone looked at the child intently. Adam gazed back at Wolstone as severely as ever and the hairs on Wolstone's arms suddenly stood on edge. The psychiatrist had backed down when he met with such defiance earlier on, but he refused to give up this time.

"Adam, do you want the nightmares to end?" asked Wolstone bluntly but with a tinge of steel in his voice.

Adam knew he did. More than anything he wanted to reclaim his sleep. Slowly, he let his icy gaze melt away.

"Yes" he replied softly.

"Then tell me what you can remember. I promise it will be okay. Nothing can harm you here. I won't allow it" advised the psychiatrist.

Adam threw Wolstone an expression that seemed to question the doctor's statement.

Wolstone had to admit, he was starting to feel a little uneasy. This entire case was pushing the boundaries of what he understood and of what he felt comfortable dealing with. He honestly did not believe that the boy would come to any harm recalling the dreams, but he was beginning to worry that the recall activity might lead to severely damaging levels of sleep disturbance. He mulled it over for a while but, as Adam started speaking, the psychiatrist brushed his concerns aside. It was a ludicrous worry. He'd been practicing for over forty years. He could handle this. At least, that was what he kept telling himself.

Place: Constantin Linder Estate

Date: 1909

Time: night

Adam blinked his eyes a few times as he tried to figure out where he was. Scattered bits of food remained on fine porcelain in front of him. Candles were lit. A turkey, mostly picked apart, sat in the middle of the table. Across from him were Constantin and Helene, both with ever more streaks of grey in their hair. The children were all older now too. Mandi, who was gazing out the dining room window, looked to be maybe sixteen, Erno seemed to be eighteen and Aulis was now a young man in his mid-twenties.

"It looks like four on horses and nine, no ten, on foot" said Mandi as she squinted her eyes.

"Do you think they know?" Constantin asked Adam.

Know what, pondered Adam. What was happening here? What were they discussing?

"I don't think so" he replied, allowing the words to flow with the memory.

"And our people?" asked Constantin.

"I have spread word that they are here" replied Adam, still clueless as to what they were talking about.

"Just as well" complained Erno, "It's no good lying when they've got so many more guns than we do."

Helene's hands clenched into fists and her face twisted into a scowl as she glared at him.

Now Adam remembered. The Russians were getting wise to the growing resistance in Finland and installing soldiers in the towns to make sure people were speaking Russian, giving their children Russian names, and discontinuing Finnish traditions. If he remembered correctly, the soldiers were only making matters worse by further angering the Finns and galvanising the resistance.

"Erno! What have I said about those comments?" Helene responded with severity.

"Yes, I know" the boy answered in annoyance, crossing his arms and sinking back into his chair.

"Mama, may I be excused?" interrupted Mandi, stepping back from the window.

"Not just yet darling" said Helene. "Constantin, Adam, I know the soldiers are making you nervous, but if you remember, we arranged this feast for a reason" she said.

"Right... Yes. Aulis, we have got something special for you..." said Constantin.

Constantin lifted up a letter from the side of the table and handed it over to Aulis.

"Your application to join the college of surgeons has been accepted" smiled Adam.

Aulis' jaw dropped as he read on, eyes glowing with enthusiasm.

"I think you'll be the youngest to ever attend. I am very proud of you son" said Constantin, reaching his hand and holding Aulis' shoulder tightly.

Helene did her best to smile in support, but there was no denying that something was eating at her.

"Is something the matter mother?" asked Aulis, feeling the tension in the air.

Helene slowly let the smile slip from her face.

"Helene, please, it really is not the time" said Constantin, holding up his hand.

"No, I think he has a right to, err, I mean he needs to know" she replied with agitation.

"Aulis, while I am aware that you are going to be at the college of surgeons, the rising tensions in Helsinki scare me and I was thinking, well, perhaps, you might defer for a year until things settle down a bit" Helene explained.

"Helene, the protests in Helsinki have been quite minor. The governor general has things well in hand" advised Constantin.

"Three people were shot in Helsinki just last week Constantin" whispered Helene.

"They were traitors to the socialist cause Mother. They deserved what they got!" argued Erno.

"Don't be stupid! You can't call someone a traitor just because they don't agree with your view of how our country should be run or because they refuse to speak a language that they don't even understand!" lectured Mandi.

222

"Erno! That's enough of that!" shouted Helene before turning back to her eldest son and begging "Aulis, please consider deferring!"

"What? Stay here? That makes no sense at all! Honestly, there are also tensions in our streets and you know it is not just the Russians. We have plenty of moronic Finnish reds who are all too eager to see us become some sort of socialist paradise." he shouted back.

"That's crap! You only say that because you don't want to share our wealth with those who were born with nothing!" screamed Erno.

"Aulis, Erno enough! These matters are not to be spoken about, certainly not at the table!" yelled Constantin.

The din was becoming overwhelming. Adam did not feel he stood a chance of getting a word in edgewise, so he simply stood up, walked to the window and looked out at the snow. As if on cue, the group at the table grew quiet.

"Aulis, Mandi, Erno. Leave us" commanded Constantin.

Without debate, the two younger children stalked out. Aulis was slower to follow, taking his time to properly push in his chair and kiss his mother good night. It all, on the surface, seemed the actions of a well behaved youth, but as Aulis departed, Adam caught sight of an expression that hinted otherwise. It left Adam unsettled, but he remained in the dining room anyway. Somehow, deep inside, he felt that it was a decision he would regret.

"Whether we like it or not, Aulis is right" advised Adam as he looked down at the Russian soldiers in the streets below.

223

"Helsinki, Joensuu, Oulu, Tampere… he will be in danger when the revolution comes… no matter where he is. We all will" Adam continued.

"But let him go to Helsinki? Now?" asked Helene with a rising tone of panic in her voice.

"For years we have tip-toed around St Petersburg's regulations, quietly breaking rules when necessary and resisting the Russian drive to turn us red with the hope that they would just give up. It hasn't happened. A fight is coming. Maybe not today, maybe not tomorrow, but soon" cautioned Adam.

"Exactly! All the more reason to get our young man trained up as a surgeon as soon as possible" said Constantin.

"But Constantin!" cried Helene.

"No Helene. Constantin makes a fair point. Aulis has a gift that I cannot nurture further, certainly not here. He needs real doctors in a proper hospital to take him the rest of the way" advised Adam.

The mention of real doctors left Adam uneasy. The expression that Aulis had on his face when he walked out from the dining hall started to bring the pieces in his mind together. Adam felt his blood run cold. He needed to get back to his chambers.

"Please excuse me" he said as he stepped out the door and down the hall.

As he had suspected, Aulis was in his room. The secret compartment in the side of the desk was open and the leather-bound book was in the hands of the young man.

On the desk was the bronze box. It too was open, revealing an unusually shaped syringe, a few eerily familiar vials and some tubing. Adam could feel his heart racing; the bitter taste of adrenaline flooded his mouth.

"What are you doing?" Adam asked, doing all he could to keep his composure.

"A question came to my mind after dinner and I thought I would check the book that you always check" replied Aulis in a nonchalant manner.

"This book is not yours. It is private!" hissed Adam, stepping closer.

"Yes, of course" said Aulis, "but I don't understand something. The opening entries in this book on organ transplants and tissue cultures are not in your script. They are all signed off with the name 'Victor.' Who is he?"

Adam could feel the muscles in his body tensing up, as if preparing him to pounce like a predator. He marvelled at the haughty arrogance of his own son.

"He was a man who died a very long time ago" answered Adam curtly.

Aulis scanned Adam's face carefully, clearly deciding how much further to press the matter.

"Was he your mentor?" asked Aulis.

"Somewhat" replied Adam, drawing closer and growing angrier by the minute.

Aulis took a step back and stopped with his back against the wall.

"But how can that be?" he asked, "The entries in his script are dated between 1805 and 1810. How could you possibly have been trained by someone conducting research over a hundred years ago?"

In a predatory burst of ferocity, Adam seized the book, slammed it shut and turned towards the young man. Aulis scrambled to the side but he was far too slow. Adam grabbed him by the collar and lifted him off the ground with ease.

He was about to berate the boy but the image that reached his eyes forced him into silence. His arm was covered in a ghastly patchwork of swollen purple scars and his muscles were bulging beneath a thin layer of skin that could barely conceal their ropey nature. His hand was the hideous blue of a fresh bruise. He felt extraordinary strength and terrible fear.

Shaken by what he was seeing, Adam dropped Aulis to the ground. Their eyes briefly met and, in an instant, Aulis was fleeing down the hall. Adam turned towards the window and caught a faint reflection of himself in the glass. The scars and welts were not limited to his arms, they were everywhere. On his shoulders, his neck, even his face. His lips were black, his teeth were pearly white. Suddenly, an eye of sickly yellow sitting in the socket of his head, reflected back at him, forcing a surge of bile into his mouth.

Adam stumbled backwards in shock, breathing hard. What was happening? He was sucking in air and seemingly unable to get enough. A pain grew in his chest. His hands and legs started to feel numb. The breaths came in futile gasps and he fell to his knees.

"Try to realise it is just a hallucination!" said a voice.

"It can't be. It is so real. My skin, it feels like ice!" replied Adam, still gasping.

"But it is an illusion. It is a figment of your imagination. Concentrate. Remember who you are and look back at your hand" advised Wolstone.

Adam shook his head in a panic.

"Think about all the good in the dreams" explained Wolstone, "You saved Helene from running away and potentially leading Nikolay to be hanged, you adopted and protected Elsa, you protected those children when their grandmother died. No matter what this nightmare tells you, must remember that you are not a monster!"

Adam did as he was told and tried his best to focus on the positive. It was difficult, there were dark demons fighting for control of his thoughts, but as he put his mind to it, the fear and self loathing started to fade away. Astonishingly, the blue was already beginning to recede and the scars were vanishing right before his eyes. His panicked breathing slowed down.

"I don't understand. What is this all about?" asked the boy.

"That remains to be determined, but I think it best if we find our courage and carry on after having already come so far" said the doctor.

Adam rubbed his hands against his face, rose to his feet and looked into the window again. His blue eyes were back where the yellow ones had just been. He shivered ever so slightly as he recalled the ordeal he had been through.

"Where do we go now?" asked Adam.

"It won't be easy, but I think we will learn much if you try and recall the night of the revolution" advised Wolstone.

Adam shuddered as he leaned his head against the window. The psychiatrist was right. It was not going to be easy, but as he put effort into recalling the event, the memories came flooding back with remarkable ease.

The seasons flashed by and suddenly, he was there.

Place: Constantin Linder Estate

Date: 1918

Time: day

Adam lifted his head back from the window and glanced out at the plaza below. The winter sun was riding low in the sky. It was midday but it looked like early evening. He could just make out a number of young men in the square speaking with a pair of older men with red bands wrapped around their upper arms. One of the older men appeared to be revealing how the different parts of his rifle functioned as he was taking it apart and allowing the others to examine the bits and pieces. The other older man was passing around a bottle of some sort of liquor. Adam squinted his eyes to look at the group more closely and noticed as Erno took a swig from the bottle.

"It is getting worse" said Helene.

Adam had not even heard her creep in to his room. Her face was becoming more finely chiselled with age and her chestnut locks turning silver.

"I know" he replied, still staring out at the plaza.

"Constantin told you then?" she asked.

"About the riots in Helsinki? Yes" he replied.

The lines of her face creased and drifted into sadness.

"I am sure Aulis is being sensible" said Adam, trying his best to console her.

"It is not Aulis who I worry about so much" replied Helene.

She stared out at Erno and her eyes grew glassy as she reached out for Adam's hand. His fingers met hers and she gave him a gentle squeeze.

"Give him a chance" he murmured, "I am sure he will grow beyond this. It is just a phase."

They stood together, hand in hand for many minutes before they heard footfalls in the corridor. The door opened and their hands broke apart.

Constantin held an unopened enveloped and a letter in his hand. His face was full of worry and desperately pale.

"Shots are being fired in Helsinki. Many are dead" he said.

"How many?" asked Helene.

"Dozens" said Constantin referring to one of the letters, "Social democrat factory workers are standing in open rebellion against the idea of an independent Finnish state. They are far more organised than we expected and advancing north. Worse, St Petersburg is openly arming them and sending troops to us to bolster the red effort."

"Civil war" said Adam.

Place: Constantin Linder Estate

Date: January, 1918

Time: night

Adam, Helene and Constantin stood by the dining hall windows staring out at the moon-lit horizon like statues. A dozen rifles and sabres sat behind them on the dining table.

"They knew where to go to light the fuse" asked Constantin.

"Oh yes, they were there at the stables when I laid it out" answered Adam.

"I don't remember" asked Helene, "where did we get all of those explosives from?"

"Cartridges for the cannon St Petersburg sent" replied Constantin.

"But I thought the cartridges never arrived?" questioned Helene.

Adam leaned back and smiled broadly.

"I see" she answered dryly.

"And all our people know?" asked Constantin.

"About the ruse?" asked Adam, "Yes, all of them."

"I don't understand, what is taking so long?" asked Helene.

Suddenly a flash of fire flared at the edge of town. In seconds, the sound of the blast shook the estate. For a minute, there was only silence, and then there was a rifle shot... and another... and then there were many.

"Adam, please tell our guards at the windows to begin their orders" advised Constantin.

Adam knew where he was needed, and headed for the stairs. As he entered the sitting room he found the estate's loyal guards precisely where he had left them earlier in the day. All were prominently wearing the red arm bands sent to the estate by Helsinki.

"Gentlemen, take your positions and remember, keep your shots few and far between until I say otherwise" said Adam as he took his place by a boarded up window with just a tiny peep hole exposed.

As the minutes passed, he could see a group of men wearing white arm bands emblazoned with the Finnish coat of arms taking cover behind barrels on the other side of the street. They took aim at the estate and fired at its walls. Several Russians soldiers were approaching from another road on horseback.

"A few shots at the whites please" asked Adam.

As the guards fired, Adam watched as the Russians leapt out of their saddles, took cover behind the statue in the central plaza, and aimed at the whites. He could make out seven other Russian soldiers alongside many men with rifles wearing red arm bands over plain clothes riding swiftly down another road to join their allies.

"Sir" asked one of the guards, "Shall we change targets now?"

Adam had to admit, the three Russians by the statue were so vulnerable. Even so, he knew their trickery would only work once and wanted to claim as many reds and Russians as he could with the ruse.

"Not yet" cautioned Adam.

The reds and the seven additional Russians dropped behind the statue and opened fire on the whites as well. One of the whites from behind the makeshift barricade of barrels fell to the ground with blood pouring out of his chest.

More reds came rushing in from a side street to protect the estate. They dropped behind Constantin's carriage on the street with their backs to Adam and opened fire on the whites too.

"Now?" asked another one of the guards.

Adam could count thirty men. It was certainly a good number of Russians and reds to take down, but it could still be just a small fraction of the enemies in the town. Much depended upon how many they were able to kill in the sabotaged barn and he had no way of knowing that number until he had a chance to get over there and search the place for bodies.

"Sir?" asked the guard, "how many more are we waiting for?"

The guard was right. Realistically, Adam was not sure how many more Russians and Finnish reds might filter into the square to defend Constantin.

"Very well. Change targets now" Adam called out as he hefted a rifle of his own from the table and took aim out the window.

And with that, the rifles in the windows of the estate shifted from aiming at the whites to aiming at the Russians and the reds. One shot after another hit them in their backs. It only took the Russians and the reds a matter of seconds to figure out what was happening, but it was long enough for Adam and the guards to drop twenty of them.

Shards of glass and splinters of wood came flying in as the battle continued on. They had outstanding cover from their opponents, but it was not perfect. Shots were still getting through. Suddenly, one of the estate's guards just a few feet away from Adam fell backwards.

Adam looked at the man and briefly considered trying to help, but he could see blood spurting out of the upper left section of his chest. That's a cardiac wound, he thought, there's no way I am going to be able to fix that, definitely not here.

Adam hefted his rifle and fired again but his shot went wild. He could see more whites taking up position on the northern side of the square but the Russians and reds were solidifying their hold on the streets to the east near the bakery. Indeed, they seemed to be intentionally migrating there. Rather than load his rifle again immediately, Adam took a moment to look carefully into the shadows of the road where the Russians were gathering. It was awfully dark, but as a rifle shot flashed, it granted him the temporary light he needed to spot the barricade they were building and the cannon pieces that they were carrying down from the saddles of several horses. Damn, he thought, we cannot let them get one of their cannons operational.

In seconds, Adam was racing down the hall towards the kitchen in the back of the estate. As he turned a corner, he slammed into Mandi.

"Sorry!" she exclaimed, struggling to keep her balance.

"Not a worry" said Adam.

He started to dash off again when he saw the bag of fluid filled glass bottles that Mandi was carrying in the bag slung over her shoulders.

"What have you got there?" he asked.

"Mother is making them in the cellar with a mix of kerosene and vodka" replied Mandi rather brightly. "She's calling them Russian Drinks!"

"Where are you taking them?" asked Adam.

"To the guards on the roof" she said, "Why?"

"I think I've got a better use for them. Come with me" he answered, motioning for her to follow.

There was no way the estate guards were going to be able to hit the cannon or the troops behind the barricade and he knew that if the Russians finished building their cannon it would be the end. They'd blast a hole in the estate wall and it would all be over in minutes.

"Where are we going?" asked Mandi, as she raced to keep up with him.

"You know how the alley out back goes right past the rear entrance to Hildur's" he asked as he dashed into the kitchen.

"The bakery?" she asked, "Sure."

They crossed the kitchen together and came to the back door. It was locked.

"When did this get locked?" asked Mandi, "We never lock this door!"

"Yesterday" replied Adam, as he produced the key.

"Your father and I didn't want any unexpected guests getting in" he explained, "I had no idea we were going to be the ones having to make use of it though."

He took the lock off and opened the door ever so slightly, realising for the first time that he had left his rifle in the front of the estate with the guards.

"Mandi, would you…"

Seemingly reading his mind, she hopped across the kitchen and pulled out a butcher's knife from the cutting block.

He glanced out again and was relieved to see that the alley was clear.

"Come on" he whispered.

Together, they crept through the shadows down the narrow passage and stepped over to the back of the bakery. Adam tried the door and, as he expected, it was locked. He looked it over and considered just how strong it might actually be. The hinges certainly did not look too

236

tough. With that thought in mind, he handed the butcher's knife to Mandi, took a few steps back and rammed his shoulder into the door. The wood by the hinges started to crack. He rammed into it again. More cracks. On his third attempt the hinges broke apart and the door came crashing down in a cloud of dust. Amidst the terrible din of rifle fire coming from the plaza, the noise of the collapsing door barely registered.

The bakery was deserted. Adam wasn't surprised. Hildur and her husband hated the Russians with a passion. He was certain they were amongst those fighting in the streets.

Adam and Mandi climbed the stairs and stopped when they came to a bedroom with windows facing out to the plaza. Gingerly, Adam pulled back one of the shudders. Glancing down, he realised he was in the perfect spot and not a moment too soon. The Russians were directly below and loading their small cannon. In a matter of minutes they would have it aimed directly at the estate's front doors and be ready to blast.

"Hand me a few of those will you" he asked Mandi.

She passed him a bunch of the bottles. Adam was impressed. Helene certainly knew what she was doing when she designed them. The bottles each had an alcohol-soaked strip of cloth sticking out of the top. They'd light easily, likely remain lit in a freefall, and then explode in a cloud of fire when they ruptured. They were exactly what he needed.

"Mandi, I am going to light these, and as I do, I just want you to drop them out the window" he explained. "No need to throw them and don't expose your arm or head.

Just quickly drop them and stay well clear. Can you do that?"

She nodded.

"Here we go" he said as he struck a match and started lighting the pieces of cloth.

Mandi was quick and, in seconds, the courtyard was alight with flames. Adam could not see exactly what the cocktails were doing, but he could guess from the agonising screams that the opponents below were burning. Mandi started to peak over the edge, but Adam pulled her away.

"There is no way we got all of them and it will not take the survivors long to figure out where we are. We have to get out of here" he said as he pulled her along with him.

Hand in hand, they ran down the stairs and, as they stepped into the alley, they found themselves caught between a pair of Russian soldiers.

One was between them and the back door of the estate. The other was further down the street and approaching fast. Both lifted their rifles to fire but Adam was quicker. In an instant, the butcher's knife was flying out of his hand. The soldier between them and the back door dropped his rifle and grasped at the blade lodged itself in his throat. He made a sickening gurgle and sank to his knees as he clutched in futility at the blade. They raced towards the door as the other soldier fired. Adam felt no pain and assumed the soldier had missed, but as he reached the estate he realised he was wrong.

"Adam!" she screamed.

Just ten steps behind him was Mandi, breathing heavily and bleeding profusely from her shoulder.

The soldier was still a way off but reloading fast. Another, an officer it seemed from his uniform, stepped in from the street behind and lifted up his rifle as well. Mandi was struggling to climb to her feet, but Adam knew there was no way she would get inside before one of the two soldiers managed another shot. He also knew that one more shot would be her end.

With a mixture of courage and fear, he leapt over to Mandi, lifted her off the blood-soaked ground and did his best to shield her with his own body as he raced away from them.

Daring a glance back as he ran for the estate, Adam caught sight of the officer aiming his rifle and firing. Adam braced for the ripping pain but all that followed was a pitiful cry. As Adam got to the door, he watched as the soldier next to the officer fell to the ground with a bloody hole through the centre of his chest. The Russian officer had shot him! And he was now running towards the estate himself.

Thoughts went racing through Adam's mind at a lightning pace. Who was this? A Russian traitor? One of the local rebels in disguise? In the darkness, it was difficult to determine, but as the officer came close and started looking at the severity of Mandi's wound, Adam heard a voice that he never thought he would be so happy to hear again.

"We had better get her inside and fast" whispered Aulis.

The brass candlestick holders clattered to the ground as Aulis cleared the table. Dripping with her blood, Adam laid Mandi out. Helene followed, looking desperately nervous.

Aulis dumped his pack on the floor and pulled out a medical kit.

"Mother, get towels, clean towels! Adam, keep the pressure on and try to lift her legs!" he shouted so he could be heard amidst the cacophony of rifle fire outside.

Helene dug through one of the drawers, throwing fine cloth towels to Adam.

"Adam, pull back so I can take a look" advised Aulis.

He did so and Aulis dove in. His fingers were quick and nimble, moving the bloody tissues out of the way to get a better look at the wound. Mandi flinched in pain, clenching her teeth hard. Adam was no expert, but, bloody as she was, everything actually looked in tact.

"Is she going to be alright?" Helene asked.

"I think so. She's lost some blood, but the bullet seems to have gone out of its way to avoid hitting anything vital" explained Aulis.

"Adam, can you hand me the needle and thread from my kit?" Aulis asked.

He handed them right over.

"It was lucky you turned that corner when you did. I thought we were dead" said Adam.

"That fire bomb in the plaza might as well have had your signature on it" Aulis laughed. "The reds should have taken you into account when they were working out how many men to send to Joensuu!"

Aulis began stitching up Mandi's wound.

"When I saw the troops scramble towards the back alley, I had a hunch you were going to need help" explained the young doctor.

"And the lieutenant's uniform?" asked Helene, "Wherever did you get it?"

"Courtesy of Grandpa Nikolay's old secretary" smiled Aulis.

"Speaking of Nikolay, how is Helsinki?" asked Adam.

"Horrible and getting worse" said Aulis darkly. "I was genuinely surprised by how many Finns decided they prefer the comfort of Russian socialism over the risk presented by the possibility of establishing our own democracy."

Aulis was working extremely quickly. Adam marvelled at how talented the young surgeon had become.

"I've never seen that stitch pattern before, it looks very effective. Much stronger than the technique I taught you" marvelled Adam "You have gotten good at this."

"It comes from spending every day and night in a hospital next to streets where people are shooting at one another" he replied with a wry grin. "Great for training. Bad for sleep."

Suddenly rifle shots rang out from just down the hall.

"What the devil!" gasped Adam as he ran over to take a look down the stairs.

The smoke flying upwards was thick, but he could see just enough to catch sight of Constantin. The regent's arm was red with blood.

"What has happened?" called Adam.

"We've been betrayed! Someone let them through the entryway in the servants' quarters! They've got inside" the regent shouted back as more bullets flew by.

Helene ran to Adam's side.

"Constantin come up here!" she screamed.

"No. We have to hold them. Get to the cellar tunnel! Go to the safe point, like we agreed. I'll follow as soon as I can" Constantin yelled.

Helene hung at the edge of the stairs, staring down at the scene.

"Go! Go now!" Constantin shouted, as he lifted his rifle to take another shot at the intruders as they pressed their way through the downstairs living room.

A powerful explosion shook the building violently. Plaster came falling down and glass shattered. The cannon, thought Adam, they had finally got it working. He grabbed Helene by the arm and pulled her close.

"Get your bag and meet me in the dining room!" he said.

She ran into her room and Adam dashed into his own. He hurriedly opened the secret compartment in his desk and slid both the leather-bound book and the bronze box along with a few other objects into a knapsack waiting on his bed. He threw it over his shoulder, strapped on a sword belt, grabbed a rifle by his door, and raced back to the dining room.

The smoke was growing ever thicker. Mandi looked up at him as he came in. She was pale, but well bandaged and standing. Aulis had done a marvellous job. In a moment, Helene was with them too, rifle in hand and a sword strapped on to her belt.

"Grab your things, we're going" Adam ordered as he loaded his rifle.

Together, the four of them made their way down the stairs. The ground floor hall was a disaster area. One of the curtains was on fire, half-broken bricks were scattered across the floor, and numerous pieces of furniture were overturned and being used as makeshift barricades. Two guards who had been loyal to the family for years lay dead with grievous wounds to their heads. While Adam could not see either the Russians or the reds, he could hear them down the hall and firing from the servants' rooms. Worse, he could see a sizeable hole in the front wall; he had no doubt that it was the work of the cannon.

Three guards and two servants knelt behind the barricades and fired back. Four others, with Constantin amongst them, were still by the windows taking aim at enemies in the street. Suddenly, the front door and part of the wall near the cannon hole exploded. Fragments and wall debris went everywhere, throwing several of the

243

guards backwards. From the smoke emerged a troop of Russian soldiers and reds with their rifles ready.

Constantin stepped forward with his rifle aimed at them.

"I am the regent of this town. We are loyal to St Petersburg. Stand down!" he yelled at them in Russian.

Erno, carrying a rifle of his own and wearing a red band on his arm, came forward from the smoke and stood next to the soldiers. He pointed his gun at Constantin and gazed at him darkly. Instinctively, Adam pulled Helene and Mandi behind the banister for cover.

"He is a traitor. They are all traitors" said Erno in near perfect Russian as he fired a shot into Constantin's chest.

The soldiers followed with shots of their own.

Constantin fell backward with the force of the impact and struggled to crawl behind a table. Mandi shrieked in anguish.

The servants and guards hid behind what furniture they could, and returned fire.

"Adam, get them out of here!" yelled Constantin as the blood flooded out of him.

"Constantin!" screamed Helene.

Adam dragged Helene down the stairs with Aulis and Mandi close behind. Shots continued behind them and, in moments, Adam could hear the sounds of boots coming down the staircase.

Together they ran down the underground corridor. The door to the cellar was not far off, just around the next turn in the passage. Aulis grabbed one of the lit lanterns hanging on the wall as Adam pulled his keys out of his cloak. Just as they were turning a corner, a shot ricocheted off the stone. Adam could see the cellar door just ahead.

"Helene, catch" said Adam as he tossed her the keys.

Looking back around the corner, he could see five of the soldiers running through the hall after them. With no cover for them to hide behind, Adam realised he could drop at least one of them before they could return fire. He hefted his rifle and took a shot. One of the five fell to the ground as Adam's bullet spilt the man's skull in two. The others scattered to the sides of the corridor, drew their rifles and fired back.

"We've got it Adam!" called Aulis as Helene pushed the door open and he and Mandi went through.

"Helene, give me your gun!" shouted Adam, "I haven't the time to reload."

She ran it over to him and he readied it as another bullet came flying.

"Get out of here, I'll catch up!" he yelled.

"But Adam!" she said with tears in her eyes.

"Go. I'm going to be fine" he said.

Their eyes met for a moment, and, in the chaos of the battle, their lips met briefly once more.

"Now go!"

Helene ran for it as Adam stuck his head around the corner. He was forced to dodge back just a soldier fired another shot. Damn, they were creeping closer. Adam poked around the corner again and fired but the shot missed. Three of the soldiers shot back, almost hitting him. There was no way he was going to win this, he thought, and with that in mind, he pulled back and ran.

In the cellar, Aulis and Helene were shifting a storage rack to the side. As it moved, a service tunnel came into view.

"Hurry, they are getting closer!" shouted Mandi.

With the tunnel nearly open, Aulis ran forward, lantern in hand. Adam, Helene and Mandi followed. Adam dared a glance behind once more and found the soldiers entering the cellar. Three were reloading as they ran after them but one was already taking aim.

The shot was deafening in the narrow tunnel. The force of the impact knocked Mandi off her feet and blew her right arm straight off. She screamed in agony. Shards of bone flew outwards and blood came gushing out of the wound.

The other three soldiers charged forward, quickly closing the distance and drawing their swords.

Helene abruptly turned as her daughter fell. Gone were fear and anguish from her face. All that remained was the ferocity of a mother standing between danger and her daughter. With grace and power, she drew her sword.

The soldiers were upon her in moments. With considerable skill she deflected an attack and handily stabbed the sword's wielder in the heart, dropping him to the ground.

Adam pulled his bag off his shoulder and quickly drew his own sword.

"Aulis, take this and go!" he said as he threw him the bag.

"But Adam, I can help!" shouted Aulis, as he started to draw his own sword.

"Get out of here and meet me at the rendezvous. We will need you alive to stitch people up!" yelled Adam.

Without a second glance, Aulis did as he was told, grabbed the bag and fled as Adam turned back to the battle.

The two remaining men were slashing at Helene with cool and professional precision. There was no question that they were well trained. In contrast, while Helene was passionate, she did not have the skills. Parrying wildly, he could see her tiring fast. Worse, the third remaining soldier was behind and reloading his rifle as fast as his fingers would allow.

Adam could feel the monster roaring to life within and, for the first time in his long life, rather than fear it, he willed the beast to take hold. He could see the thick scar tissue spreading across his body, sensed his shoulders crackling as his muscles strengthened and felt no sense of fear as he gripped his sword with a jaundiced hand of mottled grey. The cold of death enveloped him and, perversely, he found himself savouring it.

Helene gasped as one of the soldiers stabbed deep into her flank. She dropped her sword as the other followed through with a fierce cut to her neck. They grinned with pleasure at having downed their opponent, but their grins were soon replaced with open-mouthed terror as the monster approached.

The first soldier lunged, but Adam was too fast and too strong. With a powerful parry, he knocked the soldier's sword out of his hand and then, with inhuman strength, struck him hard with his fist. The man flew backwards seven feet and slammed into the wall. The sickening snap of his back as it hit the stone echoed down the hall leaving any question of his survival settled. The second soldier slashed at him, but Adam was quick and managed to ram the hilt of the sword into the soldier's face. Teeth went flying and blood came flowing from the man's mouth. The soldier staggered backwards and dropped his weapon in fear as Adam's fist came crashing down on his head. Skull bones cracked and splintered as the man crumbled.

Then came the shot. Adam sensed the impact, but felt nothing. He looked up and saw an expression of shock as the soldier with the rifle stared at him for a moment. As realisation set in that Adam was not going to fall, he frantically started to load his rifle once more. It was all for nothing. In a second, Adam closed the distance between the two of them and locked his hands around the man's throat. The soldier did all he could to try and pry the dead hands off, but it was no use, in moments, Adam had crushed the life out of him.

For a moment, the monster within lingered and his fingers remained wrapped around the man's throat, but as it dawned upon Adam that the fight was over, the rage faded and warmth started returning to his limbs. The scars faded as did the strength. Sensation returned to his body and he could feel both the pain of his bullet wound and the blood soaking his shirt, but he paid it no mind as he ran to Helene and Mandi. Mandi was unconscious and bleeding heavily from her arm, she still had a pulse but it was weakening fast. On instinct he wrapped a tourniquet around the stump that remained of her arm and turned to look upon Helene. She was far worse. With a terrible chest wound and a horrendous gash in her throat, Helene's face was paler than he had ever seen it and her eyes were growing glassy.

"Adam…" she gasped as she reached out and grasped his hand.

"Helene!" he replied desperately, clutching her blood soaked fingers tightly.

"I… I will see you in Heaven" she whispered as the light left her eyes.

He buried his face in her hair as tears poured down his cheeks. Time seemed to stop as her loss overwhelmed him, but the peace did not last long. Adam was suddenly brought back to attention as a shot flew by from far down the tunnel. He glanced over his shoulder and saw a dozen reds swarming in. On instinct, he threw Mandi over his shoulder and ran as fast as his legs would carry him.

During the minutes that followed, he turned from one tunnel to the next, following the path through the underground labyrinth exactly as Constantin had told him to. Sewer rats scurried away as he splashed through the fetid puddles. Horrible as the journey was, Adam was certain the labyrinth would take the soldiers an hour to navigate.

Exhausted and weakened, Adam emerged from the tunnels and found himself on a hill among two dozen whites from the town engaged in a rifle fight with a regiment of reds approaching Joensuu from a road down below.

A grenade thrown by the reds fell short by a few dozen feet and blew up behind a boulder. It rocked back and forth menacingly with the force of the explosion. Adam quickly scanned the crowd for Aulis. He spotted him in the back of the group administering first aid to a few of the injured. Adam ran over and laid Mandi down. The young man looked up at Adam.

"Where is mother?" he asked.

Adam shook his head sadly.

"I couldn't get her out, there were just too many of them" replied Adam.

Aulis frowned deeply as his eyes filled with tears.

"I wrapped her arm in my cloak to try and stop the bleeding, but I think she is still bad" Adam explained as Aulis took a closer look at Mandi, putting his fingers to her neck.

"She has a pulse. It's weak, but it is still there" said Aulis.

He grabbed a backpack and pushed it beneath her legs to get her in shock position.

"This will help, but she's going to need blood" advised the young surgeon.

Adam watched as a white nearby reached into his bag and prepared a grenade to throw back at the reds. His gaze shifted to the boulder that had just been rocking about and he suddenly had an idea. Adam ran over and put his hand on the young rebel's shoulder.

"No, not at them!" Adam advised.

"What?" asked the young Finn.

"They are too far. Throw it behind the boulder" explained Adam.

Following Adam's advice, the rebel threw it behind the boulders and the well placed explosion started a rockslide. Boulders went bounding down the hill, crushing the reds at the front of the regiment and forcing the rest to scatter. Adam turned back to Aulis.

"Where the hell are we going to get blood?" he asked impatiently.

Aulis slapped the soft side of his arm to expose the veins and handed Adam a cloth tourniquet. Adam's eyes widened as Aulis stuck himself with a needle and connected it to a tube.

"Tighten that around my arm will you and hand me that jar!" commanded Aulis.

This stuff was straight out of Victor's notes, thought Adam, he was certain of it. His mouth filled with bile at the prospect of participating in such a horrific activity.

"Aulis!" said Adam with fear and menace in his voice.

Aulis glanced up and gave him a look indicating he knew exactly what his old mentor was thinking.

"Do you want her to die or what?" argued the young doctor.

Biting his lip in frustration, Adam reluctantly handed the jar over and tightened the cloth around the arm. Slowly, Aulis' blood started flowing in.

"Since she is my sister, the chances are good that she should be able to tolerate this" advised Aulis.

Adam knew the science well from Victor's notes. Foreign blood often proved lethal. Aulis was right; his blood was the best chance that Mandi had. Even so, it killed him to see Victor's work in action like this.

Five minutes later, Aulis patched himself up, stuck a needle into Mandi and reversed the flow from the bottle. As his blood flowed into her, the moon slipped away behind the hills and the impenetrable blackness of the night consumed them all.

Place: Kaivanto Bridge, 10 miles southeast of Tampere

Date: February, 1918

Time: day

The red regiment was approaching quickly from the south but Adam knew he need not be afraid, he remembered this moment. He glanced down at himself. He was dressed in the lieutenant's uniform that Aulis had arrived in months earlier. To his side he saw a handful of the villagers who he had come to know so well from Joensuu. They too were in uniform to complete the trap's illusion.

"What news?" asked the red captain as he neared.

"Tampere is holding well and the white attackers from the north are beginning to falter" replied Adam.

"Good to hear! Tales abound of what crafty bastards they are, putting up a savage fight" said the captain.

"They were, but the upper hand is ours now. Commander Salmela expects to have the whites fleeing from the towns north of here within a matter of days. I wish we didn't have to man this bridge. It would be nice to have some of the war spoils for ourselves" Adam lied as convincingly as he could manage.

"I will try and save some for you!" laughed the captain as he motioned for his troops to follow.

As a unit, the reds rode out across the bridge.

Adam almost felt bad as he looked down at the icy lake below. He and his men would not even need to fire a single shot. Hypothermic shock would set in as soon as the reds hit the water. They would never even make it to the snow-covered shore. And with that thought, Adam watched as a fuse running from a nearby copse of trees sparked and sizzled its way over the cliff and down to the bridge supports. He motioned to the others and ran for cover as the explosion blew one of the bridge beams out of place. Like ants running from water, the reds scrambled to save themselves, but it was all for nothing. The bridge quickly shifted sideways and, in moments, the men were falling to their deaths in the lake.

Adam stared into the dark waters churning with dying soldiers and in them, he saw battle after bloody battle during the revolution. There were so many they made his head hurt. At every one, he walked away unscathed. At least, that was his physical condition. With the swirling images of battle also came memories of sleeplessness and haunting nightmares.

This is where it started, he thought, this is where his long past started blending with shadow. This is where it became impossible to discern dream from reality. As he pondered this last thought, he found himself standing in a tent filled with blood.

Place: White Camp, Tampere

Date: March, 1918

Time: day

The place was like a meat factory. It was filled with stretcher after stretcher of wounded men writhing in agony. The air was thick with the scent of iron and medical grade alcohol. Outside, Adam could hear a camp that had to be made up of nearly a thousand whites, bustling with activity.

The man directly in front of him on the stretcher was coughing badly and had a bloody gash in his upper chest.

"Sometimes you won't see the hole in the lung itself. Scan for bubbles" said Aulis, standing nearby in full surgical gear and working on a patient himself.

Adam was confused. Scan for bubbles? Why? He carefully looked over the wound. Suddenly he saw them. Bubbles. The memory quickly came back more solidly.

The soldier was coughing from a wound to the chest. This hinted that there might be a rip in one of his lungs. That was what Adam was looking for so he could stitch it up before cleaning and closing the external wound. He followed the bubbles to their source and got to work on the lung. Out of the corner of his eye, he saw two people enter.

They were polite enough to leave him to his work, but it was obvious they needed to speak with him as they quietly stood nearby. Minutes went by as he cleaned and

255

closed the man up. He quickly washed his arms and turned to find Mandi and a man with a fierce part down the centre of his light brown hair. Mandi was looking well. Losing an arm had clearly not hindered her overall health much, if at all. The man eyed Adam carefully.

"He says he needs to speak with you and only you" advised Mandi.

Aulis washed up in a soapy bucket and moved on to yet another patient.

"Hjalmar Frisell, captain of the first brigade" the man said crisply in Swedish.

"And what business does the Swedish army have with those fighting for Finnish independence?" asked Adam, also in Swedish.

"You are Adam Adlerberg" asked the man.

"Adam Adlerberg? No. I am Adam Korhonen" said Adam.

The man threw an awkward glance at Mandi and back at Adam.

"But I was told…" said the man.

"I was an advisor and friend to Nikolay Adlerberg. I lived upon his estate and was entrusted to look after his daughter and her husband's activities in Joensuu…" Adam trailed off as thoughts of death circled his mind.

"Ah, I did not know. We had you listed as family" said the Swede.

An awkward   silence followed.

"I trust you know of Helene's death" Adam said sadly.

The Swede nodded sombrely.

"Yes. Many of us mourned her passing. While St Petersburg has long been a threat, few in Sweden held any animosity towards Adlerberg or his family" explained Hjalmar.

"But I did not come to discuss such sorrowful things. If you are who you say you are, then I am told you will be able to read this" explained the soldier, handing him a note.

Adam looked it over. It was written in a mix of Latin, French, German, Polish and Swedish. What the devil? He slowly worked his way through the wild linguistic obstacle course.

"God declares that... the sport... is sacred and that I will... end up in a fiery pit... for having never tried it... all swear fealty ... to tennis" read Adam slowly.

The soldier's eyes brightened as Adam translated the note aloud.

Lord almighty, Adam thought. This had to be from Gustaf. He started to smile in spite of the grim surroundings.

"We must speak in private" said Hjalmar quietly, putting a gloved hand on Adam's shoulder.

Moments later they were alone in a tent with a small table and a map set out in front of them.

"We are hidden in these woods" explained the Swedish commander.

"Four hundred of you?" asked Adam.

"Yes. And three dozen Norwegians" advised the Swede.

"You will attack independently?" asked Adam.

"No. King Gustaf does not want war to risk angering Russia. An invasion by them would be our end. We are to integrate ourselves amongst your ranks. We are to function as if we are simply part of your forces. As you know, many of our people speak some Finnish..." explained Hjalmar.

"And many of our people speak Swedish, so that should not be a difficult ruse to pull off" added Adam.

"What are your plans?" asked the Swede.

"Well, the last major red force is well fortified in Tampere. They have some battle-hardened Russian units with them, but we have now stolen the weapons and food meant for these soldiers twice and General Mannerheim thinks they are weakening. We were going to wait for more whites to arrive from Oulu, but with you and your men here now..." Adam trailed off.

"Attack in the morning?" proposed Hjalmar with a grin splitting across his broad features.

"We damn well should! I will send a messenger to the general immediately" said Adam.

The evening came far faster than Adam would have liked. The Swede had gone to rally his troops and Adam had passed along the message of the planned joint attack to the northern camp. After pondering the battle map on the table for a few more minutes, he stepped out of the

258

command tent and strolled over to a brightly burning pit fire.

Five whites lay dead on the icy ground. Nearby, Aulis sat on a stone and was cutting open the now dead body of the patient who Adam had treated for the hole in the lung earlier in the day. Not hearing Adam's approach, Aulis looked intently at the organs in the man's chest.

"We lost him?" asked Adam quietly.

Broken from his thoughts, Aulis looked over at Adam slowly, warily.

"Yes" he replied.

"I'm so sorry" said Adam solemnly. "What was it that I did wrong?" he asked.

"That is just the thing. It is so frustrating. I checked him over and you fixed his lung perfectly, exactly as I taught you last month. It was precisely the way to repair a pneumothorax, almost as if you had studied medicine at a hospital yourself. And now I'm looking, and everything else is fine. He has all his organs in tact, the heart is uninjured. It kills me to see a healthy young man die just because the spark of life has sputtered out" Aulis said miserably.

"I guess it was just his time" advised Adam. "Perhaps we should both take solace in knowing he is with the angels now?" he whispered.

"You know I do not" Aulis replied sourly.

Adam sighed to himself in quiet frustration.

"Victor didn't either" added the young doctor.

259

Adam grimaced, feeling the verbal knife digging into his side. He thought about letting it go, but his exhaustion got the better of him.

"What have we discussed about that?" said Adam sternly.

Aulis turned away and stared into the warmth of the fire.

"Are you really certain the book is lost?" the young doctor asked.

"Yes. I have not seen it since we fled Joensuu. And even if I did have it, I would never try to use the information held inside. The spark of life is God's territory, it is not for us to meddle with" advised Adam calmly.

Aulis looked towards Adam with a face full of sadness. Adam felt for the young man, but, in truth, losing the book took a great weight off his shoulders. It had already led him off the path of principle too many times. With it gone, the temptation to use the material within would come to an end. In many ways, he was glad to be rid of it.

"Come on. Try and get some sleep. We attack at dawn" said Adam.

Place: Psychiatry Office, Boston, Massachusetts

Date: April 27th, 2018

Time: 1:34pm

Wolstone leaned back in his chair and sighed deeply.

"And I suppose that if I asked you for a description of the battle for Tampere you could give it to me in detail?" asked the doctor.

"Would you like me to?" asked the boy with a brightness in his exhausted eyes that had not been present earlier.

"No thank you. I believe you. But I am curious about the book you keep mentioning. Is it written by you or by this Victor?" asked Wolstone.

"In the battle I have this memory of the Red flag being torn down and of the Finnish flag being hoisted up in its place. I think I played a pivotal role in that moment" Adam rambled.

"Adam, could we stick with the question that I asked? I am curious about the book you keep mentioning. Is it a book that you actually wrote?" asked the psychiatrist.

"I really don't know" answered Adam.

The doctor looked at Adam's face carefully. It was astounding; the child was lying to him outright, but with such expertise. It was almost as if he was in negotiations with a professional politician. That thought hung in his mind for a moment. Now that was unnerving. He quickly banished the idea as insane and moved on.

"You keep telling me about the words 'I Victor' in the first pages of the book" continued Wolstone.

"Yes" answered Adam.

"Are they in your handwriting?" pressed the psychiatrist.

Something in Adam snapped. He could not answer that question.

"I don't know" he lied.

Wolstone was both frustrated and pleased. The lies were annoying, but at the same time, they indicated that the boy was consciously aware of a piece of information that he was actively shielding. The book was critical to this case. Of that much Wolstone was now certain.

"Does the book come from 1805?" asked the doctor.

"After the battle for Tampere, I have this memory of being decorated and becoming a foreign secretary for the state. I think Mandi even runs for the Finnish parliament" explained Adam.

"Does the book come from 1805?" repeated Wolstone calmly.

Adam felt the pressure. He desperately wanted to give the psychiatrist the information. He wanted his life back but a fragment of his mind refused to give up the fight. Adam considered the situation for a moment. If his own mind would not surrender the information associated with

1805, might he be able to give the doctor another pathway there?

"I have this memory of looking for the book" said Adam quietly as pins and needles flooded his fingers.

Wolstone immediately spotted the lead for what it was. The child, aware of the barriers in their communication was trying to help.

"You mean looking for the book in 1805?" asked Wolstone hopefully.

"No" replied Adam, losing himself in thought.

"In what year then?" asked the psychiatrist.

"1921, I think. I have to go somewhere, but I feel a sense of urgency" explained Adam.

"An urgency to search for the book?" asked Wolstone.

"Yes" responded Adam.

It wasn't 1805, but it was at least about the book. Wolstone figured he ought to take what he could get.

"Can you tell it to me?" he asked.

And with that, Adam started to weave yet another story from his memories.

Place: Helsinki

Date: 1921

Time: evening

All was silent. Adam looked up and several medals flickered in the light of the nearby oil lamp. He was seated, at a desk with numerous formal government documents set out in well ordered piles. One was open and directly in front of him. It closed with "Adam Adlerberg, Foreign Secretary." He felt like he was about to sign the document as his eyes drifted to his hands. His skin was getting so wrinkled. The thought of his age drove him to put his pen down and consider his mortality. Something about the thought of death made him feel uneasy in a way he had never felt before.

He pushed his chair out from the desk and stepped over to a closet. It just had to be there somewhere, he thought. Everything from Joensuu had been sent over. Everything. He remembered he had stuffed both the book and the bronze box in his knapsack when he fled Constantin's estate but his memories, even his recent ones, were becoming less and less reliable. Was he sure he had packed them?

Adam's body felt heavy and he knew it wasn't just age. Sleep deprivation from the nightmares was taking its toll, both mentally and physically. The nightmares of ice and darkness were getting worse. His hands started to throw open boxes ever more frantically. Where was it?

The gong of the city's bell tower abruptly broke him from his search. He opened a pocket watch and realised he had to be somewhere soon. He closed the closet, put on a coat and stepped out the front door.

The gas lamps at the docks flickered warmly as the evening grew darker. Several servants carried bags from a coach down to a ferry as Adam approached. He immediately spotted Aulis nearby looking over a handful of identity documents. Adam wasn't exactly sure how old Aulis was now, perhaps in his late thirties? The past was becoming murky and he was having ever greater trouble keeping his grasp on reality.

"You look terrible" smiled Aulis.

"Thank you" replied Adam sardonically.

"Honestly, your eyes, the bags beneath them look darker than I've ever seen" said Aulis more seriously.

"It comes with the job" answered Adam, trying to smile in spite of how tired he was.

"Too much time travelling to visit Gustaf" asked the doctor.

"That and more. They had me in France last week. And the week before there was that independence parade. I wouldn't have missed it for the world, but damn was it cold. I want to find the idiot who scheduled that for April and have him shot" said Adam.

"I know. I nearly froze my hands off. By the way, did you see, we made it into the newspaper?" said Aulis.

"What was that… the tenth time?" laughed Adam.

"I'm losing count. But tell me truthfully, is it really the job that is depriving you of sleep or are you having those dreams again?" asked Aulis sincerely.

"Hmm... yes. Sometimes I hate that you are so discerning. I have to admit, the past is haunting me" replied Adam.

"Do you want to talk about it?" Aulis asked.

"I would, but I can never remember the dreams that are waking me!" replied Adam.

Aulis studied his face carefully.

"You know I could prescribe something, maybe a sedative" suggested the doctor.

"No good. I don't have any trouble falling asleep. It is the sleep itself that is the problem" explained Adam.

"There is a doctor in the city who is doing some work with dreams. Speaking with patients and trying to help them come to terms with upsetting thoughts. Maybe you could talk to him and see if he can help?" offered Aulis.

Adam appreciated the concern but was fairly certain it would be of no help. More than anything, he felt he just needed family contact.

"Can I not convince you to just stay and practice medicine here? You know how busy Mandi is at parliament and how consuming my own work is, I mean, we are both certainly going to miss you" said Adam.

"I really must go" replied Aulis.

"That desperate to experience the British cuisine?" mocked Adam.

"Hah! No. Just that desperate to get away from all this fanfare" laughed Aulis.

He suddenly broke from the laughter and looked at Adam more severely.

"You know, you could come with me. You may not have a proper medical license, but you definitely know your way around a medical clinic. I spoke with Charing Cross and they have already advised that the funds are available for me to hire a few assistants. You could..."

"What? And spend my remaining days in a British hospital?" scoffed Adam with a smile.

"Well, it was worth a try. Father always said your English was good" added Aulis.

A moment of silence followed as the two men considered one another.

After all these years, he still does not know, thought Adam. Constantin was dead. Helene was dead. Adam looked down at his wrinkled hands and considered his own advancing years. He was not that far off from the grave. What harm could telling Aulis the truth at this point have now?

"You know, Aulis, about, about your father..." Adam stammered.

"I know. He was involved in the resistance from the beginning. Even from before he met mother. She didn't drive him to do what he did. He had Finland in his heart from the very beginning. I read the article last week vindicating him from all of the past propaganda suggesting that he had been a Russian puppet. I kind of always knew, but now that it is out there, I have to say, I am more proud to have been his son then ever before" said Aulis.

Adam smiled sadly and briefly considered whether it really mattered to him that Aulis actually knew. He was pulled from his thoughts as the ferry sounded a whistle. Aulis gave him a quick embrace and then started off towards the ferry.

"You be careful. I've heard dreadful things about the English weather" shouted Adam.

"Worse than the Finnish winter? Hah! That I will have to see! Keep Finland running while I'm gone! And I will see you again. I promise" he shouted from the deck of the ferry.

Adam stood there in the darkness for what felt like ages as the ferry drifted off into the night. Eventually, as the chill dug into his bones, he made his way back to his home. The streets were no longer thick with snow, but the water in the gutters was still freezing solid at night. Winter was finally fading, but its chill would linger for weeks.

He sighed and his breath came out in a foggy cloud. Another summer alone. Another summer to immerse himself in his work and forget about the past. Without paying much attention, Adam turned the corner and made his way towards the stairs leading up to his apartment when he noticed something stirring in the darkness nearby. He looked closer and saw an elderly woman stepping out of the shadows.

"Hello?" he asked nervously.

The women said nothing. Adam stepped backward, concerned. But fear rapidly turned to joy as the light of the gas lamps streaked across the face inside her cloak.

"Pekka? Is it really you?" asked the aged voice.

Shock poured through his veins as he took in the sight before him.

"I'm sorry, but with your face in all of the papers... I had to know" she asked, gazing at him closely.

Her raven-black hair had gone white, her once athletic body had gone thin and frail, but the sparkle in her sapphire eyes made her identity undeniable. It was Elsa. Somehow her fire and faith had endured these many years. Emotion started to overwhelm him.

"Elsa... I am so sorry" he said as tears started to run from his eyes.

"No. It is I who should be sorry. The farm... Pekka, I know I drove you away."

"I was a coward. I should never have run" sobbed Adam as he embraced her with all the love he could muster.

"I have never stopped loving you" she whispered.

They stood, holding one another, whispering and crying in the chill of night as the last flakes of winter fell. After what felt like hours, Elsa pulled back slightly.

"But I am curious, why did you change your name to Adam Adlerberg?" she asked.

Adam's eyes fixed on the flames of the nearby lantern.

"Did you fear I'd search for you?" Elsa asked tenderly.

"Not at all. It was... it was..." he stumbled, refusing to reveal the truth to either Elsa or himself.

"It was more a matter of honouring a man who I much respected" he said, immediately realising the lie to only be a partial one as he had in fact publicly adopted the Adlerberg name to honour Nikolay and Helene.

Elsa looked deeply into his eyes and nodded slowly.

"Adam died only a few months after you left... I miss him too" she whispered as more tears started to trickle down her face.

"You actually have his eyes" she added as they closed into another embrace.

Place: Psychiatry Office, Boston, Massachusetts

Date: April 27th, 2018

Time: 1:48pm

The emotion became overwhelming and drove Adam to tears.

"She had come back! I had not been able to love her as she wanted, but she never lost her love for me. She came back" he sobbed

Wolstone opened a drawer and pulled out a box of tissues. He handed it to Adam and, as the boy wiped his face, the doctor tried to work out where to go next. Wolstone badly wanted to continue pressing Adam on the matter of the leather book, but this reappearance of an ancient character from dreams that Adam was dating to so much earlier also seemed important. That she was eliciting such a powerful emotional response and was challenging him about his own identity in a way that no other characters in the dreams ever had also raised numerous questions in Wolstone's mind.

"It is okay Adam. Remember that all of this is just recall, it is not actually happening" said the doctor, feeling increasingly uneasy as he said the words.

"It feels so real" said the boy.

"I know" said Wolstone.

Adam nodded.

"Do you feel comfortable if I ask you a few questions" asked the psychiatrist.

Adam breathed in deeply. It had felt strangely good to cry so much. He was tired but also keen to help the psychiatrist in any way that he could.

"Sure. What do you want to ask" asked Adam.

"I want to talk about how Elsa perceived you because I think I am a bit confused. You said Elsa thought that you were Pekka, the boy whose life you saved in one of the earlier dreams. You know, the one that took place on the farm?" explained Wolstone.

Adam was not entirely certain what the doctor was asking.

"I am always just me" said Adam.

"Yes, I know, but you said Elsa thought you were Pekka" said the doctor.

As the psychiatrist pointed this out, Adam too suddenly felt confusion.

"I know. I don't understand it either. It is as if she thinks I am the young boy who I saved from the wolves" said Adam.

"So I understood you correctly when you said that she thought you were Pekka" said Wolstone.

Adam nodded.

"Does she always mistake you for Pekka when you have that dream?" asked the psychiatrist.

Adam thought about it for a moment, but he wasn't sure.

"To be honest, it's been such a long time since I've had that dream I can't remember. Now that you've helped me to recall it, it seems like it was only yesterday when I last dreamed it, but I know that isn't so. I think she has always mistaken me for Pekka, but I can't be completely sure of it" said Adam.

Now it was Wolstone's turn to nod. He had long realised they were going to run into this sort of trouble as more and more deeply buried dreams started getting dug up. Even so, he found it fascinating that Adam was mixing the identity of the child who had died of fever in rural Finland with his own.

"And you have dreams of living in old age with Elsa?" asked Wolstone.

Adam concentrated and they came flooding back. He was suddenly awash in good memories

"Yes. Now that you've helped me to think of them, I realise that I have many" replied Adam with a small smile.

"Do you have any sense of how long?" asked the psychiatrist.

"Eighteen years" said Adam, confident that he was now remembering things correctly

"And during this time you still dream about yourself working as foreign secretary for Finland?" asked Wolstone.

Adam nodded.

"To what countries?" asked the doctor.

"France, Germany, Britain, Sweden, Denmark, Belgium, and Poland" said Adam

"And if I asked you about these diplomatic visits now, you would be able to recall the details of them?"

Again, Adam nodded.

A knock came at the door.

Wolstone looked at the clock. Goodness, it was already two. There were so many more questions that he wanted to ask, but they would have to wait for another time.

Once Adam had left, the doctor flipped through the last few notes he had jotted down. The presence of identity swapping was really throwing him. During his years of experience, Wolstone had seen identity mixing normally only happen when a dream involved some horrible activity that the dreamer did not want to be directly engaged in.

He saw it all the time with veterans having dreams about killing people which were, in fact, really buried memories of actual field experiences that the soldiers' minds were desperately trying to push away. More often than not, they would dream about the violent event but dream that they were, in fact, someone or something else not directly involved in the heinous act. It was a sort of protective mechanism and perfectly explained why Adam kept viewing himself as a monster of sorts when he was dreaming about violence. The wolves, the conflict with Aulis in the bedroom, the fight with the soldiers where Helene was killed... It all made perfect sense, but what flummoxed Wolstone was why Adam was experiencing another form of identity confusion in a dream where there was, in fact, no violence at all. Was it some sort of reaction to the presence of a long term romantic relationship? Could the boy not come to grips with the idea of such a thing? He certainly had significant tension associated with romance but the doctor just wasn't sure that was it.

Wolstone shook his head in frustration. It bothered him greatly that, after three long sessions with the child, he was no closer to understanding the source of the dreams than he had been during their first ten minutes together. If there was any patient he wanted to help, it was Adam. Never before had he worked with anyone who had such a full life laid out before them and so much to lose if his work did not succeed.

He briefly looked over at his pile of paperwork and considered losing himself in it. The medical school and ethics board applications still beckoned. Wolstone started to reach over to them but saw the distraction for what it was. He still had time on those, but felt that if he did not make some sort of breakthrough with Adam soon, he might never be able to.

Part 4

Place: Faculty Pub, Imperial College, London

Date: November 26th, 2017

Time: 1:11pm

"Are you sure?" asked Dixon, eyeing his student and soon-to-be colleague carefully.

"I am. I know how much you want me to stay, but it is a lot closer to home" said Ida as she took another bite from her sandwich.

"Because with the kinds of waves our *Nature* paper is going to make when it publishes next month, Imperial's funders are just going to be throwing their money at you" he said with a grin.

"Thanks, Dr Dixon. That means a lot coming from you, but Harvard's offer is incredibly generous and I really do value having a two hour flight home rather than an eight hour one" she replied.

He paused for a moment and looked around cautiously to make sure nobody else was listening in.

"Any idea if their ethics committee is going to be okay with what you've got planned?" he asked.

"I had a chat with the director of their medical school and he seemed up for it. I mean, he was cautious and told

276

me that the members of their ethics board would have to review the experiment, but you'd kind expect that with this sort of thing" she replied.

Dixon leaned in closer.

"Have you already found a potential candidate?" he asked quietly.

Ida smiled ever so slightly.

"Three years old. Severe cerebral meningitis" she explained in a near silent whisper.

"Do the medical records indicate that there is definitely no chance of recovery?" he asked.

Ida nodded ever so slowly.

"So you are just going to transplant one of the neuron cultures and see if it takes?" he asked.

"That's the plan, assuming we can get through all the red tape that I am sure is going to crop up as news of this gets out" she said.

"Wow, if you get approval, well... golly that is going to be something else. Keep me posted" said Dixon.

Place: Psychiatry Office, Boston, Massachusetts

Date: May 12th, 2018

Time: 3:57pm

"Adam, the children's magazines are over there" said Catherine as they waited outside Wolstone's office.

Adam just could not be bothered to continue the charade of looking like he was interested in the infantile material in the far corner of the room. He was too tired.

It had been another two weeks of almost no sleep and, worse, the nightmares were often following him into the daylight hours. He prayed that this was the darkness before the dawn.

As he put his head in his hands, his eyes fell upon the *Nature* issue he'd started reading a few weeks earlier. He lifted the journal up as the door to the doctor's office opened.

"It is good to see you both again" said Wolstone.

Catherine stood up while Adam remained reading the scientific journal.

"Ah yes, you wanted to speak with me for a moment. Do come in" said the psychiatrist to Catherine.

Adam stayed put in the waiting area while Catherine and the doctor had words in private. He didn't understand why their conversation had to exclude him. He already knew the problem, Catherine wanted the sessions to end and he did not. It was infuriating having her lecture him on

278

whether the therapy was doing what it was supposed to do. After all, she wasn't a psychiatrist. She wasn't even sitting in on the sessions. Exasperated, Adam tried to put the thought of it out of mind by giving the article in front of him some attention.

He was tired, but he still had enough energy to scan a few pages. The journal once more flipped open to the article about using biological batteries made out of electric eel cells to light a Christmas tree in Japan. Not again thanks, he thought. He turned the page and read an article about a research team that was growing a human liver in a bottle from stem cells. Exhausted as he was, the wonder of what they were doing drove him on and his eyes moved to an adjacent article about a lab grown neuron network that proved even more interesting. Adam let out a yawn as he read on and found the sleep deprivation leading his mind to wander.

He knew that Dr Wolstone was speculating about him incorporating information collected from materials like those in this journal into his dreams but the thought left him wondering... after reading this, might he now start having dreams about livers or brains being grown in jars? Something about that seemed wrong. He could not remember reading history books about the Finnish revolutionary war or about the naval battles that took place during World War II off the coast of Norway. No, the doctor's speculations had to be incorrect. He could not be picking up the details from his dreams from reading material.

The door to the psychiatrist's office opened and Catherine stepped out looking more than a little upset.

"I promise you Catherine, it is going to start getting easier soon" said Wolstone as he walked her to the exit.

"I sure hope so" she said.

She turned towards Adam at the door.

"I'll see you in two hours" she said as she waved goodbye.

"Please, come in" said the doctor to the boy.

Adam stepped into the office with the journal in hand.

"Were you reading anything interesting in there?" asked Wolstone, pointing at the copy of *Nature*.

"Nothing much, just some interesting cellular biology stories on page 10" said the boy, putting the journal down on the psychiatrist's desk as he sat down in his chair for the session.

Wolstone closed the door.

"I'm sorry if she is giving you trouble. I told her not to" said Adam in a manner that was decidedly inappropriate for his age.

"It is understandable. If you are losing weight, missing school and feeling dizzy so often, these are things worth worrying about. Particularly if you are a parent" said Wolstone.

"But you said things would likely get worse before they got better" said Adam, trying to smile in spite of the dark circles beneath his eyes.

"I know I did, but 'worse' comes in degrees and things seem to be getting quite terrible for you at the moment. I'm inclined to try and change tactics" said Wolstone.

"No. Please don't!" begged Adam.

Wolstone was surprised by the intensity of the child's response.

"You want to continue even with things getting as bad as they are?" asked the psychiatrist.

"Yes. Definitely yes!" said Adam.

"But why?" asked Wolstone, intrigued.

"I can't explain it, but accessing the dreams in the way that I do with you is helping me to understand things that I never understood before. I know I am sleeping worse and that I am more distracted during the day than I ever have been before, but I want to continue. It is really important. I'm certain of it" pleaded Adam.

Wolstone drummed his fingers on his desk as he looked at the child. It bothered him. As much as he had not wanted to do it, he had promised Catherine just minutes earlier to change his therapy methods for the sake of Adam's health. It was either that or Catherine was going to end the sessions altogether and he didn't want that. Especially not for this patient. He desperately wanted to pull through for this kid.

"Dr Wolstone, please" said Adam with utter sincerity.

To hell with it, thought Wolstone. This patient has been more courageous than many of the toughest soldiers I have ever treated. The least I can do for him is muster my own bravery and give him the treatment that he really deserves. And if I get fired or sued for it, I will have gone down doing the right thing. I can live with that, he thought.

"Okay Adam. What happens after eighteen years?" asked Wolstone.

Adam was relieved and jumped right in to give the doctor the information he was seeking. Eighteen years, Wolstone was asking about the eighteen years of diplomatic duties and living with Elsa in old age.

"Elsa dies" said the boy, feeling a tinge of sadness upon recalling that dream.

"And you remember mourning her?" asked Wolstone solemnly.

"No. There isn't any time. It is 1939 when she passes and war is starting to spread …" said Adam as the dream took hold once more.

Place: Royal Palace, Stockholm

Date: November, 1939

Time: 14:28pm

"The Russians are demanding freedom of movement for their troops through Finland in preparation for possible German invasion."

The words came floating out of Adam's mouth before he was even aware of the space he was in. His heavily wrinkled hands were leaning heavily on an ornate chair of velvet and gold.

"That is, of course, entirely sensible considering the German invasion of Poland. But, even so, you cannot allow it" said a voice that Adam knew all too well.

He looked up, and there, sitting across from him, was Gustaf resting his back against a lavish sofa. He too looked old, possibly now in his seventies.

"Yes, we are well aware that we cannot permit them to move their troops across our land as if it were a Russian motorway, and they know that" said Adam, still trying to digest what he himself was saying.

"They are giving themselves an excuse to invade" said Gustaf soberly.

"Yes" replied Adam with a grim expression on his face.

He looked up at Gustaf with hope.

We need Sweden to stand with us" he said, realising
was, at last, delivering the request that the Finnish
Parliament had sent him to make.

Gustaf sighed deeply and ran his hands through his
long grey hair.

"I want to help. I really do. But our own parliament has
clipped my wings. The people of Sweden cannot aid you"
said the king.

"But Gustaf! We only just threw off the Russian chains"
answered Adam, realising that the help he hoped they
could have would not be coming.

Suddenly, there was a knock at the door.

"We're busy!" said Gustaf.

"I'm sorry your majesty, but I have an urgent telegram
for your visitor" said a young voice from outside.

"Very well then, enter" replied the king.

A servant entered with a telegram, quickly handed it to
Adam and left.

The telegram burned in his fingers, as if his flesh
somehow knew that it bared bad news. Adam looked up at
Gustaf with enquiring eyes.

"Go on old friend, read it" he said.

Adam put on his glasses and felt his heart sink as the
words became clear.

"They are attacking" said Gustaf, clearly reading the
expression on Adam's face.

"Yes. Russian tanks are already approaching our south-eastern border" he replied sadly

"Look, our parliament won't budge. They don't want to get between Russia and Germany, and while I disagree with that decision, I can understand why it is being made. But there may be an alternative" said Gustaf with a smile.

"Yes?" replied Adam despondently.

"I spent a day with Hitler at a recent tennis tournament and found him to be a rather amicable man of business, so I mentioned your predicament" explained the king.

"You did?" asked Adam cautiously.

"Yes, and he advised me to tell you that he would be willing to supply mortars, grenades, rifles and machine guns to help Finland in its time of need" explained Gustaf.

"That is gracious, but he offers this help for nothing?" asked Adam.

"No. As I said, he is a man of business, so he is expecting payment. He requests that 30% of the iron ore coming out of Lapland be re-routed to Germany in return for the weapons. Oh, and he also requests that Finland's Jews be sent for re-education at a training camp in Poland" said the king

"Pardon?" asked Adam.

"Pardon what? I thought it a good deal" said Gustaf.

"It is, but I am confused by the bit about the Jews" said Adam.

"Oh, that. It is nothing, he just feels the Jews need to learn new ways and wants to re-train them. I thought it a small price to pay for such considerable help" explained Gustaf.

The concept did not sit well with Adam. He remembered how Bismarck tried to convert the Poles and the twenty years he endured of St Petersburg trying to 'Russify' the Finns. Now the Jews? Nikolay had been close to his Jewish cantonists for years and, during Adam's many encounters with them, they had always proved themselves to be honourable. Indeed, during the revolution many of them had rebelled against the reds and fought alongside him and General Mannerheim for independence.

"Adam, I have friends who are Jews. Some are great tennis players. There is no threat here. It is nothing that Hitler is asking" said Gustaf, sensing his old friend's hesitation.

"What about increasing the ore supply?" asked Adam

"What? Give Hitler more than the 30% he is asking for?" asked Gustaf with incredulity.

"Yes. We are pulling out far more iron in Lapland than we could ever use. If we gave 35% or even 45% it would still have very little effect on us" explained Adam.

"Increasing the iron request instead of handing over a few thousand Jews? Are mad?" asked Gustaf, aghast.

"They are Finns first and Jews second. I am not going to watch even a fragment of our population be treated as second class citizens again and certainly will not allow any of our people to be deported because of who they pray to" explained Adam   with kind conviction.

286

"And you think your parliament will agree with this decision?" asked Gustaf.

"Many will, but it doesn't matter. They are not going to know. I haven't any intention of even mentioning that this ridiculous request was put on the table" said Adam.

Gustaf nodded and waved his hand at Adam with a grin.

"Fine. Fine. I know well when it is not worth arguing with you. I will take this counter offer to Hitler for you. I am sure he will take it" said the king.

"Thank you" said Adam as he threw on his cloak and turned towards the door.

"Godspeed my friend" called Gustaf as Adam stepped out into the hall and started plummeting into yet another dream.

Place: Parliament Building, Helsinki

Date: March, 1940

Time: morning

Adam suddenly found himself packed with dozens of parliamentarians in the back of the main hall. They were certainly riled up about something as many were booing the senator speaking at the front.

"While our barricades and regiments have held the Russian forces at bay, our resources are gravely depleted. Almost all of our ammunition and replacement weapons are coming from Germany and it is unclear whether we will have enough to endure another onslaught" she said.

Adam had to give her credit, in spite of the hostile reaction; she was keeping everyone's attention with a loud and crisp voice.

"Moreover, our spies reveal that the Russians are preparing for another assault. In light of this, we are considering the telegram received yesterday from Chairman Molotov" she explained.

Many more parliamentarians in the room booed her and the senator waved her arm to try and quiet everyone down. It was then that Adam noticed. The senator was missing her right arm. Recognition immediately followed. Of course, this was Mandi. She had fought her way through the political ranks and made it into parliament not once, but during two separate elections.

"The president and I agree that surrendering our eastern lands in return for peace is, at this time, our best course of action" explained Mandi to a chorus of ever louder jeers.

Raising her voice, Mandi continued "We know it is unpopular, but before you vote against this tomorrow, please be advised that we have counted our people and know we have the votes. I know it will be hard but try and put your partisan bickering aside and think instead of Finland. Our very survival is at stake. That is all" she said.

The chamber erupted into chaotic shouting and debate as members slowly made their way to the exits. Adam stayed where he was and remained like a statue against the back wall. He felt for Mandi having to endure one angry encounter after another at the podium. At least, he thought, she is not alone. Dozens of other members of her party were engaging in fiery debates of their own with those who opposed the treaty. Ten minutes went by and as Mandi stepped down the stairs, her eyes made contact with his. He walked around the hall and put his hand on her shoulder. She looked as exhausted as he felt.

"You look like you could use a nap" said Adam.

"I'll sleep when we get this done" she said looking up at him fondly.

"I don't want to give you more trouble, but it is a really bad deal. Neither your mother nor your grandfather would have gone along with this" he said, trying not to come across harshly.

"You think I do not know this?" she asked. "The problem is that under these circumstances, a bad deal is better than none, there are much bigger fish to cook" she said quietly.

"Bigger fish? How do you mean?" he asked.

Mandi looked from side to side, making sure nobody was nearby.

"Our agent in Berlin got in touch with the intelligence committee yesterday. We are preparing to tell the wider parliament tomorrow. Hitler is looking North" she said with a whisper.

"What? Towards us? That would be madness, we are holding the line against Stalin!" he replied.

"Hmm... that is what I thought initially. Those of us on the committee agree that he probably is not looking to invade us. It would make no sense. Instead, we are thinking that he is considering either Sweden or Norway" Mandi replied.

"Gustaf?" asked Adam nervously.

"Maybe. Since we are supplying iron that the Germans badly need, there are some in my office who are speculating that Hitler is looking to lock down the rest of the Nordic region and prevent any allied interference with his trade" she explained.

"To make sure his iron lifeline is not disrupted..." said Adam, understanding the gravity of the situation.

Mandi looked at him intently. He could sense the words sitting upon the tip of her tongue and knew what was coming.

"What do you need of me?" he asked solemnly.

"My mother was always for Finnish independence and in her name I want to get Finland out from under Hitler's thumb. I would rather our iron supplies go to forces more honourable" she said.

"We did make a deal with him though. He's going to be angry if we cut off his iron as soon as we sign a treaty with Russia" he said.

"It does not matter. I cannot abide the idea of him using weapons crafted from our iron to slaughter the Swedes or the Norwegians. Can you?" she asked.

Adam grew silent as he considered the matter.

"You want me to approach Britain." he stated as realisation struck.

She nodded.

"Discretely, ask what they and their allies are willing to offer in return for our iron and see if you can make sure that mutual protection gets put on the table" she explained.

Her eyes started to fill with tears and she gave him a warm embrace.

"I know it is a lot to request, but can you make this one last trip for us?" she asked.

"For you and the memory of your mother, I could make fifty" replied Adam.

"We will make sure your transport is ready first thing tomorrow" said   Mandi.

He wrapped his arms around her in return and, as he did, another dream hit him like a breaking wave.

Place: The Lannistumaton, Finnish Transport eight miles off the Norwegian Coast

Date: April, 1940

Time: 2am

The world went sideways and Adam felt himself falling out of darkness. The floor hit him hard in the face. Glass shattered and wood splintered. He put an arm out to steady himself, but it was no use. The ground was rocking about violently and nothing he could do would stop it. His aged body went rolling out of control into a wall. He both heard and felt the crack of his own ribs. And then the arctic cold of salty ocean water splashed into his face. Spitting it out of his mouth, he reached up again with his arms and found the door.

Flinging it open he stumbled into the transport's corridor. The water was ankle deep but rising fast. The emergency lights were running, but only just. Clearly they had been damaged by whatever it was that had hit them in the middle of the night. Suddenly, the ship tilted hard to the aft again and the water came pouring violently towards him.

Breathing hard and feeling winded, Adam braced himself against the doorway as a wave of blood and debris washed past his hips. He could not help but grimace as the broken body of one of the guards accompanying him to London swept by and smashed into a wall. Another explosion shook the boat, knocking cables loose from the ceiling and causing sparks to fly everywhere. Fearing that each breath he drew might be his last; he staggered his way up the stairs and climbed on deck.

The situation was bad. The back of the boat was on fire and, while several sailors were doing their best to get control of it, Adam could tell they were fighting a losing battle. He wasn't sure where the fuel tank was on this transport, but judging from the size of the flames, he guessed that it was going to explode at any moment.

"Leave it and abandon ship!" he shouted as loud as he could amidst the chaos.

He tried shouting again, but found his voice cut off as he gagged on the foul smoke blowing towards him.

Clutching his chest, Adam realised he was having trouble catching his breath. He simply couldn't draw in enough air to yell. His fingers made their way to his ribs and palpated. The pain was significant and he immediately knew. Not only were some of his ribs broken, at least one of them had punctured a lung.

At the edge of his vision, Adam spotted a raft dangling precariously by a rope from the side of the boat. He looked at it more closely. Unlike the rest of the ship, it looked to be in tact. He tried waving his arms at the remaining sailors but, between the flames and the smoke, catching their attention proved hopeless. Without a second thought, he kicked the clamp open that was holding the raft and it fell into the ocean.

At first he was pleased to see it land right side up, but as he prepared to jump, he realised there was no way for him to safely make the distance, it was entirely too far away. He paused for a moment, spotting the ice floating in the water and noticing the swift current. The raft was caught right in it and moving away. He looked back at the growing fire and realised that if he did not leap immediately, it would all be over. He sucked in the deepest breath he could manage and took the plunge.

The crushing cold assaulted every fibre of his being. It consumed his arms, enveloped his legs and strangled his throat, but in spite of the anguish, he fought back and reached the surface. The raft was only a short distance away. It should have been easy to reach, but with no feeling in any of his limbs and almost all of his strength drained away, the few strokes that he swam proved nearly impossible. And yet, through force of will, Adam managed them. Half dead and delirious from hypothermia Adam dragged himself over the side of the raft and collapsed on its floor.

It was not a moment too soon. Within seconds, the transport's fuel tank ruptured and a fireball as large as the ship broke it into pieces.

Shivering more violently than he had ever thought possible, Adam mumbled a simple Latin prayer before dropping into the sweet oblivion of unconsciousness.

Place: HMS Warspite

Date: April, 1940

Time: uncertain

Bleary images around him started to sharpen. There were wounded soldiers on tables across from him and a half dozen nurses moving swiftly between them. His first thought was that this was a hospital, but then as the room swayed gently with the waves, reality became clearer. This was not a hospital, but a warship with a medical chamber. Adam managed a brief glance down at his body.

There were several needles stuck into his arm. They were drip-feeding him pain killers no doubt. And his chest was a mess. He could not make out exactly what his injuries were, but he was clearly in bad shape. Forceps came down and plucked a sharp piece of metal out. He felt no pain, but grimaced just the same. He looked up and saw Aulis in deep concentration.

"Aulis!" gasped Adam through his aged cracked lips.

"I had intended on us meeting again, I just had no idea it would be in this hell" muttered the surgeon.

"What are you doing here?" Adam asked weakly.

"Well, I've been trying to keep Norwegians alive in the wake of Germany's invasion, but for the past few hours, you've been my little project" he said with a dark smirk.

"I thought you were at a hospital?" said Adam.

"I was. But then the war happened and, well, the British needed surgeons for their ships, so here I am!" Aulis replied with worrying levity in his voice.

"How bad is it" asked Adam seriously.

The surgeon's face was unreadable.

"Just try to get some rest" he said.

And with that, Adam succumbed to the drugs and dropped back out of consciousness.

Place: HMS Warspite

Date: April, 1940

Time: later?

Adam was not entirely sure how many hours had passed, but when he came to again, all was quiet. He couldn't quite sit up, but he had the strength to look around and what he saw was dark stuff indeed.

Across from him was a soldier attached to a respirator and dreadfully pale from lost blood. His nail beds were blue and his lips purple. There was no question that this was a patient who was on the verge of death and yet, there was Aulis, breaking into his chest and examining cardiac tissue.

That alone was disturbing, but what proved horrifying was the realisation that this was a room filled with men on respirators who were all on the threshold of death. Worse, Adam knew he was among them.

"Why... do so much... for the dying?" asked Adam weakly.

Aulis closed up the patient he was working on and tossed his bloody gloves into a bin as he walked over towards Adam. There was a confidence in his movements that was concerning. A kernel of fear arose in Adam's heart when he realised that Aulis was the only member of the ship's medical team present.

"Because, as I have told you, there is so much to be learned from those on the edge" explained Aulis as he leaned over Adam's bed.

"They are people… not…" gasped Adam, far too weak to put up much of an argument.

"Not experiments? Yes, you have always said that, and I have always thought it was because you were somehow more broadly studied than I, somehow wiser. That you had a firmer grip on ethics and understood matters of life and death better. I'll be honest; I have never understood a single one of your arguments. If they are going to die anyway, it should always be worth trying to learn as much as we can from them before they go. Because within them lies the truth, the ultimate answer, and the path to immortality…" the surgeon stopped in the midst of his words and looked at Adam with a glint of anger in his eyes.

He leaned close to Adam on the medical table and whispered into his ear, "but I don't need to lecture you about immortality, do I?"

"No…" was all Adam could mutter in his current state.

Aulis stood up straight once more and began pacing next to Adam.

"My mother told me that at the age of twenty-three you spoke eight languages, could read and write Latin and German, and knew more about European geography than most veteran Russian diplomats. When I studied under you, I was routinely amazed by your understanding of biology in spite of the fact that you had spent your entire life working as a political advisor" explained Aulis with confidence.

Adam found himself thinking of a jackal circling carrion as the doctor continued walking back and forth.

"It baffled me for years. I was even jealous at times, but then, after we fled Joensuu, I finally had a chance to spend a lot of time looking at these" said Aulis as he turned to a table and lifted up both a bronze box with a strange looking syringe in it and a leather-bound book.

"I couldn't understand them at first. Really, much of the material in this text initially read like fiction and I figured it had to be something by the likes of Verne or Wells, but as I looked closer, I realised it was no fantasy. It has taken me over a decade of study and experimentation but now, after having read Victor's journal in detail and having explored the uses of this marvellous equipment that he left behind, I finally understand" explained Aulis.

Adam struggled to lift himself off the operating table but it was entirely impossible. His wounds were too great and his limbs far too weak.

"Your brain cells must be the same ones that Victor animated in 1810, it is the only explanation" said Aulis as he pulled the needle-like device out of the box and prepared it for use.

The horror was overwhelming. With the loss of Victor's equipment and the disappearance of the book, Adam had come to accept that death was inevitable. He had been looking forward to embracing it as a welcome rest after a long and often painful life. His mind screamed for release but his body would not move.

It was just a small pin prick in the lower back of his skull, the pain was nothing, but the reality of it all was more of a torture than anything else he had ever experienced.

"My brain cells, when transplanted to other cell cultures, do not generate new networks like other tissues in my body, but yours are different. Take them out and put them into a new culture with the right nutrients and they replicate to fill the space. Insert a small sample of them into somebody else's brain stem and they overrun the native cells that are already present. I do have that all right don't I?" asked Aulis rhetorically as he shifted the needle into place.

"No..." was all Adam could weakly gasp in protest.

"You've been using this specially designed device to transfer your neurons between human bodies for years haven't you? Yes. Adam the ethical... Adam the noble... Adam the holy... You had everyone fooled. Nikolay, Mother, Mandi, Constantin... Everyone except me... Frankly, I don't know how you can look yourself in the mirror after doing what you have done. Inserting your cells inside the skulls of the young... Knowing your cells' regenerative abilities would allow them to replicate and destroy an already existing soul. You were sending your victims to a fate worse then death, driving their minds into nothingness and consuming the lives they had built for themselves. And, all along, you had the fucking gall to lecture me about what was and was not God's territory!" spat Aulis.

Adam could do nothing but writhe in pain as Aulis continued his work.

"That such incredible regenerating brain cells were created over a hundred years ago is simply amazing. I

301

would love to see you perish for what you have done, painfully if possible, but for the sake of science you must be preserved. Yes, you cannot be allowed to die, at least not before we can fully understand how Victor managed to accomplish all that he did" said Aulis coldly.

Adam felt the needle as it was removed and watched as Aulis carefully decanted the sample into a Petri dish. He placed the collection needle down and picked up a syringe.

"But as you heal up, I can't have you causing me any trouble either" explained Aulis as he plunged the syringe into Adam's neck.

Adam could feel the sedative seeping into his body. It was numbing every nerve and quickly clouding his mind. As it spread, he fell back into darkness.

Place: HMS Warspite

Date: April, 1940

Time: night

Adam felt a growing warmth around his body and sensed light beyond his eyelids. His muscles were fatigued, but the excruciating pain that he had experienced before was completely gone. Slowly, he tried moving a few of his fingers and was relieved to realise he had control of them once more.

"Oh, good, he is coming to. Can you hear me Lieutenant?" asked a female voice with a thick British accent.

"Don't ask him to speak yet" said a Scottish female voice from further away in the room.

"Right. Sorry" said the first female voice.

Adam opened his eyes and found a young nurse looking down upon him. Her face quickly broke into a grin as their eyes met. She raised her hand in front of him and lifted up a finger.

"Lieutenant, just try to follow my finger with your eyes" said the nurse.

It was easy enough, he was tired, but not in pain.

"That's lovely" she said.

"He's tracking me jolly well too, what do I do now?" she said with enthusiasm to the other nurse.

Adam managed to look from side to side. He was no longer in the morgue-like lab that Aulis had stuck him in before. This was a proper hospital space, similar to the one he had first found himself in. He felt the boat lurch sharply to the side and then bob back again. There were obviously large waves outside.

"Oh for God's sake Emily" said the other nurse, walking closer and coming into view.

Her elderly face popped up over his bed and smiled gently. She then lifted up a medical form that was attached by a string to his headboard to look something over.

"Michael, if ye hear me, can ye blink twice please?" asked the nurse.

Adam did as he was told but he was confused by the title and name. Lieutenant? Michael? What was going on?

"Bloody unbelievable... This is the second patient I've found today who was being over-sedated" she muttered.

"Hey, wait a minute Rita, maybe he was being sedated for a reason. Perhaps he's an enemy combatant?" ventured Emily, grasping Rita's arm.

"Nonsense lass, all of them are being put downstairs. And besides, he's understanding me English just fine!" replied Rita.

"What, you don't think there are Nazi's who speak English?" asked Emily.

"I am not a Nazi" said Adam in the best English he could manage.

He started to sit up and was surprised that it was not actually all that difficult. Wait a minute, something did not feel right. He glanced down at his arm and made a gruesome realisation. This was not his body. His was the arm of a young man, maybe not more than seventeen years old. The shock hit him hard and he started to feel light-headed.

"Careful there. Try not to take things too fast. You've had a rough time of it" cautioned Rita as she reached over to support him.

His mind raced as it tried to grasp the reality of the situation around him. His eyes caught sight of the sheet attached to his bed. The name on it read 'Lieutenant Michael Varchild.' Aulis had obviously been successful. By God, Aulis, the thought of him having access to all of Victor's work was frightening. Where was he?

"The doctor…" he stammered.

"Easy there Lieutenant" advised Emily, you've been comatose for a long time.

"The doctor, where is he?" asked Adam more clearly.

"Out cold in his room down the hall. He was on the coast for the past few days, helping to evacuate Norwegian troops. Hard at work he's been. Lots and lots of wounded. To be honest, I'd really rather not wake him. Is there something I can do for ye" asked Rita.

Adam caught site of a uniform neatly folded by the end of his bed as the ship tilted hard to the side once more.

"No. I'm fine, just want to get back to my post" he lied as he cautiously stepped out of bed and reached for the uniform.

"Oy! Ye can't just go wandering off like that!" said Rita.

"Sorry, I really have to" said Adam, throwing on the trousers and truly feeling fine.

"Unbloody believable. Just like the old one we saw earlier. What did he call himself? Callum? Adam?" asked Rita.

Just like the old one? He turned around half-dressed and looked the elderly nurse straight in the eye.

"Are you saying there was an older man named Adam who was also being over sedated and got up in a hurry?" he asked.

"That's right" said Rita, looking a bit nervous.

"We tried to stop him. With the storm blowing and all, we didn't want him running off, but he seemed determined" added Emily.

"Do you know where he went?" asked Adam.

"No idea lad and really, ye should lie down for a rest yourself" advised Rita.

Adam threw on the uniform's jacket and started walking away.

"Sorry, I've got something urgent that I have to deal with" he said, as he ran off.

He could hear the nurses behind him, calling his name. Asking for him to return, but he knew that would be foolish.

What he needed was to find the officer's quarters, but asking the nurses would be pointless. Then a thought drifted past his mind. The nurse had said he was 'out cold down the hall.' Of course, a ship's doctor would naturally have his quarters near the sick bay. Adam immediately turned his attention to the doors nearby and started scanning them for the name 'Linder.'

He went from one corridor to the next and suddenly came face to face with himself. It was deeply unnerving, but there, standing in front of him, was the elderly body of Pekka that he had come to identify with for nearly a lifetime.

Noticing him staring, his old body, disguised in an ill fitting stolen uniform reached for the pistol that it carried on its hip.

"No, no" cautioned Adam, "I'm a friend" he said.

The face on his old body looked at him carefully and its eyes widened as realisation dawned. The boat pitched to the side and both braced themselves.

His elderly self stepped forward carefully and reached a wrinkled hand out towards Adam's face. He stroked the youthful cheek softly.

"Then he did it?" his elderly self asked.

"Yes, I'm afraid so" replied Adam.

"I'm so sorry. I wanted to bring it to an end" said his elderly self.

"I know, I was there with you. I look at my hands. I see the youth, but I don't feel it. It kills me to think of what Aulis is going to do" said Adam.

"Damn it! I should have destroyed that book decades ago" said his elderly self.

"Why? So we could watch Elsa starve herself to death as Pekka wasted away in a coma? We were not channelling Victor when we transferred into Pekka" said Adam.

"But Victor was evil" emphasised his elderly self.

"Yes, but the science is not. Not on its own. He chose to abuse what he had at his fingertips. We never did" replied Adam.

The corridor shook violently again as waves crashed against the outside of the boat.

"We could end it though. Now. Once and for all" suggested his elderly self.

"That was my plan. I'm sure if we find his quarters we will find both the book and the box" said Adam.

"I've already been down that corridor. He has to be somewhere along here" said his elderly self pointing down the adjacent hall.

"Then let's go this way" said Adam, already starting to walk.

Together they turned a corner and caught sight of a stairway going on to the deck. Water was dripping down from above. The floor had ample places for the water to drain off, but it was still a soggy mess. Ahead of them, on the left, Adam spotted a door with the name 'Linder' on it. He pointed to it so that his elderly self would notice. Suddenly, a guard turned the corner.

 Without missing a beat, his elderly self stepped forward to engage the guard in conversation. Adam tried his best to act natural and walk calmly in to Aulis' quarters. The door was unlocked, just as it always was in this dream.

Inside, Adam found things as they always were. A bed, a small table, a trunk and Aulis' pale face sound asleep beneath a thick wool blanket.

He made quick work of the lock on the trunk at the foot of the bed and found both the leather-bound book and the bronze box exactly where he always remembered them. He snatched them up swiftly and quickly snuck back to the door. Peering around the corner he saw his elderly self still engaged in conversation with the guard.

Thunder crashed in the distance and a chill wind blew down the hall, blasting moisture into his face. The corridor grew darker and colder and time seemed to slow down. Now was the moment that he had come to dread so much.

He made his move for the stairs leading to the deck and, as he did, he felt his left foot begin to slip on the wet floor as the boat lurched to the side. He tumbled and, as he did, the book and the box crashed to the floor. The guard immediately came running, but Adam's elderly self came after him.

"Thief!" shouted Aulis' voice from his cabin.

The guard reached for Adam as he scrambled to get up but his elderly self caught hold of the guard first. Adam grabbed the box and book and raced for the stairs, managing a brief glance behind as he got there.

His elderly self was wrapping his arm around the guard's neck, forcing him to gasp, when a shot cracked through the air and a burst of blood erupted from the chest of the body he had inhabited for so long. A fiery rage emerged in his old body's eyes as he turned, revealing Aulis with a revolver just outside his chambers. Adam watched as Aulis fired another three shots into the chest of Pekka's elderly body before he fled up the stairs and onto the deck.

The rain was pouring down and the lightning streaking through the sky. Thunder rumbled ominously as he ran to the end of the deck. He briefly looked into the sea and considered the option of swimming, but he knew that would be suicide.

Suicide. The idea had appeal. He had not wanted this life; he had been ready to end it all. Indeed, he had wanted to.

"Stop!" shouted Aulis, as he emerged from below deck, aiming his gun carefully.

"It's over Adam. Come away from there!" he ordered.

"Why? So you can keep me in a cage like a lab rat and spread the misery of my condition" asked Adam as a wave splashed across the deck.

"No! To give everyone the gift of immortality that Victor gave you" he shouted back in the heavy rain.

"Gift! You think this is a gift? Victor cursed me from the day he created me!" Adam shouted back.

There was not going to be any reasoning with Aulis. He had to make sure this came to an end, and soon. Adam turned towards the railing and prepared to throw the book and box overboard.

"Throwing them overboard will accomplish nothing. I've copied everything and will just transplant your brain tissue when I have you captured!" shouted Aulis.

Adam smiled, knowing the weakness in the surgeon's logic. He was ready. In fact, he welcomed what was to come. He wanted to be with Helene. And with that, he closed his eyes and started to climb the railing.

A shot rang out, forcing his left arm to lose its grip. Adam came crashing to the deck. The book and box went tumbling away from him. Aulis dashed forward and pulled the trigger of the pistol once more only to hear it click.

Realising he was out of ammunition, Aulis struck at Adam's head with the back of the gun, but was too slow.

Adam was on his feet in an instant and seized Aulis by the throat. As he lifted the pale-faced surgeon off the ground, he could see the necrotic blue tissue of his arm, the stitches, the scars, his nearly purple finger nails. The electricity that birthed him surged through his muscles and he suddenly felt more alive than he had in decades. The pain of the bullet wound in his arm vanished.

In a rage, Adam threw the doctor across the deck like a rag doll. He hit the side of the boat hard. Bones cracked but Aulis struggled to stand nevertheless. As Adam came towards him, Aulis frantically tried to reload the pistol, but

Adam was far too fast. He swatted the weapon away like an insect, grabbed Aulis again and lifted him high off the ground by the neck. The surgeon desperately struggled to break the grasp but it was impossible.

"But… Victor's legacy!" he pleaded.

"Dies with you" said the monster.

The rain and spindrift sprayed across them both and, as another bolt of lightening lanced across the sky, Adam's ice blue fingers crushed the life out of his son's throat.

Place: Psychiatry Office, Boston, Massachusetts

Date: May 12th, 2018

Time: 5:02pm

The psychiatrist hadn't realised he had been holding his breath until Adam finished reciting the dream. Fiction blended with historical fact, this changes everything, Wolstone thought. After checking so many of the details in the child's dreams, he had come to assume that everything Adam was telling him was based upon astonishingly accurate historic records that the boy had somehow learned, but now he wasn't so sure. While the dates, events and even the characters like Gustaf and Nikolay all matched up with his casual searches on Google, he didn't need the internet to know that Victor was most certainly not real. He couldn't be. Moreover, his lab work was entirely the stuff of fiction.

As he thought things through, Wolstone found the boy gazing at him with a face devoid of colour and eyes that looked as if they had just seen a ghost.

"You've been very brave Adam" said the psychiatrist gently.

The child smiled weakly.

"But there is one more thing. If I were to ask you now…" asked Wolstone.

"About the monster?" interrupted Adam.

"Yes. About the monster" said the doctor.

"It will not be easy" said the boy.

"I know, but remember, you are not alone. I will be right here with you. Nothing bad is going to happen" advised Wolstone.

Adam nodded, meekly, nervously.

"Now... tell me about Dr Victor Frankenstein" said the psychiatrist.

Place: Ingolstadt, Germany

Date: 1810

Time: night

There was a surge of heat and then everything went cold. Very cold. Adam could feel his body lying against something solid but, as he tried to move his arms, he found them to be exceptionally heavy. Cautiously, he opened his eyes.

The room was large and dark. Candles were scattered about, but they granted precious little illumination. It was almost as if the space itself did not wish to be lit. Adam started to lift his arms once more but struggled with restraints clamped onto his wrists. Suddenly, he caught sight of movement to his right. Smiling broadly in rapture, a thin man with greying hair, intense eyes and a scar over one eyebrow came into view.

"I was right. I cannot believe it! I was right" gasped Victor.

"They said it could not happen. They said reanimation was impossible. But here you are, proof. The proof I needed!" said Victor.

As Adam looked towards Victor, the man's smile transformed into a grimace of horror and fear filled his eyes.

"By God, what a wretch you are. What have I done" whispered Victor.

Adam tried to rise once more and this time, he broke open the restraint holding his right arm. Finally able to sit up, he planted his free hand against the work bench and broke the restraint holding his left arm as well. He started to rise, putting his legs on the ground, but sight of his arms gave him pause. They were covered in purple scars and stitches. His flesh was the mottled purple and blue of a fresh bruise. His chest was the ghastly yellow of jaundice. His body was one of corpses. His lungs were those of dead men. As the realisation hit him, nausea roiled up within his abdomen, paralysis struck his limbs and the air in the room became heavy.

Victor gasped in horror, backing away towards his desk as Adam's inhalations grew shallower. Adam's own fear became overwhelming, driving his knees to buckle. The crushing darkness of the place came down upon him as he fell. He'd been here before, he realised. This was the dream that had hospitalised him years ago and he could feel his heart racing at the same speed as it had last time.

Then came a hand shrouded in light.

"I've got you" said Wolstone, as he reached out and grasped the monster's arm.

Adam regained his balance. Feeling stronger, he took in the scene once more.

Victor was frozen in time, staring at him in revulsion. The nightmare usually ended here, with him writhing on the ground in agony. Yet Adam was now standing with Wolstone by his side.

"I don't understand, what is happening here" asked the monster.

"You are taking a big step forward and learning to access the memory without actually reliving it. This is a pivotal moment for all who suffer from post traumatic stress" explained Wolstone.

"The memory, but I thought these were dreams" asked the monster.

"That's what I thought too initially, but your sense of self in these is far too strong for them to merely be dreams" said Adam's image of the psychiatrist in the dream.

"Do you mean to tell me that this scientist, that this lab and that this body were all once real?" asked the monster.

"No. Not at all. However, for one reason or another, your mind has stored the Frankenstein narrative, shaped it, and moulded it such that it is somehow viewed as something that you were once a part of. So, while it is not real, that fact is irrelevant. It is real to you" explained the psychiatrist.

The monster's eyes caught sight of a familiar leather-bound book on the desk behind Victor.

"That's the notebook that I have in all of my dreams" said the monster, walking over to look at it.

However, as he gazed down upon the pages, the text was nothing more than a blur. He could only see the words "I Victor." Nothing more could be read.

"Why can't I read anything in this?" asked the monster.

Wolstone pointed to the space where Adam would have collapsed had he not intervened.

"Your perspective is limited by the dream. You have only seen this space from there, on the ground where you collapsed after first being given life. You would never have seen what was in this book at this time, so your mind fills the text of the book with the only information that you know was written in it at the time" explained Wolstone.

Adam looked at Victor again.

Wolstone watched as the monster's hands balled up into fists.

"Adam, there's no point in..." said the doctor as the monster threw a fist into the scientist's face.

The fist sailed right through. In a fury, the monster attacked again, but the man was entirely unaffected.

"You can't alter the path of the memory. You didn't harm him then and so you can't harm him now" explained Wolstone.

"But, but I want to so badly. You have to understand!" spat the monster.

"I do" replied the psychiatrist sympathetically.

"How can you?" raged the monster. "How can you possibly understand!"

"I've seen soldier after soldier in my office for decades. I've walked with them back onto the battlefields where they saw houses burned, women raped and children murdered. I watched them in desperation try to halt the death and destruction that took place so long ago. I've watched them transform into monsters and try to rip apart murderous opponents responsible for the very worst of crimes, but they cannot change the past. Nobody can" replied the psychiatrist calmly.

"Then if I can't change any of this, what is the point? Why bother bringing me here!" screamed the monster.

"Because what we do have the power to change, is you. Working together, we can help you look upon these memories differently than you ever have before" explained Wolstone.

"I don't see how that is possible. Did you see him? Backing away from me in terror as I was falling to the floor in anguish. I was his son! I was suffering and, and, he abandoned me!" seethed the monster.

"But were you really?" asked Wolstone.

"Really what?" asked the monster.

"You are so quick to claim him as your father and to designate yourself as his son, but do you really think that is a fair assessment?" asked the psychiatrist.

"How do you mean?" asked the monster with a tinge of menace in his voice.

"What exactly is a father?" asked Wolstone.

The monster's harsh yellow eyes softened somewhat at the simple question.

"You obviously know your biology well, so why don't we start with the scientific definition" suggested the psychiatrist.

"The male that contributes his sperm to the egg during sexual reproduction" answered the monster.

"I would agree. So with that definition does Victor classify as your father?" asked Wolstone.

"No" said Adam, turning a feral expression towards the fictional scientist.

"But there is more to a father than his biological contribution" growled the monster.

"And I would agree" said Wolstone.

"There should be care. Affection" said the monster.

"And you never got this did you?" asked the psychiatrist.

"I came close" whispered the monster as the laboratory around them dissolved away, revealing a forest.

Place: Val Thoiry, France

Date: 1810

Time: afternoon

"Victor fled and, after walking the halls of Schloss Frankenstein for several days, I went wandering the world in hopes of finding compassion elsewhere" said the monster.

"So you found comfort in the isolation of the forest" speculated Wolstone aloud, not entirely remembering the plot of Mary Shelley's novel.

"No actually" said the monster. "Do you see that there?" the creature said pointing at a small log cabin in a clearing a few hundred meters away.

"Yes" answered Wolstone.

"I was the guardian angel of the family living in that cabin for several seasons" explained the monster.

Wolstone wracked his brain for the details of the narrative. He vaguely remembered the monster having an interaction with a child at some point, but could not remember any family.

"I lived behind a copse of trees nearby and watched them every day as they went about their business. They seemed so happy, so full of joy. All I wanted to do was good so I gathered wood for them by night and left it on their doorstep early in the morning. I prayed that one day they would show affection towards me for the kind deeds" he explained.

321

Wolstone watched as the family went about their activities near the cabin. There were children and two adults. Then an old man came hobbling into view. He had his hands out in front of him, as if he was having trouble keeping his balance.

"What is the situation with the old man?" asked Wolstone.

"That's the grandfather, De Lacey. He was blind and that was what led me to approach him first" said the monster.

"You thought that if he could not see you, you might stand more of a chance of being accepted?" ventured Wolstone.

"Precisely" said the monster, feeling the dream guide his feet towards the door of the cabin.

"You don't have to do this Adam!" said Wolstone nervous that the boy was allowing himself to relive the nightmare once more.

The melancholy music of a lute emanated from beyond the door of the cottage.

"I came to the grandfather one morning when everyone was away" explained the monster as his hand knocked on the door.

Wolstone could see Adam's respirations increasing.

"Who is there? Come in" said De Lacey.

The monster's hand opened the door and its legs carried him in.

"Pardon this intrusion. I am a traveller in want of a little rest. You would greatly oblige me if you would allow me to remain a few minutes before the fire" said the monster.

"Of course. I will try in what manner I can to relieve your wants, but unfortunately my children are away and I am blind, so I am afraid I will find it difficult to procure food for you" said De Lacey.

"Do not trouble yourself, I have food. It is only warmth and rest that I need" said the monster.

With that, Wolstone watched as Adam sat his hulking body down next to the fire and wrapped his arms around his knees like an insecure child. The movements were astonishingly similar to those that he had seen made by the boy in his office.

"By your language stranger I suppose you are my countryman. Are you French?" asked De Lacey.

"No, but I was educated by a French family and understand only that language" replied the monster.

"I take it you are actually talking about De Lacey and his family here?" asked Wolstone.

The monster nodded towards the psychiatrist.

"Ah, I see, you learned from them while watching and listening to them from afar" added the doctor, now recalling more of Shelley's story.

A silence fell between the monster and the blind man.

"I am now going to claim the protection of some friends whom I sincerely love" offered the monster.

"Are they Germans?" asked the old man.

"No. They are French" replied the monster.

More silence and more tension.

"I must admit, I am rather nervous. These friends of mine have never seen me before and know little of me. I am full of fears because if they do not accept me…" the monster's voice trailed off.

"Do not despair. To be friendless is indeed to be unfortunate, but the hearts of men are full of brotherly love and charity. Rely on your hopes" advised De Lacey.

"Oh, they are kind. They are the most excellent of people, but unfortunately they are prejudiced against me. Where they ought to see a feeling and kind friend, they only behold a detestable monster" said the creature.

"That is indeed unfortunate, but if you are truly blameless, is there any way you can undeceive them?" asked the old man.

The monster took in a deep breath.

"I am about to undertake that precise task" said the monster.

"If I may ask, where do these friends reside?" asked De Lacey.

"Near this spot" replied the monster carefully.

With that, the old man paused and thought the matter over carefully.

"If you don't mind confiding in me the details of your situation, perhaps I might be able to help you? I may be blind, poor and an exile myself, but there is something in your words that seems quite sincere. I'd like to help if I can" said De Lacey.

"That would be wonderful. You are raising me out of the dust with your kindness and I do believe that with your aid, I will not be driven away by my friends when I meet them" said the monster.

"Heaven forbid. Now, may I know the names and residence of these friends of yours" asked the old man.

Wolstone watched as a cloud floated in front of the sun and the space grew darker. He could see Adam's muscles growing tense and his eyes growing wide with fear. Thunder rumbled in the distance.

"Breathe Adam, breathe" cautioned Wolstone.

Suddenly, Wolstone heard footfalls outside and watched Adam throw himself at the old man's feet.

"Save and protect me! You and your family are the friends whom I seek. Please do not desert me in my hour of need!" begged the monster.

But it was all for nothing.

A young woman at the door passed out in shock upon seeing Adam's visage as the old man shouted "Great God! Who are you?"

In seconds, the young man of the family was upon Adam, striking his hideous form with a log from the fireplace.

After a moment of flinching under the relentless attack, Wolstone was pleased to see Adam calmly stand himself up as the young man continued to attack the space he had occupied.

"That's it. Very good Adam. Remember, it isn't real" said Wolstone supportively.

The monster turned towards Wolstone calmly as the chaotic scene continued to play out in front of them both.

"Not true. It is real. At least, it is real to me. But that doesn't matter. The important thing to keep in mind is what you said earlier. I cannot change what happened, but I can change how I view it" advised Adam.

A small shiver went down Wolstone's spine at the comment but he decided to shrug it off. What mattered was that Adam was finally pulling himself out of the dreams and looking at them objectively.

"I was wrong here. I should have written to them first. Introduced myself in a situation where I would not run the risk of such a catastrophe following" commented Adam.

"You mustn't be so hard on yourself" said Wolstone, worrying that he was starting to treat his patient as if these fictional events had actually happened.

"No. You are right, I shouldn't" said the monster, "because there are far worse things that I have done."

And with that, the cabin bled away.

Place: Geneva, Switzerland

Date: 1811

Time: afternoon

Wolstone found himself standing beside the monster in a gorgeous alpine meadow. He was not exactly well travelled, but he had been around enough to know the peak of Mt Blanc when he saw it.

"This is Switzerland" said Wolstone.

"Yes. A meadow not far from Geneva" replied the monster.

"I'm confused" said Wolstone, "What sort of thing did you do here that you are ashamed of?"

"Come with me" said Adam, walking across the meadow.

They walked together for a few moments before stopping at the body of a small boy lying in the grass.

Wolstone knelt down and looked closely at the child, he was freshly dead and, from the look of things, his death had been by strangulation. Closer inspection revealed extraordinarily long finger marks along the child's neck... long fingers that could only belong to the inhumanly large monster standing beside him.

"You killed him?" asked Wolstone aghast.

"Yes" replied the monster simply.

"Why?" asked   the psychiatrist.

327

"My intention was to kidnap him. I hoped that since the De Lacey family would not adopt me, perhaps I could make a young child grow to love me" explained Adam.

The Shelley story started to come back to Wolstone. Yes, this was the child he remembered from the story.

"I understand that you were lonely, but why would you kill your would-be companion?" asked Wolstone.

The monster smiled in a way that left the doctor feeling deeply uneasy.

"As I grappled with him he threatened to tell his father, a man named Frankenstein, on me. He told me that Frankenstein was powerful and would punish me for my actions" explained Adam.

"Victor had a biological son?" asked Wolstone feeling rather confused.

"That's what I thought initially, but as I learned later, this boy was William, his youngest brother" said the monster.

"So you killed him because he was a Frankenstein?" asked Wolstone.

"Yes. I killed in vengeance. And it was only the beginning" said the monster.

He looked towards the mountain and grew pensive.

"I begged Victor to create a companion for me. He told me he would, but it was all a lie" spat the monster.

"For his treachery I went on to kill Victor's dear friend, Henry Clervil and then his wife Elizabeth" explained Adam quietly. "You could even go so far as to say I killed Victor himself."

The wind whipped past them both bringing an icy breeze and, in seconds, snow enveloped the landscape.

Place: Svalbard

Date: 1814

Time: day

"I don't understand. Where are we? Is this Finland again?" asked Wolstone.

"No. It's the frozen ocean, not far off the coast of what is today Svalbard" explained the monster walking towards the horizon.

"Norway? But why here?" asked Wolstone.

The monster pointed to a ship locked in the ice in the distance.

"Victor was furious about me destroying his family and swore to chase me to the ends of the earth. After years of him hunting me, this is where I led him" explained Adam.

"You were unaffected by the cold?" said Wolstone.

The monster nodded solemnly.

"But it made Victor very weak. He became quite ill" explained Adam.

Side by side, the psychiatrist and the monster walked towards the ship. Snow devils blew past their ankles and, periodically, the ice beneath their feet cracked. In a short while they were climbing the side of the boat and making their way down a staircase.

Adam opened a cabin door and approached a body wrapped inside a   sheet.

"Adam, you don't have to do this" advised Wolstone.

"But I want you to see. I want you to know" said the monster as it untied the knot holding the sheet closed and drew it back. There, curled up in a sad pose of death, was Victor's pale corpse.

Wolstone didn't even know the man, but he felt for him. He glanced at Adam and was not entirely surprised to see a tear streaking down from his gruesome yellow eyes.

"I did not kill him, not with my own hands, but I was responsible" said the monster as it slowly lowered itself to its knees.

"Do you really think you are being fair to yourself?" asked Wolstone.

"Yes I do. I killed the ones he loved. I goaded him into hunting me" said Adam.

"But Victor had many opportunities to set things right. He could have summoned up the courage to be kinder. He could have created a companion for you. Sure, you escalated the situation by lashing out, but you were what, two years old at most? Frankly, it has been a long time since I've read Mary Shelley's book, but I do remember thinking that it was Victor who was the monster, not you!" said Wolstone

The creature looked the psychiatrist in the eye and laid one of his ghastly arms on the doctor's shoulder.

"Thank you Dr Wolstone. It means a lot to me hearing that from you" said the monster.

"I only say it because it is true. But I am curious; this is the end of the story as I know it. What happened next?" asked the doctor.

"Well, after realising that in my search for love and companionship I had spread nothing but death, I resolved in this very place that I would destroy myself" said Adam.

"But that's not what happened is it?" asked Wolstone.

"No. I did go to nearby Svalbard and I did build a large fire, but as I stood over it, I found that I could not make my body enter. No matter how hard I tried, I could not allow myself to come to an end. Ultimately, in misery, I wandered off. I travelled to Sweden, Denmark, Belgium, France and Switzerland, but ultimately my feet brought me back to the place of my creation" said the monster.

Place: Ingolstadt, Germany

Date: 1815

Time: night

In an instant, the two of them were back in Victor's study. Piles of books lay open upon the desks. Some on science, some on literature.

"For five years I pored over the notes and books left behind by my maker. I found that the words 'it' and 'creature' haunted me, so, with time I became more and more determined to become an 'I.' This bible became my guide and, having no name of my own, I decided to call myself Adam after the first man created by God" explained the monster as he showed Wolstone the piles of texts.

"You read all of this?" asked Wolstone.

"Most of it. And I made my notes here" said Adam, pointing to the leather-bound book at the side of the bible.

Wolstone caught sight of glassware at the far end of the room. Beakers, test tubes, burners and a range of medical devices were set out; some of the burners were actually lit and bubbling fluids around the intricate systems that had been laid out.

"I don't suppose that was all still running when Victor left?" asked Wolstone.

"No. This was my work" said the monster.

"Your work?" said Wolstone with astonishment.

"After reading all of Victor's notes, studying all of his drawings and analysing the various cell cultures that he had grown, I came to a rather remarkable discovery" explained Adam.

"And what was that?" asked Wolstone, truly baffled.

"My learned creator was wrong. He entirely misunderstood his own achievements. What he had managed was not re-animation of dead tissue, but replication of stem cells that would transform into neurons and maintain their synapse structures whenever they were transplanted. The brain in my head was not a re-animated brain, as Victor believed, but a brain grown from a few cells that had not yet died inside the skull of a freshly dead individual. As soon as Victor gave those brain cells oxygen and glucose, they replicated until they filled up the available cranial space, forming a new neural network. They effectively created a new brain" explained the monster.

Wolstone looked over all of the medical equipment with incredulity.

"You doubt what I am saying?" asked Adam.

"Well, it has been a while since I took biology, but I'm fairly certain that human cells cannot just keep replicating forever" said Wolstone.

"That is what we once thought" said Adam, "but not any more."

"What are you talking about?" asked Wolstone.

"In 1951 a woman named Henrietta Lacks was treated for cancer at Johns Hopkins in Maryland. She didn't last long, dying shortly after diagnosis, but the doctors working with her collected some of her cells and noticed that even after her death, the cells kept on replicating so long as they had all of the necessary nutrients. They are still replicating and found in laboratories all over the world. I haven't run the experiments yet, but I will bet that the HeLa cells, which are what her cells are now called in her honour, are very similar in nature to the brain cells that Victor collected and nourished when he created me" explained the monster.

"So are you telling me that using your understanding of Victor's work, you transferred your replicating brain cells..." said Wolstone.

"...into others over the years" explained Adam.

"So the man in the Austrian fields who ultimately made his way to Prussia and befriended Elsa was who?" asked the psychiatrist.

"An Austrian soldier who had been shot and nearly killed by a septic infection that followed" answered the monster.

"And from him you transferred into Pekka during that night when he was dying" said Wolstone, realising how the pieces of the puzzle fit together.

"The transfers all depended upon extracting a precise sample of brain tissue in a suspension of cerebro-spinal fluid and inserting the mixture with a precise injection into the upper spine. Then, as my brain cells replicated within the foreign skull, my awareness was replicated" said Adam.

335

"And this body that Victor gave you? I suppose you are going to tell me it is still out there somewhere?" asked Wolstone.

The monster closed its yellow eyes in sorrow.

Adam remembered standing nearby as the hideous form climbed up on top of an unlit funeral pyre. His eyes met those horrific ones that had once been his. The creature reached out and their hands held one another for a moment.

"Do it. Be free of me. Be free of Victor" said the creature.

And with that, Adam watched as his own arm lifted up a nearby torch and lowered it into the centre of the pyre, setting the wood and his old body ablaze.

Place: Psychiatry Office, Boston, Massachusetts

Date: May 12th, 2018

Time: 5:58pm

Adam inhaled with a touch of sadness in his voice.

Wolstone was curious about the particulars of the monster's death and was just beginning to formulate a question to explore the matter when an abrupt knock at the door brought both he and Adam back to attention.

"Come in" said the psychiatrist.

Catherine carefully stepped in as Wolstone sighed deeply, feeling years older than he did just two hours earlier.

"Have you made any progress?" she asked.

"Indeed we have. Haven't we Adam?" replied the doctor.

Adam nodded.

"We were actually just finishing up. Would you mind giving us one more minute?" asked Wolstone.

"Of course" replied Catherine, stepping back out again.

"So what do I do now?" asked the child.

"How do you mean?" asked Wolstone.

"Am I supposed to just tell myself that none of this is real when it wakes me up in the middle of the night?" asked Adam.

"I would not tell you to do that" replied the psychiatrist carefully.

"Then, you think the dreams are real too?" asked the boy quietly, looking at the doctor with a sense of hope.

Wolstone considered the matter carefully and, as he did, his eyes fell upon the issue of *Nature* that the kid had brought in from the waiting room. Right there was an article on the page that Adam had been reading just two hours earlier all about a research team in London that had grown a neuron network in the lab. As far as Wolstone was concerned, that was the silver bullet.

The dreams were all just fantasies carved from material read by a very bright child. Exactly what horrors he had been exposed to early on in his life remained to be determined. They might forever be a mystery, but Wolstone was certain that Adam was using a mix of historical details and fiction to come to grips with the terrible experiences that still haunted him.

"I think they are real for you and that is enough of a reason to treat them as memories rather than fantasies. When they come to mind, don't dismiss them, but celebrate the good ones while pushing the bad ones aside. We can work on that together as we meet in the weeks ahead" advised the psychiatrist.

Adam's head fell into his hands, leaving Wolstone immediately regretting his words.

A moment passed with the two of them left in uncomfortable silence. The water of the clock dripped away and, sensing that their session was over, Adam got up and made his way to the door.

"Thank you Dr Wolstone" the boy said softly.

"You are welcome. See you again in two weeks" replied the doctor, still feeling depressed at having let the child down.

As Adam closed the door behind him, Wolstone leaned back into his chair and pulled the issue of *Nature* up to give it a proper read.

It was exactly as Adam had described from the dream. A team was placing stem cells into a nutrient rich environment and monitoring them as they rapidly replicated. The article had references to Henrietta Lacks and noted how these cells were utterly different from hers in that they transformed on their own accord into neurons and naturally developed into a complex network that resembled the neuron networks found in the human brain. It was unbelievable; the boy had read this and spouted off the information during their session nearly word for word. Fascinated, Wolstone read on.

The cells were from a single line that had been cryogenically frozen and stored at Charring Cross Hospital in 1947. They were found and identified by Ida Whittle of the biochemistry department at Imperial College, London during a routine identification of old items in storage. Dr Whittle was the lead author of the new paper.

Ida Whittle, thought Wolstone, that name rang a bell. He was certain he had heard it before, sometime recently. Sitting up, he turned to his pile of paperwork and started digging through it until he found what he was looking for. He flipped open the cover of the ethics committee folder and paged through the various applications until he got to the last one, the one that he had been delaying dealing with.

Request to transplant stem cells into a comatose patient being made by Ida Whittle, PhD - Department of Biochemistry, Harvard University.

Following the success of our lab studies with the self replicating AdAd subventricular cells, we have reason to believe that, as they produce neurons and these neurons develop into a network, they are building complex structures that reflect the neuron network that existed in the brain of the person from who they were originally sampled in the early 1940's. These structures, may even be encoding information. We have secured a four-year-old child who, due to severe cerebral meningitis suffered nine months ago, is effectively brain dead but still otherwise healthy and in tact. With the permission of the university ethics board, we wish to transfer a sample of the AdAd subventricular cells to the ventral telencephalon of this patient and monitor the activities of the neurons that they produce. Due to their robust behaviour and tendency to create neural network structures that are very similar to those found in the human brain, we suspect that their insertion may either reactivate the remaining brain cells in the patient or lead to the development of novel structures.

Wolstone's mouth went dry as he digested the proposal in front of him. His eyes started scanning the piece for mention of where the name "AdAd" came from. There was no way, he thought. No way. And then he found it in the "Additional Notes" section.

AdAd: the stem cells are named in honour of the patient whom Charring Cross Hospital has in their records as being the donor. A member of the Royal Navy who died aboard the HMS Warspite during the battle of Narvik. His name was Adam Adlerberg.

The psychiatrist's eyes flashed to the *Nature* article. It was impossible, utterly impossible. Did the *Nature* article mention where the cell line name came from? If that was the case, it was feasible that the boy had just made up the surname Adlerberg to be in line with the article and that there was just a bit of dumb luck in him having the same first name as this World War II seaman, thought Wolstone.

He scanned the article but didn't see any mention of an Adam Adlerberg. Nothing at all. He looked back at the ethics board application. It was a confidential file. It had been sealed until recently and locked in his office. Only a handful of other academics at the university had a copy of the same ethics request and none of them would have shared it with others, let alone a child.

Overwhelmed by the thoughts that were rushing through his mind, Wolstone flew up from his chair and ran over to his window. There they were. The boy and his mother were walking across the street to the parking lot next to the university campus garden. In seconds, Wolstone was out the door and dashing down the stairs as fast as his old legs would carry him.

"Wait, wait!" he called to the child and his mother as he sprinted across the crosswalk in the midst of a green light.

Catherine stopped and looked at the doctor in confusion.

"I... I..." the doctor said completely out of breath.

"Dr Wolstone, are you okay?" asked Catherine.

"I... I'm fine. I just a need a quick moment with your son, there was, there was something I forgot to ask during our session" explained the psychiatrist.

Without even waiting for any response from his mother, Adam started walking away into the campus garden on his own.

"Well, I guess I don't really have a say on this one" muttered Catherine with exasperation as Wolstone stumbled after the boy.

The spring flowers were out in force and newly growing vines were rapidly making their way up the arches that ran over the path. Wolstone walked behind the child for what felt like ages as he sucked in air from his sprint and then, abruptly, as they came to an isolated fountain in the centre, Adam turned to face him.

His eyes were brighter than Wolstone had ever seen and his face was filled with hope.

It had to be a grand and elaborate fantasy, thought Wolstone, it had to be, but his doubts were increasing rapidly and he had to know. With that, Wolstone decided to give the inexplicable a try.

"After two hundred years of life, what is it that you really want now?" asked the psychiatrist.

The boy studied the man's face carefully, for any sign of doubt and was pleased to find none.

"It is the same thing I have always wanted" said the boy.

"And what is that?" asked the psychiatrist.

"I just want to live one normal life. Beginning to end" he replied quietly.

Wolstone knelt down onto the ground and looked the child in the eye.

"And what of the syringe?" Wolstone asked in rusty Finnish that he had not used since his mother had passed many years earlier.

A glimmer of a smile formed on Adam's lips as he heard the psychiatrist's words.

"Normal lives do not usually involve the tools of immortality do they?" he replied in perfect, if not slightly antiquated, Finnish.

"No, I suppose not" answered Wolstone, feeling the weight of realisation come crashing down on his shoulders.

"Houva homenta" said the boy fluently as he walked back down the garden path to his mother.

Place: Psychiatry Office, Boston, Massachusetts

Date: May 12th, 2018

Time: 11:29 pm

After several stiff drinks and a long slow wander around the campus, Wolstone sank back into his desk chair and pulled Ida Whittle's ethics committee proposal form over. He gave it a good hard look one more time but knew that reading it again was pointless.

The neurons she was tinkering with had been through enough, that much was clear. To insert them into yet another life would just create another mind full of fractured thoughts and nightmares. With help, the boy that he was already seeing might have a chance at the normal life that he so desperately sought, but Wolstone couldn't guarantee it. Nobody else deserved what he was going through.

Wolstone's pen hovered over the disapproval check box for a mere second before he put an 'X' in it. He glanced at the comments section and questioned exactly what, if anything, he could possibly say that would lead anyone to understand his reasoning without suggesting that he be committed to a psychiatric institute.

He pondered the matter for a few moments longer before writing:

Consider Shelley and you'll know why.

Factual Notes

HMS Warspite

Was a British battleship that fought in both world wars. During her long tenure she sailed through the Atlantic, Indian, Arctic and Pacific Oceans and earned an extraordinary number of battle honours. In April 1940, Warspite was on course for the Mediterranean when Germany attacked Norway. She was immediately commanded to turn around and support the Norwegians and, on April 13th, the vice-admiral of the Royal Navy hoisted his flag on Warspite. Under his command, she led a group of nine destroyers to sweep mines off the Norwegian coast and engaged in battle with the Germans at the port of Narvik. She remained off the Norwegian coast until April 28th when she returned to Scotland for a brief period before being redeployed to the Mediterranean.

Johann "Gregor" Mendel

Mendel lived at St Thomas' Abbey in Brno, Germany throughout the 1850's and 1860's. He conducted experiments with pea plants in the abbey gardens and discovered that selectively cross-breeding the plants had remarkable effects upon future generations. More specifically, he worked with traits like plant height, seed shape and pea colour and discovered that when a yellow pea plant and a green pea plant were cross-bred they produced offspring that were always yellow. Then, in the next generation, he found that green peas reappeared at a ratio of one green pea for every three yellow peas. Mendel sensed that there were invisible factors controlling plant traits and is widely considered the father of modern genetics.

Between 1856 and 1863 Mendel worked tirelessly to understand the rules of heredity. Unfortunately, his research was badly disrupted by administrative responsibilities when he was elevated to the rank of abbot in 1868 and at this time his scientific work largely ended. However, he never lost his passion for science, spoke with others frequently about his findings and speculated about the ways in which heredity might be used to shape plants and animals.

Finnish Famine of 1866-1868

A very wet summer in 1866 caused vitally important root vegetables, like potatoes, to rot in the ground long before they could be harvested. The weather also made it difficult to sow grain during the autumn months. These factors, combined with a very harsh winter that lasted until May 1867, forced Finns into a desperate situation and led to mass starvation by the autumn of 1867. In 1868, the weather was better but infectious diseases that had spread widely during the time of famine continued to kill many. Throughout the catastrophe thousands of Finns ended up begging and dying on the streets of Helsinki.

Hayflick Limit

This is a real phenomenon whereby the telomeres, which are effectively the caps on either side of each DNA strand, get shorter and shorter each time a cell replicates. Eventually, they get too small to be functional and replication can no longer continue. The limit makes it impossible for cells to replicate more than 60 times before the shrinking telomeres cease to function.

HeLa Cells

These are immortal cells that are widely used in research. They originally were found and taken without permission from a patient named Henrietta Lacks who died on October 4, 1951 from cancer. The cells produce a compound known as telomerase that shields telomeres from becoming shorter after each replication cycle and allows the cells to evade the restrictions presented by the Hayflick limit. They are extremely aggressive and, if placed in cultures with other cells, they readily grow over and destroy them. To date, researchers around the world are estimated to have grown twenty tonnes of HeLa cells

Neuron Transplants

Up until 2016, all attempts to help stroke patients by implanting pluripotent stem cell-derived neurons into brain tissue failed. A major reason for this was because the implanted neurons never gained the sort of spatial organisation that is required for them to form a functional nerve network. Then, in 2017, research took a major leap forward.

A joint effort made by biomedical engineers, neuroscientists and stem cell biologists at Rutgers University and Stanford University revealed that it was possible to program neurons generated from stem cells to form functional networks by growing them on scaffolds made from microscopic polymer threads. Crucially, the team was able to take their lab-grown neural networks and successfully graft them into mice that were suffering from brain damage and dramatically improve their mental health. The work has not yet been applied to humans but, what works in mice, stands a decent chance of working in people.

To date, no neurons have been found that can form networks spontaneously in the absence of polymer threads. However, just because we have never seen cells that can do this does not mean that such cells are not out there waiting to be discovered. After all, until HeLa cells were found, it was deemed impossible to break the Hayflick Limit.

Nikolay Adlerberg

Adlerberg was born into a Swedish noble family living in Saint Petersburg in 1819. His father was a good friend of Tsar Nicholas and this helped set Adlerberg on course to gain great favour with the rulers of Russia. He became a skilled military commander and, after fighting in wars in the Caucasus and Hungary, he became a colonel. Later, during the Crimean War, he attained the rank of general.

Aside from all of his military activities, Adlerberg was intensely curious about the world and thoroughly enjoyed meeting people from other cultures. In between his military campaigns, he travelled extensively in Greece, Egypt, Italy and Palestine and wrote a book about his journeys "From Rome to Jerusalem" which was ultimately published in 1853.

His experiences left him with a soft spot for those who followed faiths that were different from his own. He was noted for having close friendships with many of the Jews, known as cantonists, who were forced into military service by the Russian state.

Adlerberg had tremendous enthusiasm for theatre and wrote extensively on the subject. He was responsible for leading the construction of the Helsinki Theatre in 1879 which he built in honour of Tsar Alexander II.

He served as Governor General of Finland from 1866 to 1881 and is widely considered to have been the most benevolent and learned man to hold the post. He died of natural causes in 1892.

Helene de Fontenilliat

Helene was the grand-daughter of Nikolay Adlerberg's second wife Amelie. Helene's grandparents played a major part in raising her in Helsinki and arranged for her to be married to Constantin Linder in 1873. Helene's politics and social interactions remain poorly recorded.

Otto von Bismarck

Bismarck and Adlerberg did not like one another. Observations reported in memoirs written by Prussian civil servant Friedrich von Holstein detail how Adlerberg obtained skilled artisans from Bismarck to work on the theatre in Helsinki and then reportedly failed to pay an appropriate fee for their services. Bismarck went over Adlerberg's head and took up the matter directly with the Russian tsar. This enraged Adlerberg and the tensions were plainly visible when Adlerberg and Bismarck ultimately met in person at a reception given by the French Ambassador to Prussia at the Palais Beauvryé.

Bismarck disliked the Poles and used numerous tactics to weaken and Germanise them. Polish was not taught in schools and Polish settlements were often given German names. Poles were blocked from attaining positions of political power and intentionally given poor farmland.

Constantin Linder

Linder was a nobleman who dominated Finnish politics from his manor in Joensuu. He was married to Aderberg's beloved grand-daughter Helene. After Nikolay Adlerberg left office, Finland faced subsequent governor-generals who were increasingly rabid about crushing Finnish culture. Linder strongly believed that the best strategy for dealing with this threat was to follow the Russian policies as slowly as possible without engaging in open resistance.

King Gustaf V

Gustaf ruled Sweden from 1907 until his death in 1950. He was an enthusiastic athlete and fell in love with tennis during a visit to Britain in 1876. After years of practice, he became an excellent player in his own right and ultimately represented Sweden at the 1912 Olympics in disguise as the mysterious Mr. G. During a visit to Berlin in 1939, Gustaf is noted to have gone straight to a tennis match with the Jewish player Daniel Prenn after meeting with Adolf Hitler.

The king was friendly with Germany and, in some cases; he has been accused of being a Nazi sympathiser. Counter arguments have been made that his warm relations with Hitler were diplomatic and aimed at helping the Nazi's to crush "the Bolshevik pest" that threatened Finland. It is debated whether he tried to use his good relationship with Hitler to soften the German treatment of the Jews.

According to notes made by Swedish Prime Minister Per Albin Hansson in 1941, King Gustaf threatened to abdicate if the Swedish government did not approve a Nazi request to transfer an infantry division through Swedish territory to support troops in northern Finland fighting against the Russians.

Russification of Finland

Between 1899 and 1917, Russia made a concerted effort to sabotage Finnish autonomy and weaken the country's culture such that the Finns would ultimately be assimilated. The Finnish language was widely banned, the Russian Orthodox Church was made the church of state, the Finnish army was incorporated into the Russian Imperial Army and all Finnish currency and stamps were removed from circulation. These policies stoked hatred of the Russians in Finland and were a key reason for Finland eventually declaring independence in 1917.

Finnish Civil War

The collapse of Russian power following the October Revolution of 1917 pushed the fledgling Finnish state into an identity crisis. There were essentially two factions: the reds and the whites. The reds were those who saw socialism and close ties to Russia as the future of the state. The whites saw a representative democracy and independence from Russia as the best option for Finland.

While foreign nations did not formally give support to either side during the war, roughly 10% of the red army was made up of members of the Russian Imperial Army and roughly 15% of the white army was made up of members of the Imperial German Army. King Gustaf arranged for a Swedish brigade of a thousand men disguised as Finns to quietly support the whites during the battle for   Tampere.

Hjalmar Frisell

Frisell was a master marksman and competed for Sweden in the 1912 Olympics where his clay pigeon shooting team finished in fourth place. He attended many Swedish sports events where he would have unquestionably met King Gustaf in his disguise at "Mr. G" but it is unclear whether Frisell ever learned of the tennis player's secret identity. During the Finnish Civil War, Frisell was chosen to command the Swedish Brigade that fought in the battle of Tampere and helped the Finnish whites to win their independence. It is unknown whether a relationship with King Gustaf played a part in his being nominated for this leadership position.

Finland and World War II

At the start of the war, Finland was invaded by the Soviet Union. In spite of the fact that the Soviets had three times as many soldiers, thirty times more aircraft, and a hundred times more tanks than the Finns, they struggled to conquer the small country. While fighting began in November and was expected to quickly end in Finland's defeat, the Soviets were still struggling to make progress in February. During this conflict Finland begged Sweden for help but this was refused. Sympathetic of their situation, King Gustaf communicated with Adolf Hitler and arranged for support in return for access to iron ore from Lapland. A further request was made for Finnish Jews to be handed over to the Germans but the Finnish General Carl Gustaf Mannerheim declared "While Jews serve in my army I will not allow their deportation" and all further attempts to send Finnish Jews to concentration camps failed.

Finland signed a treaty with the Soviet Union in 1940 that surrendered a portion of the country's territory in the south east. However, the treaty did not last long. As soon as Germany declared war on the Soviet Union, the Finns declared war as well and fought to take their lost territory back. The Finnish theatre of war is the only known instance where Nazis fought alongside Jews and were forced to tolerate the presence of a field synagogue operated by a rabbi of the Finnish army.

Mandi Hannula

Hannula initially worked as a schoolteacher but eventually developed a keen interest in politics and joined the National Progressive Party. She served in the Finnish

Senate from 1919 to 1930 and then again from 1936 to 1945.

Printed in Poland
by Amazon Fulfillment
Poland Sp. z o.o., Wrocław

53955183R00211